The Wind Dragons Motorcycle Club Series

Dragon's Lair

Arrow's Hell

TRACKER'S END

CHANTAL FERNANDO

Gallery Books

New York London Toronto Sydney New Delhi

G

Gallery Books
An Imprint of Simon & Schuster, Inc.
1230 Avenue of the Americas
New York, NY 10020

First Gallery Books trade paperback edition August 2015

GALLERY BOOKS and colophon are registered trademarks of Simon & Schuster, Inc.

For information about special discounts for bulk purchases, please contact Simon & Schuster Special Sales at 1-866-506-1949 or business@simonandschuster.com.

The Simon & Schuster Speakers Bureau can bring authors to your live event. For more information or to book an event contact the Simon & Schuster Speakers Bureau at 1-866-248-3049 or visit our website at www.simonspeakers.com.

Cover design by Patrick Kang
Cover photograph © Gabriel Georgescu/Shutterstock

Manufactured in the United States of America

10   9   8   7   6   5   4   3   2   1

Library of Congress Cataloging-in-Publication Data is available.

ISBN 978-1-5011-0621-7
ISBN 978-1-5011-0623-1 (ebook)

Have you ever met someone and they instantly feel like family?
I have.
And her name is Rose Tawil.
Love you, honey!

*   *   *

The best people possess a feeling for beauty, the courage to take risks, the discipline to tell the truth, the capacity for sacrifice. Ironically, their virtues make them vulnerable; they are often wounded, sometimes destroyed.

—*Ernest Hemingway*

ACKNOWLEDGMENTS

As always, I'd like to thank Abby Zidle and Gallery Books. This experience has been so amazing, and I've been so blessed to be surrounded with such wonderful people.

My agent, Kimberly Brower, thank you for always believing in me, and pushing me to work harder.

Arijana Karcic—I don't think I can ever thank you enough. You're one of the best people I've ever had the pleasure of knowing. Thank you for being you. Your dry humor gets me through the day.

Thank you to my family, I love you all and appreciate your help.

Tenielle—My sister, my best friend. You know how much you mean to me. There's nothing I wouldn't do for you, nothing.

Sasha Jaya—You're the best friend a girl could ask for. And lucky for me, you're my blood too. Love you always.

Brent—Thank you for answering all my extremely personal questions and allowing me a peek into the male mind. You're kind of great. Okay, more than great, you're amazing. And also a huge pain in the ass.

To all the bloggers that support me on a daily basis, I adore each and every one of you! Tara Lynn—Thank you for your hilarious messages, I'm flattered you love my heroes so much.

Natasha Awkar—I adore you woman! Thank you for always being there for me.

Thank you to all my beta readers, and all the girls in Chantal's Alpha Male Support Team, especially Eileen Robinson, who is such an amazing lady.

Aileen Day—Books brought us together, and now you're one of my best friends. Thank you for being so wonderful.

To my three sons. Thank you for inspiring me to be a better person, for giving me a reason to fight. I love you infinity.

PROLOGUE

ANNA, who is this?" a blond god calls out.

I step closer to my best friend. When Anna moved back into town, I'd never have guessed I'd be thrust into a world of motorcycle clubs and insanely hot yet dangerous bikers. Nothing is going to be boring around here from now on—that's for sure. The man who approaches us is probably the most handsome guy I've ever seen in my life, and I'm not even exaggerating. Playful blue eyes, angular features with a strong jaw covered in stubble, I can see tattoos peeking out from his white T-shirt. I can also see a muscled arm that I imagine wrapped around me.

Yeah, maybe I will start hanging around here more often.

Like, every day.

"Tracker, this is Lana." Anna introduces us, explaining, "This is one of Rake's friends."

I'm still getting used to hearing Anna's brother, Adam, being referred to by his MC name. I've known Adam—I mean, Rake—since I was a young girl. He wasn't in an MC while he was in high school, but he still caused trouble wherever he went.

At heart though, he's a good guy and cares about his younger sister.

"Nice to meet you, Tracker," I say quietly, glancing shyly at him.

He smiles slowly. "Pleasure is all mine."

I have to remind myself to breathe.

"So you're Anna's partner in crime?" he asks, moving closer.

I glance at Anna, then back at him. "No. I'm usually the one trying to keep her out of trouble."

He laughs, rubbing his chest absently. My eyes follow the movement, unable to stop staring at the way his shirt clings to him. "I can see that. Only known her for a while, but I can already see how she starts trouble."

Anna gives him the finger.

Tracker gives me a look that clearly says *See what I mean?*

A small smile forms on my lips. "It's usually her mouth that gets her in trouble."

"Traitor," Anna fires back good-naturedly.

"Or because she thinks I need protecting."

Tracker studies me. "You are kind of small. Cute. It's hot."

I duck my head shyly.

"Don't embarrass her," Anna chastises, then pauses. "And don't flirt with her. You have a woman, remember?"

I'm surprised by my disappointment at hearing he's taken, but I brush it aside. This is not the kind of guy I can trust, that is clear. His flirty, friendly demeanor is clearly a well-practiced act—it's probably worked on countless women in the past. It won't work on me though. Nope.

I try to keep my expression impassive as Tracker studies me for a moment, a thoughtful expression on his face. As if coming to a conclusion, he nods and moves his gaze away from me. "Just being friendly."

"Well, don't," Anna replies. "Come on, Lana, we better get going."

"Okay," I murmur, following behind her.

I can't help myself. I turn around to look back at him.

But he's not looking at me.

He's staring at the ground, lost in thought. He almost looks confused, his eyebrows drawn together, as though he doesn't understand whatever is on his mind.

I wonder what he's thinking about. I wonder if he's thinking about me. Not that it matters. He isn't available.

And I'm probably not his type anyway.

My thought is proven correct when a beautiful woman walks up to him.

His beautiful woman, I realize as she puts her hand against his chest with a seductive look on her face.

She's everything I'm not. Tall, slim, and dressed in tight leather pants, a black top showing off her toned flesh and shiny red high heels, she's the epitome of a biker chick.

I look down at my worn jeans, graphic T-shirt, and flip-flops and I keep walking.

I may not be oozing sex appeal like that woman, but that's just not me. Sometimes you have to know who you are, and who you're not.

ONE

TRACKER

I SEE her.

As usual, she's standing a little behind Anna, almost hiding. Fuck, she's shy. It's cute as hell. Women are usually forward with me—the same way I am with them. But Lana? Her gaze avoids mine as much as it can. I know she wants me. I know lust when I see it; but with her, there's something more there. She wants more than a fuck. She *deserves* more. For the last year I've tried to stay away from her. I didn't think I was good for her— oh, and I wasn't really single either.

I'm still not good for her.

But wanting her—that has stayed constant since the moment I met her.

She's dressed in a blue top that hugs her petite frame, and jeans that cup her juicy ass. That ass could bring a man to his knees. Feeling myself harden, I shift uncomfortably and force myself to remove my gaze from her. I scan the room, my gaze landing on Allie.

Fuck.

The situation between me and Allie is a huge clusterfuck. A whole fuckin' mess that I went along with because it was easy. She was here; she wanted me. She knew the lifestyle. Easy.

Allie is the daughter of a fallen member of the Wind Dragons Motorcycle Club. Because of this, we let her stay in our clubhouse, and we look after her. She's hooked up with a few of the other members, I know, but when her claws landed on me, the bitch dug deep. She wanted to be my old lady, and I let her play the part for a while without giving her the official title. Looking back, I know I didn't treat her how I would treat my old lady, how I would treat Lana if she were mine. The feelings just weren't there—and they still aren't. I was looking for something in Allie that I didn't find, but I held on anyway. I led her on more than I meant to. Staying with her was me being a selfish fuck, because I should have let her go when our relationship first started going south. Which was right after it fuckin' began. I have the feeling she knows it won't work but is hopeful anyway. Whatever it is, it's a fucked-up situation that needs to be over with.

Allie is jealous, mouthy, and has a vindictive streak in her that people shouldn't underestimate. She hates Lana with a passion and is jealous as hell of her. I mean, she'd been a bitch toward Faye and Anna as well, with her snide comments and general cattiness, but with Lana it's different. Faye and Anna can put Allie in her place, but Lana is more quiet and unaware. I've seen the scheming looks Allie gives Lana, almost like she's planning something. Maybe she senses the connection I feel toward Lana. I've always tried to protect Lana from her, because I know Allie can be vicious. Whenever Lana's around, I give Allie a little more attention, just to curb her jealousy. By trying to save Lana from Allie, it pushed her away from me a little bit more each time. But it had to be done. I want Allie and me to be completely done, and I want to close that distance with Lana.

Allie does have a sweet side, a vulnerable side, which she always tries to hide. It just isn't enough for me to overlook the bad. Overall she is a hard bitch who was born to be on the back of a bike, just not mine.

But Lana . . .

I wanted her from the moment I first saw her, whether I was with Allie or not, even though I pretended that I didn't. I tried to make sure she thought I only wanted her as a friend, but I'm not sure what message I really sent. Mixed fuckin' signals for sure.

My head turns, my attention on her once more.

She's beautiful. Sweet.

Not a mean bone in her little body . . . and yet . . . she belongs on the back of my bike. The loyalty I've seen her show Anna when she and Arrow got together made me realize just how strong she is. She's so much tougher than I'd initially thought.

This one is *mine*. I wanted her then. And I want her now.

There is no more fighting it, pretending I don't want her. Trying to ignore her. Giving her the impression we don't have a chance in hell. All the games are coming to an end.

I'm going to soak all that sweetness up.

Consume her.

And no one is going to stand in my way—not even her.

She's my end.

TWO

LANA

I CAN feel his gaze on me, but I pretend to ignore him. Instead, I concentrate on the beautiful little girl in front of me. Clover is the Wind Dragons Motorcycle Club princess. Daughter of the president, Sin, and his kick-ass wife, Faye, Clover is protected by all and loved by many. With jet-black hair, hazel eyes, and the cutest smile, the six-year-old is a force to be reckoned with.

And I'm her nanny.

Today is only the second time I'm watching her, but honestly, she is a treat. It's extremely amusing to see how this little girl has all the rough men of the MC wrapped around her little finger. Hell, I can probably learn a thing or two from her. She's currently sitting on Arrow's knee, waiting impatiently as Arrow pulls a piece of strawberry candy from his pocket, unwraps it, and pops it into her mouth.

Did he just carry around that candy for her?

The girl is good.

"Don't tell your mother," I hear Arrow tell her quietly, in that gravelly voice of his.

"I won't," Clover replies, grinning.

I shake my head at her, amused. Arrow, who was recently elected the club's vice president, is Anna's man. I happen to think that they're great for each other. As long as Anna is happy, then so am I, and it's clear that she's over the moon about Arrow. Feisty and strong as she is, Anna is like a happy cat when he's around, and he's the same. He adores her and would kill anyone who tried to hurt her. I wish I had that.

Anna's brother, Rake, is also a club member, which is how she met Arrow and I guess how I ended up here.

The men in the Wind Dragons MC are intimidating, but they've only ever been nice to me, albeit a little overbearing. I know that they love Anna, and as her best friend, they also look out for me. I like to think of myself as extended family.

Anna suggested to Faye that I would be a great nanny and, more importantly, that I could be trusted. She thinks I need the money, so when Faye asked me, I accepted. Really, I just couldn't think of a reason to refuse. But then, the more I thought about it, the more I wanted to do it. Faye needed someone, and I liked her and wanted to help. It also gave me more time with Anna. Before I was Clover's nanny, I usually saw her only once a week or so. So now I can see her more often, while getting paid to be here. Win-win.

And then there was Tracker. As much as I wanted to deny it, I was looking forward to seeing more of him, even if only from a distance.

Arrow stands, putting Clover down on the couch. "Gotta go, princess."

Clover pouts. "So soon? Why?"

"Hey, I'm still here," Tracker calls out, mock hurt in his tone.

Clover turns to Tracker. "I know, Uncle Tracker, but you don't have candy."

The two men both laugh, and I join in.

"I have to go and meet Anna," he says, patting her on the head. "I'll see you tomorrow."

Arrow's brown eyes then turn to me. "You okay, Lana?"

I nod. "I'm fine."

Why wouldn't I be? Okay, so I look out of place here. I *am* out of place here. My black hair is up in a messy bun and I have on my reading glasses, no makeup, jeans, and a loose black tank top. Truth be told, I usually look better than this on a day-to-day basis, but I'm proving to myself that I do not care if Tracker finds me attractive or not.

Nope. I do not care.

Not one bit.

And neither does he.

"Call me if you need anything," Arrow murmurs, eyes darting between Tracker and me before leaving.

"I'm here if she needs anything," I hear Tracker say to him in a hard voice.

I'm pretty sure I hear Arrow mutter, "That's what I'm afraid of," as he walks out the door. With Arrow gone, Clover runs to sit next to Tracker, taking his hand in hers. Standing there awkwardly, I shift on my feet, no idea what to do with myself. With no option but to look at him, I let my eyes take him in.

Today his shoulder-length blond hair is tied up in a bun, a *much* nicer bun than the one I am sporting, and it looks sexy on him. But then again, he always looks sexy. He has a certain appeal to him that I just can't escape. And I know I'm not the only one. His blue eyes are steady on me, and slightly narrowed.

I wish I didn't find the stubble on his face so attractive, but I do. The man belongs on a magazine cover and is well aware of his charm. He's also a badass, dangerous biker—and the contradiction is extremely appealing.

"Clover," Tracker says. "Why don't you go get some coloring books and crayons?"

"Can I use one of the new ones you got me?" she asks in excitement.

"Uh, yeah!" he says, trying to match her excitement. She whoops, jumping off the couch and rushing away in search of her things.

Tracker turns to me. "Sit down, Lana," he commands quietly.

I look around the room before I sit down on the couch opposite him. "Okay."

"I'm not gonna bite," he says, flashing his sharp white teeth at me in a wolfish grin.

I think he does bite. And I want him to bite me.

Shit, I'm so screwed.

"What was that thought?" he asks, amusement written all over his too-handsome-for-his-own-good face.

"Nothing," I say with a casual shrug. I need to stop being so expressive. "Are you going to be here all day?"

Maybe I'll take Clover out somewhere. No point sitting here and being teased with something I'll never have.

"Yeah," he replies, tilting his head to the side and studying me. "I live here."

"Right," I reply, shifting on my seat.

"How is school going?" he asks, leaning back on the couch. I'm still getting my business degree. After high school, I'd worked and helped my mom instead of jumping straight into college. Because of this, I'm twenty-five and still in college. I don't mind though, I'm just happy to be studying something.

"I'm on break now," I say. "Just started."

He nods, eyes widening. "Right. Anna told me that; I forgot." He flicks his tongue over his bottom lip, and I can't help but stare at it.

"So you're going to be here every day watching Clover?"

I shake my head. "Not every day. Four days a week. While I'm on break anyway."

I honestly don't know why Faye wants me to look after Clover here. There are always people going in and out. Anna told me that during the day while Clover is here, the clubhouse is a family environment and everyone is well behaved, but when night falls, all bets are off. It still doesn't explain why Faye doesn't have me watch Clover at her own house. It would be safer and quieter, in my opinion, but Faye's the boss. I worry that maybe she doesn't fully trust me yet and wants there to be other people around just in case.

Visiting the clubhouse did have some perks, obviously. I can stare at Tracker when he isn't looking, sad as it sounds, and so far I find myself doing it at every opportunity. Anna is also here more often than not, so I'm looking forward to spending more time with her.

"That works," Tracker replies. I don't miss the way his gaze lowers to my chest, then lower, over the curve of my thighs. The tension in the room suddenly spikes. I quickly look away and am relieved when Clover comes back into the room, books and case in hand. She sits next to me and shows me all the different coloring books Tracker has bought her. I can feel Tracker's eyes on me, but I stay focused on her. Or try to, at least.

"I want to play a game," Clover says after fifteen or so minutes of coloring silently.

"What a great idea!" I blurt out. Tracker smirks, clearly aware of just how tense I am around him.

"How about hide-and-seek?" he replies, glancing down at the little girl. "You go hide and I'll come find you."

Clover grins, and I watch her dart off the couch and into the hallway. I look back at Tracker to see his gaze steady on me. "I want to ask you something."

"What?" I ask, pushing my glasses up on the bridge of my nose.

I shift in my seat again as he lazily peruses my body from head to toe once more, his lips kicking up at the corner. "You free after you finish up here?"

Am I free? I open my mouth, then close it. "Why?"

"I want to take you for a ride," he says, licking his lower lip.

"A ride?" I repeat slowly. My mind jumps to dirty things.

He nods, eyes flashing with amusement. "Yes. I want to take you out on the back of my bike."

His intense stare lets me know that this means something important. I don't understand much about his MC lifestyle, except bits and pieces I've seen for myself or what Anna has told me. Excitement flutters in my stomach at the thought of my arms wrapped around him, my hair blowing in the wind. But then I think about Allie, and the butterflies exit, my stomach plummeting. This is always the issue with Tracker.

He isn't single. Even when he says he is, he isn't. She is always there. Sometimes on the sidelines, sometimes in the forefront, but nevertheless, *there*.

Why does it have to be her? Anyone but her. I am not about

to share him, or any man. I want a man who only has eyes for me. A simple enough request, I'd think, but proving hard to find. The fact that I have a hard time trusting men doesn't help either. I am one of those suffer-in-silence, keep-everything-to-themselves type of people. I hardly ever put myself out there, which is probably why I'm still single.

"What about Allie?" I ask, curious as to what his answer will be.

Anna told me he's on and off again with her, and it's been this way for years. To me, it sounds messy. A complication I don't need or want, no matter how drawn to him I am.

I want him, badly. But Tracker is bad news. I think about him. I dream about him. I fantasize about him. But I keep my distance. Why? Because I'm smart enough to know that we have no future. My head tells me one thing—stay away—but farther south says something else—invite him in. I get wet just at the thought of him. He has that much control over me. The wanting, will it ever end? I sure as fuck hope so.

The reality is that he probably has that effect on most women. Including Allie—that's why I do what I can to discourage his flirting and persistence, which is getting more and more frequent and which I'm having a harder time refusing.

Tracker scowls, a look of displeasure entering his dreamy eyes. "Allie and I are over. I'm not seeing anyone right now."

But for how long? I don't want to be caught in the cross fire of their relationship. While he may insist that it's over with them, it's clear she doesn't think that, which suggests he's leading her on. Why would I want a guy like that? I am worth more than that.

I am at war with myself. I can only hope and pray that my mind wins over my body.

"Okay," I say slowly. "Ummm . . ."

I don't know what to say. The rejection is hard to form on my lips. The sounds didn't want to come out, my body betraying me once more.

His eyes and mouth soften, as if he senses my inner turmoil. "I thought maybe you and I could—"

Could what? Have sex?

Did he think I was a sure thing?

I mean, he had to know I was attracted to him, right? I can't stop the excitement I feel at the thought of being with him. Just thinking about his touch makes me blush and my sensuality come alive. I want to explore that side of me, with him.

Then something occurs to me. Does he want me to be his rebound girl? The thought of that hurts. As lame as it sounds, I don't want to be his rebound, I want to be his forever girl. His wife. His old lady, as I've heard Faye being called.

Yeah, I'm living in a dream world. And if Tracker knew my thoughts he would run to the other side of the country. I don't even know if he does commitment. From what I heard, he wasn't always faithful to Allie, another strike against him. Cheating is unforgivable to me. William was the first and only cheating scum I will have anything to do with. If Tracker's okay with sleeping around on a girl who cared about him—even if she is a massive bitch—then he's not someone I want to waste time on.

"I don't think so, Tracker," I reply before he can finish his sentence, looking down as I speak. The words hurt coming out, because really all I want to scream is *yes!* My resolve hardens and I push those thoughts away.

"Why not?" he asks quietly. "I've seen how you look at me."

Yep, he knows. Of course he knows.

No wonder he thinks I'd get on the back of his bike just like that.

He knows.

And I can't believe he just said that. Red-cheeked, I choose to ignore his comment and point toward the hallway. "Go and find her."

He stands, but then crouches in front of me, his hands resting on both of my thighs. "We would be so fuckin' good together, you know that, right?"

I know. We would be. While it lasted anyway.

Then I'd be left to deal with the ramifications of giving in to him.

A broken heart.

"Yeah, but for how long?" I reply, forcing a smile that doesn't reach my eyes. "I don't want to be just another woman to you, Tracker."

He studies me, eyes flashing. "I don't think I'd put in this much effort for a one-night stand, Lana."

I think about that. What am I to him? Just a game? I don't know. I wish I could know what was going on in his head, but either way I'm not ready to risk my heart with this man. I need someone I can trust, someone who I know will be faithful and loyal to me. When I stay silent, he sighs.

"Luckily I'm a patient man," he murmurs, sliding a finger down my cheek with a gentleness that surprises me. He stands and calls out, "You better have found a good spot, Clover, because I'm coming."

I try and hide my grin as I watch him roam the clubhouse, looking for Clover. She must have hidden in the kitchen, because I hear laughter—his low chuckle and her high-pitched squeals—coming from there. For a second, I imagine that this was *our* house, and he was playing with *our* daughter.

Aaaand that's why I'm a good writer. I have a huge imagination.

Shit.

"This place is huge," I comment, walking around the clubhouse. I've been here before but was never given a full tour. I stop at a wall full of mug shots. "Keeping it classy?"

Tracker laughs with Clover on his shoulders. "Wall of fame."

I look at his. "You look really young here."

He nods. "I was nineteen. It was just for fighting. I'm not a drug lord or anything."

"Good to know," I reply at the same time Clover asks, "What's a drug lord?"

I glance at Tracker with wide eyes. He stops and says, "I didn't say that."

"Yes you did!"

He lifts her off his shoulders and starts to tickle her. She soon forgets her question. He nods in approval and continues walking with me outside, to the back of the large compound, with Clover holding his hand. There's a grassy area there, and Tracker points to it. "We should sit there and have lunch."

"A picnic!" Clover calls out. "I love picnics."

I look to Tracker. "What are we eating on this picnic?"

He pulls out his phone. "Whatever you want."

"Who are you calling?" I ask in suspicion. Was he getting

some random woman to bring us food? I know that the club has groupies, because Anna told me about them. Apparently Rake is the one who gives them the most attention, but that doesn't mean Tracker doesn't. The thought makes me seriously angry.

"A prospect."

Oh, well then.

"Prospects do lunch runs?" I ask curiously. I don't really understand everyone's role in an MC. I know there is a hierarchy but have no idea what it is.

"They do whatever we tell them to do," Tracker says firmly. Yikes. That doesn't sound like fun. Why would anyone voluntarily sign up to do that?

"How does someone become a prospect?" I ask.

He studies me. "Why are you asking? Do you want to join?"

I laugh at his teasing. "I'm curious."

"Afraid I can't tell you that," he says quietly. "But I can tell you it isn't pleasant."

"Then why do they want to do it?" I ask.

He smiles then, and it reaches his eyes, almost blinding me with its force. "We're a brotherhood. A family. We have each other's backs no matter what. There's no judgment here, only acceptance. Who wouldn't want that?"

"I heard somewhere that the prospects have to fight to prove they're worthy and that's how they get accepted."

He smiles, looking amused, but says nothing.

"How about some sandwiches?" I suggest, changing the subject. "Clover likes ham and cheese."

"Okay, anything else?" he asks, pressing more buttons.

I ask Clover and she says she wants sushi. I think she's been hanging around Anna too long, and Tracker says the exact same thing.

"Don't you have work?" I ask, leaning back on my palms.

"Not today, I don't," he replies.

Thirty minutes later, we're sitting on a blanket outside, enjoying the warmth and eating the sushi and sandwiches Blade dropped off. Blade is one of the newer prospects, and Anna told me Blade is his given name, not a club name, which I found interesting. Clover is playing with her dolls and drinking a juice box. Tracker makes conversation, asking me questions about myself and hanging on my every word.

"So why did you choose business?" he asks, popping a tuna roll into his mouth.

"I'd like to own my own business one day," I say. "But it's broad enough that I can keep my options open."

He nods, looking at Clover. "Maybe you could open your own day care."

Laughter bubbles out of me. "No, I don't think so. I like kids, and they like me, but I don't think I could run a day care or anything like that. I'd go crazy."

"Really?" he asks, sounding surprised. "You're great with her."

"Thank you," I say, ducking my head. "She makes it kind of easy. I don't think all kids are as cool as her."

Clover gets up to chase a butterfly, and Tracker takes advantage of her absence, lowering his tone. "I don't think you'll get another job as a nanny though," he states, eyes raking over me.

"What? Why not?" I ask.

"Because you're too beautiful," he says with a laugh. "What woman would want you around her husband all day?"

"Faye," I point out.

"Yeah, but Sin would never cheat, and besides, we know your character," he says. "We all know you're a good girl."

"And how do you know that?" I can't stop myself from asking.

Tracker just smiles, slowly, his eyes crinkling. "I know women, Lana. Plus Anna never shuts up about you. You've been around us for a while now, we're not strangers. I know you're a good woman."

"Define *good*," I reply to him. "There are plenty of good women who like being free and open . . . sexually."

He nods. "I know that. Good to know that you do too. But not all women think of others in every equation. Just like not all men are good, not all women are either. I wasn't talking about sexually, necessarily, you brought that up yourself."

I had, hadn't I?

"Right," I mutter.

He glances at me curiously. "You're fuckin' cute, you know that, right?"

I look down at the grass between my fingers and pull out a few blades, avoiding his eyes. "Thank you."

His compliments embarrass me, but I like hearing them and I like how they make me feel.

"Don't thank me, thank your mother," he teases, then lifts my chin up with his finger. "I assume you got your looks from her?"

I move my face out of his hold and keep my eyes on Clover, who is now playing nearby. "I do look like her a little."

"I like it when your eyes stay on me," he says quietly, which brings my gaze straight back to him. In his eyes I see the honesty in his statement. He likes my eyes on him.

"Why?" I ask.

He raises his eyebrow. "You know why. You're right next to me, so don't pretend you can't feel it."

Was he always so forward?

"I have no idea what you're talking about," I lie.

He makes a sound in the back of his throat. "Don't lie to me, Lana. The pull between us is so strong it's only a matter of time before I'm deep inside you."

My eyes widen. "Tracker, you can't just say shit like that!"

"I just did," he replies smugly. "You best get used to it. I tend to say whatever the fuck I'm thinking."

"I'm starting to see that," I reply dryly. "Nothing embarrasses you, does it?"

He shrugs. "Don't care what many people think, and the ones who I do care about, take me as I am."

I smile. "Good answer. I like that."

"Good. Now tell me something about you that I don't already know."

"How do I know what you do and don't know already?" I fire back.

He glances at Clover and replies, "Exactly. It has to be something not many people know. A secret."

I look down at the grass, thinking. "The first time I saw you, I thought you belonged on the cover of a magazine."

I look up to see him smiling widely. "Don't know about that, but fuckin' happy you like what you see. When I first saw you, I thought you were beautiful. Not my usual type, but striking with all that dark hair and eyes, petite but banging body. Innocence radiated from you. You looked to Anna, and I could tell right then how close the two of you were. You aren't like the usual women I see around the club."

"Is that a good thing or a bad thing?" I ask quietly.

He just grins. "Yet to be seen."

I don't know what to say to that, but luckily Clover interrupts.

"I'm thirsty!" she says.

I hand her a juice box, helping her open the straw and stick it in the hole. "There you go."

"Thanks, Lana," she says, then looks to Tracker. "Uncle Tracker, Mama says you like Lana."

Tracker chuckles, while I feel my face heat at her admission.

"Is that what she said to you? Or what you overheard?" he asks Clover.

She sighs, guilty as charged. "I overheard."

Tracker throws his head back and laughs. "You're trouble, Clover, just like your mom. And you can tell her I said that."

"I will," she tells him with wide, innocent eyes, then returns to her playing.

"Fuck, she's cute," Tracker says, and I can hear the smile in his voice. "Do you want kids one day?"

I nod. "Sure. Two would be nice."

"Two," he repeats, tilting his head to the side. "I can work with that."

Wait, did he mean . . . ?

Deciding to choose my battles and leave that comment alone, I talk to Tracker for another hour until he gets a phone call and has to leave.

When I realize I don't want him to go, I mentally chastise

myself. Keeping my distance is going to be hard, but it's something that needs to be done.

"Do you want to go inside and read a book?" I ask Clover, packing up the blanket.

"Okay," she replies, rubbing her eyes. "Maybe we should nap too."

I love this kid.

THREE

WHEN I arrive at the clubhouse the next day, I'm dressed in a cuter outfit and annoyed that I put in the effort. I'd gone with my favorite pair of jeans and a strapless top, and my hair is down and brushed. Underneath my glasses, my eyelashes are coated in a thin layer of mascara and lined with a little eyeliner. I probably should wear my contacts, but I hate trying to put them in. I keep poking myself in the eye every time I try. Besides, I think my glasses suit me.

Faye is feeding Clover breakfast in the kitchen when I walk in. She looks up when I enter, smiling. "'Morning, Lana."

"Good morning," I tell the president's beautiful wife, then look down at Clover. "'Morning, Clover. Don't you look pretty today?"

She is wearing a pink princess dress and has a crown on her head. "Thank you, Lana!"

When I turn my head I see a book left on the countertop, the cover a dark gray. On it is an attractive shirtless man. I pick it up and examine it, goose bumps appearing on my flesh. "You like this book?"

Faye beams. "Yes! Have you read it? I'm halfway through and can't put it down. Zada Ryan is quickly becoming one of my favorite authors."

"No, I haven't." I straight out lie because I have no idea what else to say.

"You should," she says, wide-eyed. She steps away from Clover and whispers to me, "I can't believe some of the shit that's happening in the novel right now. And damn, the woman knows how to write a sex scene. I even replayed a few of the scenes with my husband. Trust me, he wasn't complaining one bit."

I feel my face heating at the thought.

Oh wow. A little too much information.

"Oh," is all I manage to say. "Sounds . . . fun."

Faye laughs in response. "The men are so dominant. It's hot. And the storylines are always captivating and unique. Do you read much?"

I nod, knowing this is a question I can answer. "Yeah, at least a book a week."

"We should start a book club," she says, nodding her head with her eyes narrowed. "Biker chicks book club. It's going to be a big thing, I can tell."

I'm not a biker chick, but I didn't bother to point that out.

"We should read a few biker books and dissect them for their accuracy," she says, grinning. "I never read them because most of them are so off base. So I stick to contemporary romances. I like the ones where the heroine is snarky and full of sass, making the hero put up with a lot of shit."

I purse my lips to hold in my laughter. "Does Sin put up with a lot of shit?"

She smiles, and it reaches her eyes. "You have no idea."

"You two are so cute!" I blurt out.

Amusement flashes on her face. "Never been called cute before, at least not to my face. I like you, Lana."

"I like you too," I reply, glancing down shyly.

"Dex—or Sin as everyone here calls him—and I grew up together. We had a one-night stand, and I ended up getting pregnant with Clover that night," she says, smirking. "Been harassing his life ever since."

My eyes widen. "That sounds like quite a story."

"You have no idea," she repeats.

"Lana!" Clover yells, demanding our attention. "How come you're not dressed up like a princess?"

I glance at Faye, confused. Why would I be dressed like a princess?

"Today is Emily's party, remember?" Clover adds, clapping. "That's why I'm a princess. I wanted to dress like a biker princess, but Daddy said no."

Right, shit. I forgot about that. Today I was taking her to a kid's birthday party.

Biker princess? I wasn't touching that one.

Faye laughs, bringing my gaze back to her. "Forgot, did you? The invitation with the address is on the fridge. You just have to go and sit there while they play, then bring her home. You okay with that?"

I nod. "Sure. Sounds easy enough."

Faye kisses her daughter. "I wish I could be there with you today, Clover, but I know you and Lana will have a good time."

"I know you have to work sometimes, Mommy," Clover replies.

"I promise: next party, I'll be the one to take you," Faye tells her daughter. "The present is on top of the TV, Lana. Call me if you have any problems. And good luck."

"We'll be fine, won't we, Clover?"

Clover grins in response.

"Here," Faye says, handing me the book. "Read it. You'll love it!"

"Oh, that's okay," I say, trying to hand it back to her. "You're still reading it."

"No, no, I insist. This is my second time reading it," she says with a laugh. "Return it when you're done. You won't regret it!"

I awkwardly take the book with a smile, feeling incredibly uncomfortable.

Mother and daughter say 'bye once more, while I tidy up the kitchen a little.

"Oh, and Lana—?" Faye calls out as she grabs her handbag. She's a lawyer and is dressed in a professional yet sexy black suit that hugs her curves. I can see why Sin chose her over all other women. "One of the men will drive you there."

"Oh, I can drive, it's no problem," I tell her instantly.

Faye shrugs, her eyes taking on an amused glint. "He insisted."

She waves and exits through the front door, leaving me standing there.

"Who insisted?" I say to myself.

"I did," Tracker says, walking up to me dressed in nothing but a pair of boxer shorts and a sleepy grin.

My eyes flare as they take in the glory that is his body.

Wow. I mean . . . wow.

Rather than being bulky, he is lean and sculpted. Perfectly muscular. Covered in tattoos, the largest begins at his shoulder and wraps around his right pec. The artistic eagle looks as though it's swooping down on its prey, hunger and death in its eyes. Smoke and clouds surround it, working with his body to create texture and dimension. It's captivating. Smaller tattoos mark his neck, and he has a half sleeve that extends from his wrist to his elbow.

I want to trace every one of those tattoos with my tongue.

"Ummm," I mutter, now focusing on his sexy V. "'Morning." Delicious.

"'Morning, Lana," he says, amusement lacing his voice.

I look up, coming out of my reverie, blushing that I've been caught staring. "Hi."

"You wanna come give me a morning hug and kiss?"

Before I can open my mouth to object, he adds, "On the cheek."

"No," I say. It takes all my willpower to resist him. "I don't think that's a good idea."

He quirks his eyebrow. I think he's genuinely surprised. I mean, of course he is. How many women would say no to *that*? Just crazy old me.

"It's just a hug, Lana."

I can tell that he's daring me. If I say no, he will know that I'm afraid I won't be able to control myself. But if I do embrace him, I'm afraid I won't be able to control myself either. My stubbornness wins.

Closing the space between us, I wrap my arms around his bare waist and rest my head on his warm chest. I'm awkward and tense at first, but my body relaxes against him. It comes naturally. He kisses my hair and I sigh. Starting to feel a little too comfortable in this position, I pull away. I stand there in silence for a moment, shifting uncomfortably.

"That wasn't so bad, was it?" he says with a smile.

"It wasn't completely unbearable."

He lets out a bark of laughter.

"Heard we're on a birthday mission today," he murmurs, blue eyes soft and sleepy.

"Heard you volunteered," I reply with a sardonic brow.

"Faye needs to keep her mouth shut," he says with no heat in his voice. "I just thought it would be a good idea if someone tagged along. Made sure you didn't get into trouble."

I roll my eyes. "It's Anna who gets into trouble, not me."

"We'll see," he says with a boyish grin. "You get the princess sorted while I take a quick shower."

I push up my glasses, images of him in the shower flashing through my dirty mind. "O-okay."

Real smooth, Lana. I hate how nervous I get around him.

Another knowing grin and he heads to his bathroom.

Of course I stand there and watch his bare back as he leaves. Some women like abs, some like nice eyes. I like those things too, but I have a thing for a sexy, strong, muscular back.

And Tracker's back is hot. Broad, tanned, toned, *and* tattooed.

The intricate dragon tattoo staring at me is fierce and symbolic.

The Wind Dragons MC.

A reminder that he's one of them.

And who am I?

Anna's friend. Clover's nanny.

I don't belong on the back of a bike. I lead a quieter, simpler life. One with privacy. But I also have a secret. I run my hand over the cover of the book Faye had handed me.

When they say it's the quiet ones you should look out for, I think they're referring to me.

People think I'm a prude, virginal, even innocent. And maybe I am, but my mind isn't.

It is uninhibited, imaginative, and creative.

Which is how I became Zada Ryan, bestselling erotic romance author.

No one but my mother knows I am Zada Ryan, not even Anna. I started writing in high school after she left, and I never stopped. I wrote about sex. A lot. My mind would run wild, and all my fantasies, thoughts, and dreams would end up on paper. I wasn't a virgin, but I wasn't exactly experienced, so I did a lot of research. I read books; I watched movies; I studied couples out in public. I'm always paying attention to those around me. I'm not embarrassed of my career; I just want to remain anonymous. It's a secret side of me that only I know about—it's mine, and I don't want to share it.

When I sent my manuscript to an agent, I never thought they'd want me. But they did. When a publisher made me an offer, I was over the moon. The money was amazing, but I would have done it for free. It was my dream. I never imagined my books would become so big. I had so many other books already written that the publisher published one of my books every other month for the last year and a half.

I paid off my mom's house. I bought myself a car. Mom and

I always struggled with money when I was growing up, so I can't describe how good it feels to be able not to worry about finances, and to help my mom after everything she's done for me. She sacrificed a lot as a single mother, working hard so I could have everything I needed, and I wanted to repay her in some way.

I didn't have much left after that, but that was perfectly fine with me. When Anna suggested I take the job as Clover's nanny, I couldn't say no without telling her how I was now earning my money. I'm currently not on any deadlines, other than those set by myself, and I really had nothing better to do with my time. The truth is, I have a bad case of writer's block. I wanted a new book idea, but nothing was coming to me, so I thought stepping back and doing something else might help. I had no qualifications or anything like that. I didn't even know many kids, but I liked them and they seemed to like me. Plus, I was responsible. So I googled what needs a girl Clover's age would have and went from there.

Besides, making an effort to get out of the house was a good idea for me, because all I normally do when I'm not at school is stay at home writing. I don't really have any friends, apart from Anna, and I've lived in this town my whole life. It sounds sad, but I'm an introvert and usually enjoy my own company. Having Anna back though has made me consider getting my own place now and branching out. It's time.

"Lana?"

I almost forgot Clover is even here. Some nanny I am. "Hi, cutie."

"I put on the TV," she says, pointing to the living room. "I am watching *Adventure Time*. Want to watch it with me?"

"We can watch until Tracker gets ready, but then we have to go, okay?"

She scowls. "Why is Uncle Tracker coming?"

My eyes widen. I know she loves Tracker, so I'm taken aback at her cute little fierce expression. "Why, don't you want him to come?"

She steps closer, placing her chubby little hand on mine and lowering her voice. "There's a boy there that I like. The boys don't get to be princesses; they get to be pirates. Uncle Tracker will scare him away. He told me so."

I purse my lips to contain my laughter. "You're a little young for boys, Clover, honey, don't you think?" I give her a wink. "In ten years you're going to drive them all crazy."

She sighs, her plump cheeks puffing in frustration. "Daddy says all boys will be too scared to come near me."

Her daddy is right. I don't think any boys or men will want to date a MC president's daughter, unless they are stupid. Sin is scary as hell. Not to mention everyone else in the MC— Arrow, Tracker, Rake, Irish, Ronan, Trace, Vinnie, and the rest of them.

I wonder who she'll end up with one day. I hope it's someone worthy of her.

"Well, you have a long time before you need to worry about that, I think," I tell her, not knowing what else to say.

"I guess," she says before giving me a cheeky grin. "Plus, Mommy will be on my side!"

I laugh, agreeing with her, before I usher her toward the living room. "Let's watch."

We watch TV for about fifteen minutes before Tracker shows up, smelling fresh and dressed in dark jeans and a white T-shirt.

His hair is damp, looking darker than it usually is, and pulled back in a bun.

He lifts his chin. "Ready when you are."

I allow myself to gawk at him for a moment. How am I supposed to put up my defenses against a man who looks so good, smells so good, wants me, and is so charming and easy to talk to?

I drag my eyes away from him. "Let's do it. Looks like I'm going to a kid's birthday party with the MC princess and a bad-ass biker," I say, then pause. "Never thought I'd ever have to say that sentence."

Tracker's lips quirk. "We don't want the MC princess to be late, do we?"

I glance between the two of them, sigh, then lead the way.

"What do you mean you don't like the way that boy looked at her?" I ask incredulously. Clover was right, Tracker should have stayed home. He's acting like an overprotective, paranoid father.

"You didn't see how he was lookin' at her?" Tracker asks, eyes narrowed. "He's older than her too, why the fuck is she hanging out with a dude older than her?"

I roll my eyes. "He's seven, Tracker. Seven."

He crosses his arms over his chest, his eyes not leaving Clover. "Yeah, well, she's only six. Where's the kid's dad? Maybe I'll scare the shit out of him just in case. Make sure he keeps his boy in line."

"In case of what? You're being ridiculous!" I place my small hand on his biceps. "Let them be; they're kids. You're overreacting. Now, I'm going to get some food. Do you want me to make a plate for you, too?"

His gaze leaves Clover then and focuses steady on me. "I'd like that."

"Okay," I say quietly, standing up and walking to the table where all the food is set out. Grabbing two paper plates, I'm placing some cold cuts on them when someone stands next to me. Raising my eyes, I smile politely at the older gentleman while continuing to load the plates.

"Hello," the man says. He's tall, well built, and has the look of a man who was very good-looking in his youth. His salt-and-pepper hair is carefully styled, and he's dressed with casual sophistication in slacks and a white button-up. "I'm Dan. Zen's father."

Zen was the kid playing with Clover.

"I'm Lana," I say, smiling and offering him my hand. "I'm here with Clover. Her mom had to work," I explain.

He nods, turning his body to me. "Yes, Faye told me she is a lawyer. Must be hard to juggle work and being a mother."

"That's why she has me," I add, grinning.

"Are you single?" Dan asks, staring at me boldly, his eyes unblinking.

Oh, wow.

I chew on my bottom lip. Yes, I am single, but I don't want him to be interested. I'm not really attracted to him, to be honest. He isn't my type, and all I have on my mind is the biker whose food I am currently getting.

"I guess so," I mumble, hating being put on the spot, then cringe, glancing up at him apologetically. "Not the most articulate answer."

"Not exactly," he chuckles, tilting his head thoughtfully. "Does that mean you're available or not?"

"Yes to being single, no to being available," I say, blushing and looking away for a second, before daring to glance back at his face. "I'm not with anyone, but I'm not looking for anything right now."

Although I'm flattered, I don't really want his attentions. I don't want to be mean either, or hurt his feelings. I'm sure he's genuinely nice and perfect for many other women out there, just not me.

He smiles knowingly. "That's when they find you, when you're not looking."

I have no idea what to say. I'm about to reply when a large hand wraps around my waist. I know it's Tracker by the smell of leather and faint spicy cologne.

"She's taken," he practically growls. "Extremely fuckin' taken."

I swallow hard, hating myself for loving Tracker's possessiveness.

It doesn't mean anything, I tell myself over and over.

Does it?

He's made it clear he wants me, but he seems like a man who wants a lot of women, gets them, conquers them, and then moves on to the next. How could I not get attached? Hell, I already am. I'm going to get hurt, I know it.

It's inevitable.

"I see," Dan replies, straightening. "You can't blame a man for trying."

He smiles awkwardly, more of a grimace, then leaves.

I feel bad for the guy as he glances back with a scared look on his face. Tracker is intimidating, with his big arm around me and a scowl darkening his features, so I don't blame him.

I step out of Tracker's arms and give him a dirty look he ignores, instead picking up our plates and walking back to our seats, me trailing behind him. He waits for me to sit down, places a plate gently on my lap, then sits down himself. I don't know why, but I find his actions charming. Chivalrous, even. He eats one of the small sandwiches in one bite, then grabs a chicken leg.

"What was that?" I ask, nibbling on a sandwich, then putting it back down on my plate.

"What was what?" he asks, eyes back on Clover, his own plate of food quickly disappearing.

I sigh, suddenly not feeling very hungry. "Never mind."

"Did you want him?" he asks me suddenly. I lift my face from my plate to look into his eyes.

"No, of course not," I tell him. "That's not the point."

I don't really know what the point is anymore, besides the fact that I am both turned on and annoyed.

"Good. Then we don't have anything to discuss," he says calmly, picking up the gummy worms on his plate and casually putting them on mine.

"You don't like gummy worms?" I ask, biting the head off a soft blue-and-yellow one.

"Nope," he says, licking his lips. "Not a fan. I like watching you eat them though."

I look away from his heated gaze, ignoring his quiet chuckle.

I shyly take another bite, not looking at him. He is a lot. A lot to take in. A lot of man.

"You're cute when you get all shy on me," he says, and I can hear the amusement in his tone. "Your cheeks go a pretty pink. It suits you."

He really is free with his compliments. Is he like this with every woman he wants? I want to believe that I'm different, but I'm not naïve enough to think so. Or at least I don't think I am.

"Glad to amuse," I reply, taking another bite and chewing slowly. I shift on my seat, feeling his gaze on me. Tracker always makes me squirm. With just a look, he can turn me inside out. How does he do that? It isn't fair.

"You more than amuse, Lana. You intrigue. Can't remember the last time I paid this much attention to a woman," he says, sounding surprised himself.

I cut my eyes to him and say dryly, "You really need to work on your pickup lines."

He chuckles, eyes sparkling with humor. "Pickup lines are for men who need to talk shit to get a woman in bed. I tell the truth. Say what you want, but at least I'm real. With me, what you see is what you get. I don't have to lie to get pussy."

"Can you not say *pussy*?" I hiss. "We're at a kid's party." I glance around, making sure no one heard. People probably think we are the worst babysitters ever.

Tracker looks down at me like I'm the most interesting thing he's ever seen. "You're so different from Anna."

I eye him. What did he mean by that? In a good or bad way?

"How so?" I ask.

"You're quiet and shy; she's not. She's blunt. Edgy. You're sweet and gentle, but strong too. It's a mix I can't seem to get enough of."

"Opposites attract," I reply, addressing his original statement. "Anna and I just get along really well somehow. She's a good friend. She's also sweet and gentle—everyone has different sides to them. There's more to me than being a little shy.

Yes, I can take a while to open up, but once you know me I don't shut up."

"That's true. I didn't mean to put you in a box, I know you're more complex than that." He pauses. "Anna is very protective of you," he says, eyes scanning my face. "Which tells me a lot."

"Like what?" I ask, interested in what he has to say.

He rubs his palm down his jawline, and I can hear the stubble rasp against his touch. I stifle a sudden urge to run my cheek along the same path. "If you inspire such loyalty, it tells me you're a good woman. Anna isn't the type of woman to just stick up for anyone. And she fuckin' adores you. Claws out, ready to swipe at just the mention of your name. She loves me and we're pretty close friends, but for you she will get up in my face ready to fight twelve rounds. I think you're the only one she'll do that for."

I smile warmly at the thought of Anna always trying to protect me. "She's my best friend. We have each other's backs no matter what. If she needs me, I'll be there and vice versa. Everyone needs an Anna in their lives, or at least someone they can trust. You have your brothers; I have Anna."

"You have my brothers too," he murmurs. "The club will always look after you."

I smile. "See, Anna just keeps on looking after me."

He nods his head slowly. "That's because you're a damn good woman."

I smile awkwardly, not quite sure what to say to that, while glancing back over at Clover to make sure she's all right. When I see her laughing and playing with some other kids, I turn my attention back to Tracker.

"And you're good with kids," he continues. "You have that

perfect mix of gorgeous, down-to-earth, and outright fucking sexy. Wifey material. Old-lady material. The type of woman who gets in deep."

My eyes widen at his description. "And you got all that from the few times we've been together?" Is this how he really sees me? I don't think any man has seen me as the type of woman who "gets in deep." He thinks I'm outright sexy? I must be hallucinating.

"I've been watching you for a while, Lana. It's not like this thing just formed overnight," he continues, cutting into my thoughts.

"What thing?" I ask, still stuck on his compliments.

He gestures between the two of us. "This . . . thing. Connection. Obsession. Fascination. Whatever the hell you want to call it."

Obsession? My head is spinning with the things coming out of his mouth. Was he serious about this? I knew there was obsession on my side, but from his? It's clear as day that he wants me, but I'm not sure about his plans for me down the road. He's not thinking love and marriage, that's for sure. Dating? How casual would he want to be? Could I do casual with him, when I was already in so deep and we haven't even been together? Can I even trust his words? I like to think so. I know he's a good man, but I've also heard stories about all the men in the MC. They aren't exactly known for being angels, and I'd be stupid not to take that into consideration. And then there is Allie. Is it really over? What does he feel for her now? So many questions!

It is the standard issue, my heart fighting with my head. Could I sleep with him and be okay with losing him after that? Knowing him, he'd ruin me for other men. I just can't win.

"Lust at first sight?" I suggest, my eyes roaming boldly over his body, trying to lighten the conversation. It works.

He throws his head back and laughs. "Yeah, there's definitely some of that. Every time I see you I get hard as a rock. It's quite fuckin' inconvenient, really."

"Tracker!" I groan, rubbing my forehead with my palm. "Children's party, remember?"

"Well, that fucker tried to pick you up at this party," he reminds me, sounding amused. "That wasn't children's party behavior. Does he come to these parties to pick up single mothers or something? Seems like an asshole to me."

"Fuck that guy," I blurt out, making him laugh even harder. His shoulders shake with the effort, and everyone around us turns to stare.

"Fuckin' hell, Lana, we're at a kid's function. Watch your mouth," he says, shaking his head.

My face hurts from smiling. I scan the party, my smile dropping. "Did that little girl just push Clover?"

I look around, gearing for a fight, my fingernails digging into my palms. "That's it. Where's that girl's mom?" She was going to get a stern talking-to.

Tracker's body shakes with laughter, he tries to contain it but he can't. "So it's okay for you to act like this but not me? Fuck it. You go after the girl's mom, I'll go after that kid's dad. Let's show everyone they should know better than to mess with our Clover."

"Oh," I say, my eyes still on them. "Never mind. She didn't push her, they're playing tag."

Tracker's eyes crinkle. "Common mistake."

The two of us laugh some more.

"No wonder Anna likes hanging around you," I say, puffing out a breath. "You're fun to be around."

"I try and make the best of every situation," he replies, shrugging his broad shoulders. "You only live once, right?"

I nod my head. "You're easy to be around; yet people who get on your bad side should run and hide."

"Best of both worlds," he teases. "I'm a bit of everything."

"I'm starting to see that," I say with our gazes locked. "It would be much easier if you were an asshole."

His smirk lets me know he doesn't take offense. "What would be much easier?"

"Staying away from you," I say lightly, even though it's the cold, hard truth.

"Trust me, you aren't the only one struggling with that," he admits quietly, scrubbing a hand down his face. "Tried to stay away, thought you didn't fit, but you do. You're just as strong, if not more so than the other women. You're fiercely loyal. It's hard to find someone like that nowadays. Most people have their own agenda."

I nod, because I know that's the truth. There are lots of good people out there, but there are also a lot of assholes. You have to learn how to weed out the good from the bad, but sometimes you just have to learn the hard way.

"I think loyalty is one of the best qualities someone can have," I agree. "I'm glad you think that of me, Tracker. That is the best compliment you've ever given me."

"I'm glad it's true," he replies easily. "No need to thank me."

I stare at his handsome profile, his jawline, the stubble on his face. The vein in his thick neck.

"Stop looking at me like that," he replies in a husky tone,

watching me from the corner of his eye. "Or else one of the prospects will come watch Clover, and you and I will be alone and doing something I can't mention at a kid's party."

I gulp. "So . . . the weather is nice today," I blurt out, inciting a chuckle from him.

"It is," he murmurs. "Beautiful, actually."

I turn to see him watching me, and something passes between us. I acknowledge the fact that he is interested in me. He wants something from me. The problem is, he doesn't know what it is yet, and I don't want to trust him with my heart. Yet. I don't want to get attached to him, but realistically I already am.

I'm just in fucking denial.

And it's a nice place.

We both watch Clover play with all her friends for the next thirty minutes.

"How do Faye and Sin do this?" he suddenly asks, watching Clover fall onto the ground and get up by herself, brushing off the back of her dress.

"I have no idea," I answer honestly. "I'm not her mother and I want to protect her from everything and anything."

"Maybe we should homeschool our kids," he drops casually.

My head snaps to him. "I'm sorry, what?" I can't stop my mind from picturing a beautiful girl with my dark hair and his blue eyes holding both our hands.

He chuckles. "You should see your face."

"Very funny," I mutter. "Are you sure you don't have any kids out there?"

His eyes narrow. "Always use protection. Trust me, there are no mini Trackers running around."

"What's your real name?" I ask.

He studies me. "Not many people know my real name."

"So? I won't tell anyone. I'll still call you Tracker."

He cringes and ducks his head. "Daniel Davis."

I grin. "Cute."

"And you will never repeat those words again."

I cross an *X* over my heart. "Your secret is safe with me, Daniel."

"Smart-ass," he replies. "Now you owe me a secret."

"Hmmmm," I think, then smile at him. "I really write porn for a living."

He laughs and mutters, "Yeah, right. I couldn't be that lucky."

Sure, it isn't porn, but I like to joke that it is. If he doesn't believe me, that's his problem.

"Okay, fine," I say. "Once, Rake and I played spin the bottle. We kissed. It was horrible."

He scowls. "That bastard."

I laugh at his expression. "It was years ago. He probably doesn't remember."

"He better not," Tracker says. "Maybe I'll have to hit him on the head a few times just to make sure."

Watching Clover, I shake my head at him. "Never a dull moment with you, Tracker."

How did he make me feel so comfortable? I was generally awkward and didn't know what to say. Instead of drawing attention to my nervousness, he just glossed over it and put me at ease. He makes it so easy to be myself. I can't deny that I love how I feel around him.

"Glad to amuse," he says, repeating my words.

"You more than amuse," I murmur, and his expression suddenly turns heated.

"Good," he replies quietly.

"Looks like Clover is having fun," I say, changing the subject.

"She isn't the only one," he replies, eyes warm.

I look down at my hands, unnerved by the look in his eyes.

"Aren't you glad I came?" he adds. "I'm saving both you and Clover from a father and son who need to be taught a lesson."

"And what lesson is that?" I dare to ask.

His smile isn't friendly. "That if you mess with Wind Dragons property, you better prepare for war."

I almost laugh, until I realize he is dead serious.

FOUR

A WEEK passes.

Tracker's here every day at the clubhouse, spending all his time with Clover and me. Apparently he doesn't have anywhere else to be. He's also extremely hard to resist. Easy to talk to, down-to-earth, funny. Sexy. Great with Clover. I overheard him singing to her and thought my ovaries were going to explode. I'm seeing him in a completely new light. I'd thought he was some kind of player with no ability to commit to a woman. And part of me still does. But at the same time, I can't deny how kind and thoughtful he is. He's so attentive, hanging on my every word. He makes me feel important. I'd never spent so much one-on-one time with him before. Our usual interactions were in a group setting or always with Anna there. Or Allie. He's different away from his MC brothers too.

Softer.

More approachable.

He's really making this difficult on me. I can say no only so many times before I'm going to cave in.

Would it be so bad to give him a chance?

Is it just the chase for him? Or is he serious about seeing how far our relationship could go? It seems like too big a chance to take. If I give in, he will consume me.

I walk into the clubhouse living room to find Clover asleep on the floor. I laugh softly at her cuteness, picking her up and laying her on the couch. I love how comfortable she feels at the clubhouse, and now I can see why Faye wanted her here. She really is safe among the club members. I pull out my laptop, intending to get some work done, when Allie walks into the room with Jess, Trace's old lady. Jess is nice enough, but kind of closed-off. I figure it's because I'm not one of "them." Allie is . . . well I don't really know what she is. She lives here but isn't at the top of the food chain, so to speak. The old ladies go in and out, doing their own thing, and the hang-ons are brought in and out by the club members when they want them. Allie is kind of in between. She isn't an old lady, but she still gets to live here and is a part of the club. I don't fully understand her role, but I do know that she doesn't like me.

Never has and never will. How do I know? Well, her face is permanently scrunched up when I'm around and her eyes shoot daggers at me. Oh, and there are the cutting remarks. I couldn't care less anymore.

"Where's Tracker?" she demands without lowering her voice.

I glance at Clover, then back to Allie. Speaking in a much softer tone than she used, I say, "I don't know. And talk quietly or you're going to wake Clover."

She laughs, an ugly sound. "Who the fuck do you think you are to tell me what to do? I live here. You're just the hired help."

"Allie," Jess says softly, but I don't miss the warning in her tone.

"What?" Allie asks. "She's not even one of us. She's a fuckin' tagalong."

"*Allie.*"

We all jump at the sound of Tracker's voice. He doesn't sound happy. He sounds pissed. Allie turns around to look into his angry eyes.

"I'm sure Faye would love to hear how you're acting around her kid."

Allie clears her throat. "I was looking for you."

"Go and wait in my room," he tells her, then looks at me. I don't miss the fact that his eyes soften, but I'm still reeling from the blow of him sending Allie to his room. This is exactly what I was afraid of—the two of them will never be over. Jess leaves the room as Tracker comes closer to me.

"Don't look at me like that. I'm just going to clear shit up with her. Be here when I get back so we can talk. You say you don't want me, Lana, but those hurt brown eyes tell me all I need to know."

Am I that transparent? Apparently so.

He gives me a gentle kiss on my forehead before leaving the room.

Luckily for me, Faye gets home early and I get out of there while Tracker and Allie are still . . . doing whatever they're doing.

He thrusts into her, slamming her against the headboard. . . .

Sitting back in my chair, I stare at the words on my screen and sigh. I need inspiration. I want a fresh, new sexy scene and for once, my head is blank and my characters aren't cooperating. A knock at my front door brings me to my feet. It is about 10:00 a.m., so it is probably my package delivery guy. While we aren't on a first-name basis, we are friendly. He is here at my house practically every day, thanks to my online shopping addiction. I don't think he's ever seen me out of my pajamas, and I'm not going to disappoint today either. Opening the door, I smile at the prospect of what I might get to open today.

"Good morning . . ." I say in surprise, not to my deliveryman but to Tracker. "What are you doing here?"

He grins and gives my body a slow perusal. "Nice pj's."

I look down, cringing. Out of all the days, he caught me when I was wearing my black tank top. It reads FRIES OVER GUYS on the front, with a picture of some french fries. The matching shorts have pictures of fries all over them too.

I'm so sexy.

"Th-thanks," I mutter, fiddling with the hem of the top.

"Are you going to invite me in?" he asks, taking a step forward.

"I suppose so," I say, stepping back so his large frame can enter. "Is there something you wanted?"

He closes the door, studying me. Today he is wearing a Harley T-shirt, light jeans, and his biker boots. "Pretty sure I told you to wait for me yesterday. Came back to the lounge room and you were gone."

I shrug. "Faye came home and it was time for me to go."

I walk into my living room and he follows. He sits on the couch and pulls me onto his lap. I perch there stiffly, scanning the room as he gently massages my shoulders with one hand, the other wrapped tightly around my waist.

"Relax, Lana," he murmurs. "I want you to be comfortable around me. You can trust me, you know?"

I slowly relax, going limp on his lap, resting my back against his front.

"Good girl," he croons. "Now this is what I wanted to say to you yesterday. I took Allie away and told her off. One, she doesn't speak to you like that, ever; two, Clover was right there, and Faye will eat Allie for fuckin' breakfast if she heard. We spoke, and then she left. That's it, all right? I don't want Allie to give you shit, and I'm trying to handle it."

I don't know what to say. I've never verbally told Tracker I wanted to be with him, but apparently that doesn't matter to him. What is happening right now? Is this his way of courting me? I blink slowly, trying to process things.

"What's going on in that head of yours?" he asks, sounding a little amused.

"I don't understand what's going on here," I blurt out. "We can't be anything more than friends, Tracker."

He turns me so I'm facing him.

Why the man looks entertained I have no idea. "Did you just friend-zone me?"

I sigh heavily. This right here is the problem. This is all a game to him, but to me, this is my heart on the line. "Why do you have to be so difficult?"

He chuckles, his body shaking. I hold on to him so I don't fall off his lap. "*I'm* the difficult one? You want me; I want you. It's simple. The result should be you in my bed, and me in yours. You're the one fighting it, not me. I'm more than ready to embrace the fact that we've been attracted to each other from the moment our eyes met."

I puff out a breath, irritated. "Are you always so . . . so . . . ?"

"So what?" he prompts. "Sexy? Charming?"

"Annoying," I spit. "Are you always so annoying?"

"Annoying because I'm calling you out on your shit?" he asks with a sexy smirk. "Most women want a man who knows what they're thinking."

"You'd have the experience to know," I mutter under my breath.

"All the better to please you with," he instantly replies, gently cupping my cheek with his palm. "Lana, you feel this. I know you do; I know I can't be fuckin' making up this thing between us. Tell me why you're pulling back; tell me so I can fix it. This shit is driving me fuckin' insane."

He makes it sound so easy, but it isn't.

It's complicated.

"Tracker," I sigh, letting my hand run up his neck. "Of course I want you," I admit quietly, my cheeks flushing at the admission. "But we want different things."

His blue eyes darken, lids lowering. "Tell me what you think it is that I want from you."

Talk about putting me on the spot.

"Ummm." I breathe. "Sex. Lots of sex."

And I'm not opposed to that.

Not at all.

He licks his lower lip, his gaze dropping to my mouth. "I want that, yes. What else?"

I shrug. "That's it, I guess."

"I see," he says slowly, eyes lifting to mine. "Let me tell you something, Lana. I know you don't want me to bring up Allie, but I want to explain something. With her, I rushed into shit without thinking. I was desperate for something I didn't even want from her, something she couldn't give, because she wasn't you. She was easy, and easy didn't work for me. Our relationship was based on sex and convenience—harsh, but that's the damn truth. Good things don't come easy; I know that now. I can be patient, take shit slow, because I know you're worth the wait."

"What do you want from me, Tracker?" I ask. I feel like he isn't telling me anything new. He isn't telling me his end game.

"I want you. For as long as you'll have me." His face is serious, more serious than I'd ever seen him.

"Tracker—"

"And you know what else?" he adds, flashing me a lopsided grin. "I know that you're eventually going to give in. And when you do, it's going to be fuckin' perfect. So my dick can wait for you, Lana, because it has your name written all over it."

My mouth drops open at that last comment, which he of course decides to take full advantage of, surprising me with a kiss. His mouth is soft, perfect. Delicious. Forgetting everything and anything, I wrap my arms around his neck and kiss him back. I've wanted this kiss for so damn long, and to finally have it . . .

It felt like Christmas morning.

His hands wander down my back and land on my hips, gripping tightly, urging me on. Feeling bold, I let my tongue explore. He moans into my mouth, sucking and nipping on my bottom lip before pulling away. Groaning in protest, I pull his head closer to me, but he still lets his mouth leave mine.

"Lana," he murmurs, kissing my forehead. I let my head fall against his chest.

"Why did you stop?" I protest.

He chuckles softly. "Because you said we can only be friends, remember? Friends don't kiss like that."

I want to slap him.

I lift my head and narrow my eyes on him. "You're such an asshole."

"Hey, it was you who slipped in your tongue, not me. I was making it as friendly as possible," he jokes.

Definite asshole.

I squirm on his lap, trying to get off him, while he tries to hold me in place.

"Keep squirming," he says. "Feels good."

I instantly stop.

I can feel his hardness through his jeans, but I'd been ignoring it, pretending it wasn't there. But now, as we both stare down at it between us, it becomes the huge elephant in the room.

And it *is* huge.

I've been with two men in my life, and neither of them had felt this big.

"That's quite a weapon you're packing," I exclaim, cringing as soon as the words leave my mouth.

Yes, I just said that.

Why do I have to be so awkward? I should just stick to writing and never use my mouth again.

Well at least for words. My mouth could still do . . . other things.

Tracker simply laughs. "All for you, Lana."

If that were true, I'd be the happiest woman in the world.

*   *   *

Tracker ends up staying over for the next few hours, just hanging out and watching TV with me.

"You kind of look like her," he says, nodding at the TV screen. We are watching *Smallville* reruns, and he is referring to the stunning woman who plays Lana Lang. "And you share the same name."

My eyes widen. "Yeah, right."

"I'm serious," he says. "Petite, dark hair, porcelain skin, and stunning features."

I still don't see it, but the compliment feels nice anyway. "Well, you don't look like Clark Kent," I say, pausing. "More like Thor."

He chuckles at that and mumbles something about having a hammer.

When he casually slides his arm around me, leaning it on the back of the couch, I pretend I don't notice. When he goes into the kitchen and makes us a snack, I feel amused. It's like he feels at home anywhere, always comfortable and confident.

I wish I could be like that.

When his phone rings, I'm snugged in the crook of his arm.

"Hey," he says, then replies with, "Yeah, okay. Give me ten. Yeah. 'Bye."

Lowering his head, he says, "Gotta go."

He kisses my forehead, then walks to the front door, calling out for me to lock it.

And I'm left sitting there contemplating.

Is it possible for me and Tracker to have a relationship after all?

FIVE

"Y OU made up an Ed Sheeran drinking game?" I say into the phone, blinking slowly.

"I did," Anna yells, making me wince. "I drank every time he sings the words *me* and *I*. I'm drunk, Lana. *Drunk.* Druuunnnkkkk. Will you come and pick me up?"

I smirk at her slurring voice. "*Me* and *I*, huh? How many songs did you get through?"

"Not many," she replies cheerfully. "Oops. Almost fell over."

I love Ed Sheeran.

"Lana, why didn't you come out? You need to get laid. I know it's been a while, but it's like riding a bike." She pauses. "But the bike is a penis."

I start laughing at that.

"I'm hungry too," she continues. "I wonder if any sushi places are open right now."

I walk to my kitchen countertop and grab my keys. "Where is Arrow?"

He didn't usually leave her side unless he had to.

"He's on a run," Anna says, sighing heavily. "I'm standing outside of Rift. Rake's inside, but he's hooking up with someone."

Typical.

"Are you busy? I can catch a cab," she says. "I told Arrow I wouldn't leave alone though."

"Give me five minutes," I tell her, and hang up.

Rift is a bar owned by the Wind Dragons MC and is pretty close to my house. My mom is at the hospital, where she works as a nurse, and I am home alone on my laptop. The call from Anna was unexpected at this time of the night, but not unwelcome. Anna had invited me out, but I'd declined. I didn't know Arrow was away on a run, and I didn't want to be a third wheel. I also had a book I needed to finish. After Tracker left my house the other day, I was surprisingly inspired, and the sex scenes I wrote were hotter than ever. Looks like a kiss from him was just what I needed.

I didn't plan on getting out of the car, so I didn't bother to change out of my black track pants and white tank top. Sliding my feet into ballet flats, I grab my purse and get into my car. Ronald, my beat-up old Honda, sits next to my new car, a black Hyundai Tucson. The seat covers are a hot pink that make me smile every time I see them. Making sure to drive the speed limit the whole way, I find a parking spot and pull out my phone to call Anna. When she doesn't pick up, I groan and try again.

Nothing.

I'm about to get out of my car, dressed properly or not, when she calls me back.

"Where are you?" she asks in greeting, slurring her words slightly.

"Parked."

She cheers. "Which car are you in?"

"The Tucson."

"Okay, we'll be right there," she says before hanging up.

We?

Guess Rake needs a ride too.

Wrong.

When I see Anna and Tracker walking side by side to my car, my eyes go big. He looks *good*. His blond hair is loose and sitting on his shoulders and he's wearing dark jeans with a shirt rolled up at his wrists. Matched with biker boots, the chain hanging from his wallet, and his cocky grin, the man exudes power and sexuality. Has it only been two days since he was at my house? Has he always looked this good? I marvel at my self-control for having ever denied him. The man is a god. Ever the gentleman, he opens the car door for Anna before sliding into the front passenger seat, flashing me a grin and leaning forward to kiss my cheek. I can faintly smell a woman's perfume on him, making me grit my teeth.

"Fun night?" I ask, forcing a smile.

"Just got better," he replies, then turns his head to look at Anna. "Made her drink some water, help sober her up."

I turn to look at her too. "How you feeling, Anna Bell?"

Her eyes are closed.

And then she starts snoring.

Tracker bursts out laughing, slapping his palm on my dashboard once.

I narrow my eyes on him. "No need to beat up my car."

His mouth twitches. "Sorry, baby."

Baby?

That is new.

And I don't know how I feel about it. The man has me confused, lost, and drowning. I want him—I don't want to want him, but I can't stop. I am a shipwreck, and he's the storm. I can see him coming, but I still don't move out of the way.

I start the engine and look straight ahead. "Where to?"

"Clubhouse," he says. "You can sleep there too."

"And why would I do that?" I ask, glancing at him from the corner of my eye. "I'll drop you and Anna off and then go home."

"I don't want you driving alone," he states. "So you're staying. You're safe; don't worry. It's not like it's just going to be you and me alone there, there's always someone at the clubhouse. We can grab some food, and by the time we get back Rake will probably be there anyway, and he sure as fuck won't be alone."

"That's just what I want to see," I reply. "A live show starring my best friend's brother."

Is that meant to make me feel more comfortable? I guess Rake is a safety net to me in some ways, because I already know him, but I don't want to see him in his element.

"You won't see anything," he says, smirking. "Just the audio. 'Ohhhhh, Rake . . .'"

I giggle. "Seriously, there is something wrong with you guys."

"You only live once, Lana," he says. "You have to enjoy it, otherwise what's the point? No regrets."

"Grab every day by the balls?"

He laughs. "Exactly."

"I suppose I could try that."

His outlook on life is infectious. He always makes the best out of every moment, every situation. I wish I could be more like him in that aspect.

"You can start by staying at the clubhouse tonight."

Why did he want me to stay there so badly?

"And if I say no?" I cross my arms, challenging him.

"Then I'll just make you."

"Unfortunately for you, there's something called free will," I reply, flashing him a dirty look.

"Yeah, but I'm bigger than you. I can carry you with one hand, so you have to do what I say."

"Bossy," I mutter under my breath.

"Not bossy," he replies. "The boss."

"You wish."

"This what you wear to bed?" he says, and I turn in time to see him staring at my chest. I'm not wearing a bra, because I don't really need one. My breasts are small, but I'm fine with them. They're perky and easy to manage. My ass, on the other hand, is large and round. I try to contain it, but the thing has a mind of its own. I am a petite girl at five foot two inches, and my backside looks like it belongs on someone with a different frame.

"Yes," I reply, shrugging, feigning nonchalance.

"Christ, woman. You look sexy in anything," he says, sliding his large hand over my thigh.

I slap it away. "Tracker!"

"Lana!" he replies mockingly. "You seem tense. I think you need a few hours of fucking. Some orgasms would do you some good. Let me help. Fuck the friends-only shit. Literally."

Is he drunk?

I nod my head, agreeing with him. "You're right. Maybe I'll

find someone to take care of that for me. There are a few guys at school who've asked me out."

Suddenly it feels like all the air is sucked out of the car.

I look at Tracker, whose blue eyes are steady on me. "You touch anyone, they die. I didn't take you for a bloodthirsty woman, but so be it."

I roll my eyes at his dramatics. "So, what? I have to stay celibate until you decide you're sick of chasing me, while you get to fuck your way through the female population?"

"Who said I'm fucking anyone else? I'm not asking you to be celibate. Trust me, that's the last thing you'll be, it will just be me in your bed every night."

I squeeze my thighs together.

"Will Allie be joining us?" I ask him in a dry tone. It is only a matter of time before they are back together again. They'd been playing this game for years, and I refuse to be caught in the cross fire.

I hear his teeth grinding.

I'm annoying him? Good, the feeling is mutual.

"I prefer not to share, but if that's what you want," he finally says in a tone that I don't appreciate.

"I think I'll pass," I say, exhaling deeply.

"How did you afford this car?" he asks, effectively changing the subject. "Faye give you an advance or something?"

My fingers tighten on the wheel. "Not that it's your business, but I had some money saved."

"Do you? Interesting. Very mature of you."

"Girl needs to protect herself," I say, my meaning obvious.

"From who? Me?" he asks, sounding incredulous. "I've never wanted to protect a woman more than I do you, and you think you need to protect yourself from me?"

This escalated quickly. I want to explain to him that I meant that I needed to protect my heart, but I don't. I don't have to explain things to him. I'm not his, and he sure as hell isn't mine. I ignore the pang in my chest at that thought, and put the car in drive, concentrating on the road ahead of me.

"So do you want to get a bite to eat?" he asks after a good ten minutes of strained silence.

"Anna said she was hungry," I say quietly.

"Anna's knocked out, but we can grab something for her so she has food when she wakes up."

That is thoughtful of him.

"Okay," I concede. "Where do you want to stop?"

"I know a place," he says.

"Is it a drive-through?" I ask, staring down at my clothes. Why didn't I just get changed?

"No," he replies, chuckling. "But no one will dare look at you the wrong way if you walk in there with me."

"Still," I grumble.

"I'll give you my shirt to put over your tank top. It will be fine."

"You're not wearing your cut," I point out.

"It didn't go with my outfit," he jokes, making me smile. That's the thing with him. He's so good at making me feel at ease, even right after a tense situation.

"You're not wearing your hair in a bun," I exclaim. "It looks sexy in a bun."

"I'll remember that for next time," he says in a low, husky tone that I could get used to.

I clear my throat. "Was Rift busy?"

He grins, looking amused by my terrible small talk. "It was packed. Place is doing great. We hired some new girls for the bar."

"Is that why you smell like perfume?"

When Tracker doesn't reply, I turn to look at him. He's trying not to laugh.

"You're an awfully jealous woman for someone who keeps rejecting me at every turn."

"I'm not jealous," I scoff.

Okay, I am jealous.

I'm jealous of every woman who ever had him. I wish I wasn't, but the man makes me lose rational thought. I am an independent woman. I'm strong, educated and have good self-esteem, but when it comes to Tracker . . .

The word *want* fails in comparison to how I feel about him.

I'm drawn to him.

If I believed in soul mates, I would have said he was mine. The way he makes me feel is incredible, but at the end of the day, I don't trust him. The truth is, I judge him for his past. I'm not naïve enough to think that I'll be the woman to change Tracker. I've dated a few men and have noticed one recurring thing: they say and do all the right things at first. But it doesn't take much for them to lose interest and seek amusement in other places. Men lie too easily. I have a hard time trusting, and Tracker's history with Allie and the number of other women he's been with doesn't make it easier for me. Maybe Tracker truly believes I'm different and has serious feelings for me. But how long will that last? I don't want to compete with other women and fight for his affection. I don't want to wonder about where he is, who he's with.

Even though I already do that, at least right now he isn't mine. He's just a fantasy. A dream I can't let become reality.

We are two different people, and if he breaks me, I don't know if I'm strong enough to come back from that.

SIX

HIS shirt is massive on me, but it covers my nipples, which is all I can ask for right now.

"Thanks," I say as I button it up.

"Anytime," he replies huskily, stepping back and taking me in from head to toe. "You look good in it."

When his gaze returns to mine, my eyes narrow slightly.

I don't miss what flashes in his blue depths.

Possession.

"Don't look at me like that," I tell him, arching my brow.

"Like what?" he asks, taking his hand in mine and walking me into the twenty-four-hour café.

"Like I'm yours and you're just waiting for me to realize it."

He opens the door for me. "That's the truth though."

That's what I'm afraid of. I roll my eyes and walk to one of the booths. He slides in next to me, his thigh pressed against mine.

"Do you think Anna's going to be okay in the car?" I ask, staring out the window to where I parked.

"She's fine," he says, picking up a menu. "Can hear her fuckin' snoring from here. If it stops, I'll go out and investigate."

I can't help but laugh at that. "Leave her alone. She's sensitive about her snoring."

He grunts. "Proof right there that Arrow fuckin' loves her, listening to that every night."

I take the menu from his hands and glance over it. "I'll grab Anna a burger. There's no sushi here."

"Be questionable if there was," he says, grinning. "What do you want to eat?"

I scan the menu again. "I'll have some nachos."

"Good choice," he replies, waving a waitress over. She practically runs to him, making me shake my head in both amusement and annoyance.

"What can I get you?" she purrs. She's leaning over the table slightly, giving us a clear view of her ample breasts.

"Hey, sweetheart," he tells the blonde, not looking up. "Can we have some nachos, two burgers with fries, and some chocolate cake? Oh, and some ribs."

I give him a sideways glance. *Sweetheart?* He's such a flirt.

He looks to me. "Drink?"

"Water, please."

He nods and looks back to the waitress. "Water and a Coke."

"Do you want the cake with the meal or after?"

"With," Tracker replies. "Thanks."

She leaves and he returns his attention to me.

"Hungry much?"

He smiles slowly. "This is just a snack."

My mouth twitches. "Insatiable appetite?"

"You have no idea," he says, staring into my eyes. "But you will."

I swallow hard. I should know not to bait him, because he isn't shy in the least. He will say anything, and it's always me who ends up embarrassed.

Tracker nudges me playfully, so I glance up at him.

"Don't go all quiet on me, I'm just playing," he says, tilting his head to the side and studying me. "What were you doing up so late? Or did Anna wake you? When she told me she rang you I was pissed. She could have called one of the prospects to get her."

"I was up; it was no problem. What about you?" I find myself asking. "Too many drinks?"

He shrugs his broad shoulders. "I had a few. I'm not drunk, if that's what you're asking."

"I didn't mind Anna calling me," I say. "If you can't call your best friend in the middle of the night when you're drunk, then who can you call?"

"A taxi service?" he supplies, chuckling at his own joke. "A fuckin' prospect is who she should've called."

"Is that what they're there for?" I ask, arching a brow.

"Among other things."

I want to ask more about the MC lifestyle, but our drinks arrive, and Tracker slides me my water bottle before grabbing his soda, taking a deep drink. I watch his throat work, my gaze dropping down his neck to the expanse of his chest visible behind his undershirt. "This isn't how I expected our first date to go, but I'll take it," he says.

I smile, shaking my head. "This isn't a date. If it is, you have to up your game, Tracker."

He lifts his head back and laughs. "You know, I think you're right. You're not what I'm used to, and before you start throwing sass around, I meant that in a good way."

We stare into each other's eyes for a few seconds.

"You're serious about this," I finally say.

He presses his thigh closer to mine. "Wouldn't mess around with something like this, Lana. I want you. It's that fuckin' simple to me."

If only it were the same to me.

"You thought you wanted Allie," I point out. "What if you think you want me, but then you realize that you were wrong again?"

Where would that leave me? Like Allie? Begging for any attention from him? Ruined for other men? Yeah, no thanks. I'd like to keep my dignity. No man is worth that kind of drama.

He takes my hand in his, then brings it to his mouth and peppers kisses all over my knuckles. The sweet move has my breath hitching.

"You're not Allie. Nothing about this is the same. Nothing. You don't have to overthink it, Lana, just let it happen."

I think that over, doing what he just told me not to do.

"You're overthinking it, aren't you?" His eyes sparkle with amusement. "Sometimes you need to just let things unfold, Lana. Don't have any regrets."

"You don't have *any* regrets?" I ask, studying him attentively.

"I never regret things I've done, only things I haven't done," he states. "Life is too short for that. No one is perfect, sometimes shit happens, but you need to get back on that motorcycle and ride the hell out of it."

I smile at that. "Not all of us are that easygoing."

He grins wolfishly. "Maybe we can balance each other out then. You rein me in a little, while I can set you free."

Our eyes stay connected, something passing between us.

"Christ, you're beautiful," he says softly. "I don't think you know just how much. The things I'd do to you . . ."

Our food arrives, thankfully shattering the moment. It's too much for me.

Too intense.

Too tempting.

Tracker eats some of my nachos and offers me some of his burger. As I take a huge bite, I realize that anyone looking at us would think we are a couple. The way Tracker's attention didn't waiver when I spoke, the laughter, sexual tension, and casual touching of hands. I can't deny that I like it. Little do they know we certainly are not in a relationship, argue more than most, and he's a member of a ruthless MC. We also aren't having sex, but I suppose they don't know that. Or would that make us a married couple? I giggle at my own joke, getting me an adorably confused expression from the big biker next to me.

"Wanna explain that cute little giggle?"

"I made a joke. In my head."

His eyebrows rise. "Wanna share?"

"Not really," I reply, stealing a fry and shoving it in my mouth.

"You know," he says, dipping his fry in ketchup. "One day you're going to trust me enough to share every one of those little thoughts and jokes of yours. One day, you're going to get out of your head, and you're going to let me in."

"Is that so?"

He nods, chewing thoughtfully. "Yep."

"And one day, Tracker," I tell him. "I'm going to ruin you for all other women."

My comment was meant to get a reaction out of him, to scare him.

But all he says is, "I believe that too."

Shit.

I drive Tracker and Anna back to the clubhouse, and Tracker doesn't take no for an answer when I tell him I don't want to stay.

"It's easier," he says. "I don't want you driving back alone in the middle of the night."

"I'll be fine," I argue. "I drove to Rift alone."

"And I didn't like that either."

"Are you serious right now?" I grumble. "You're used to getting your way, aren't you?"

He smiles what I'm sure is his most charming smile. "With women, yes."

I grit my teeth. "Maybe that's your problem. You need to be taken down a notch. Brought back to reality."

He leans closer to me almost pressed up against my body. "You going to be the one to do that?"

"No," I reply. "But I'm sure many others will try."

"Don't want them; want you."

"You can't always get what you want," I throw back at him.

"Please," he says, eyes pleading with me. "I'll be on my best behavior. Stop being fuckin' stubborn and just stay the night. Christ. I'm being a gentleman here, wanting you safe and not driving around alone when it's pitch-black out there."

I sigh. I can't deny that I want to stay with him as much as he wants me to. Maybe even more. "Fine."

He wins graciously, not rubbing it in. Instead, he gets out of the car and carries a sleeping Anna into his arms. I exit the car and follow him into her and Arrow's room. He lays her on the bed, while I try to make her more comfortable. I remove her makeup for her with a wet wipe I find in her bathroom. She stirs but doesn't wake up, so I tuck her into bed before roaming into the kitchen in search of Tracker. When I see Rake there instead, eating a burger, my mouth drops open.

"Please tell me you aren't eating your sister's burger right now," I say, grabbing a stool and taking a seat. "She's going to kill you."

Rake grins, his mouth full of food. "Was this hers? I'm hungry. If she cared so much, she should have eaten it."

"She's asleep," I point out.

"You snooze, you lose."

I place my elbows on the countertop. "Mature."

He smirks. "What you doing here anyway, Lana? Haven't seen you around here after the sun goes down. You're like a vampire." He pauses. "But opposite."

"Rake, you worry me," I tell him honestly, blinking slowly.

Green eyes identical to Anna's smile down at me. "I drank. I fucked. Now I'm eating. Night doesn't get better than this."

"Thank you for sharing that with me."

"Anytime, Lana Bear," he says, using my childhood nickname.

I wonder if my readers will like a male character like Rake. From my point of view, he isn't very appealing, although he is good-looking—*very* good-looking. Blond hair that curls around his face, a straight nose, and sparkling, usually amused green eyes framed in dark lashes. He also has a lip ring and eyebrow ring that suit him well. I just can't take him seriously though. Maybe it's because I knew him when we were younger. He was always yelling at Anna for doing something or other, but not in a mean way, just in a way that you knew he loved her more than anything and wanted to protect her.

"Until morning, when Anna smothers you in your sleep and embarrasses your bed partner."

"Bed partner?" he asks, chuckling. "You're so fuckin' proper, Lana."

"What do you want me to say?" I ask, shifting on my seat. "Your fuckin' bed partner?"

His chuckles turn into a deep laughter. "Much better. Fuck buddy will do fine though."

"What's so funny?" Tracker asks as he steps into the kitchen, freshly showered. Bare-chested, he's wearing a pair of black pajama pants slung low on his hips. "Fuck buddy?"

His eyes dart between Rake and me.

I keep my expression blank, wondering what he's thinking. He comes up behind me, wrapping his arms around my chest and pulling me back into him. "Don't think she needs to hear about your fuck sessions, brother."

Anna told me Rake was into bondage and stuff like that. As an author, I am extremely curious. How I'd love to pick his brain. But I don't think he'd appreciate that. He's pretty discreet when it comes to his sexual fetishes. Well, as discreet as he can be, considering he lives in a massive house filled with people who come and go at all hours.

Rake throws the burger wrapper in the bin, then turns to the two of us. "You with him, Lana? If he's giving you shit, call me and I'll kick his ass."

The way Rake says it, I have no idea if he's joking or not.

"You can try," Tracker replies with no heat, nuzzling the top of my head.

Rake groans. "You fuckers are dropping like flies. First Sin and Faye, then Arrow and Anna. Now you two? Fuck me, I need another drink. And some new pussy."

Charming.

He leaves the kitchen, and Tracker carries on like Rake was never there. "You must be tired. Let's go to bed."

"I'm sleeping with Anna," I say, turning around to look at him.

"In Arrow's bed? The fuck you are," he growls, then sweetens the tone of his voice. "Come on, we're just gonna sleep. I'll even spoon you."

"Tracker—"

"I'm so glad you're such an agreeable woman," he says cheerfully, taking my hand in his and pulling me toward his room.

I open my mouth, then close it, allowing him to bring me into his room and close the door. He turns on the light, while I try to calm my nerves. His room is a large space, with a massive white bed in the middle. Looking around, I realize everything is white, with splashes of black here and there. There are a few clothes on the floor, but for the most part the room is tidy. Tracker opens the door to his bathroom and disappears inside, while I walk to his monstrosity of a bed and sit down on the very end of it. He walks out a second later and climbs into bed, pulling me backward by my waist and settling me so I'm in the middle of the mattress.

"Much better," he says, yawning. "Sleep, Lana. You're safe here. When I do touch you, you'll be the one begging me for it."

I decide to ignore that.

Slowly lying back on the thick feather pillows, I get comfortable and close my eyes.

Surrounded by his scent, I fall asleep instantly.

"Lana," he groans, touching me intimately. "You feel so good."

I open my eyes sleepily, smiling at Tracker as he slides a finger inside me.

"I want to be inside you," he whispers.

"Do it," I demand. "I want you to."

"Fuck yeah," he growls, spreading my thighs and sliding into me like he's been there a million times before.

Pinning my hands up against the headboard, he slams into me over and over, the bed shaking with his ferocity.

"Yes," I moan. "So good!"

Suddenly my eyes open.

I glance around the dark room.

Shit.

It was a dream.

Tracker is next to me, our bodies touching. His eyes are closed and his lips are parted. His hair is loose, tickling the edges of his face. I resist the urge to kiss him.

I consider waking him up but then decide not to. He looks so peaceful. Almost childlike.

I guess I'll have to finish the scene on my laptop instead of in reality. Luckily my imagination is running wild, fuel for my writing.

SEVEN

WAKE up feeling warm and content. Tracker is pressed against
my back, his strong arms around my waist and his face in my
hair.

My eyes widening comically, I sit up and look down at a
sleeping Tracker.

He cuddles.

Like a fucking champ.

Opening one eye, he grins at me lazily. "It's still early, go back
to sleep."

"How do you even know what time it is?"

"I just know," he replies, his voice thick with sleep. "Come
back to me."

The man can be so sweet.

Slipping back between his arms, I sigh, wondering how I
ended up here. When I'm almost back in a deep sleep, I hear the
room door open, and a loud gasp belonging to my best friend.

I sit up.

Anna points at me. "You . . . you . . ."

She was speechless, that's a first.

"We just slept," I tell her, sliding out of Tracker's embrace and getting out of bed. I point to the door, and the two of us leave the room. She waits until we hit the kitchen before she starts with the questions.

"What the hell happened last night?" she yells, then groans, touching her head and wincing. Her hair is a matted nest, and I cringe thinking about her having to brush it out, glad it's not me. Makeup is still smudged around her eyes—apparently I didn't do a good enough job taking it off last night—yet she still manages to look gorgeous in a grunge-chic kind of way. "Okay, no loud noises."

I laugh. "I picked you up from Rift. You were drunk and fell asleep in the car."

She groans again. "Fuck, I'm sorry I woke you."

"It's okay," I tell her, smiling. "Tracker was with you. We went and got some food, then came back here and slept. End of story."

"Where is it then?" she asks, trying to tame her blond hair, which is sticking up in every direction.

"Where is what?"

"The food. Did you get me any food?" she asks, looking hopeful.

"Ummmm. I did. But Rake ate it," I tell her, cringing.

"That bastard!" she growls, her eyes narrowed.

I start giggling and she soon joins in. "When does Arrow get back?"

"Hopefully tomorrow," she says, opening the fridge and rummaging through the contents. "He, Sin, Trace, Irish, Ronan, and Vinnie are gone."

I lean up against the countertop, tying my own hair up and away from my face. "Do you know where he goes?"

"Nope," she replies popping the *P*. "Well, I know where. I just don't know why."

"And you're okay with that?" I ask carefully.

She closes the fridge and studies me. "Why? You considering getting with one of the men? A certain member with a huge pierced cock?"

My eyes flare. "Lower your voice, Anna!"

She grins cheekily. "Why? Don't want lover boy to hear us discussing his—"

"Deliciously hung penis?" Tracker suggests, walking into the kitchen and rubbing his eyes. "Christ, Anna. You yelling the word *cock* at nine in the morning isn't how I want to wake up."

Anna laughs. "Bet if it was Lana saying it . . ."

"Whole different story," he says casually, then turns to me. "You slept like a fuckin' baby last night. Admit it."

With two sets of eyes on me, one curious one knowing, I shrug and clear my throat. "I slept okay."

"Ha," he barks. "You slept like the dead. You can play it off, but I know the truth," he says playfully. "Now, to finish off the best date in the world, I'm going to make you breakfast."

"You can't cook!" Anna balks, looking at Tracker like he's grown an extra head.

"Says who?" Tracker asks, head now in the fridge.

"Me."

"And who are you? The fuckin' cooking police?"

"I could be." Anna sniffs, giving me a wink. She gives me a curious look; she's going to want answers. But what do I say? I don't even know what's going on between us. I'd been so sure I didn't want to get into anything with Tracker, but he is proving impossible to resist.

Persistent bastard.

With cheese and eggs in his hands, Tracker commands us both to sit.

"Do you like omelets, Lana?" he asks me in a much gentler tone than the one he used with Anna.

I nod.

"Good," he replies, grabbing a pan and getting to work.

"Are you cooking for me too?" Anna asks, peering into the pan with avid interest.

He sighs exaggeratedly. "Fine. But you're really ruining our breakfast date."

I know Tracker has a playful side to him. It draws people to him, because he's so easy to be around. He's fun. However, he also has the roughness necessary to be a part of the MC. I haven't seen that side yet, and I'm not sure I want to. What if I can't accept his lifestyle? Is that what I want?

My emotions are all over the place. Thank God no one else lives in my head, they wouldn't be able to keep track of all my thoughts. I overanalyze everything and second-guess myself a lot. I also tend to replay conversations trying to find hidden meanings in other people's words.

I'm not as adventurous as Anna. I live through books rather than reality. I don't know how I'd deal with being kidnapped like she was last year, or if men broke into the clubhouse when I was here. Sounds crazy, but these things have actually happened. This is their reality. I can say no to Tracker all I want, but he knows.

He knows.

One look at me, and he knows.

I do want him.

I have since I first laid eyes on him.

He's made his move, showed me his cards.

He wants me. For how long, I don't know. I'm not the kind to take risks. But maybe for once I should live a little, take a chance.

If I did, I could get hurt.

Burned.

Ruined.

Or . . . I could find what Anna and Faye have.

The gamble seems too large, but the feelings are too strong to deny.

As I watch Tracker try and make an omelet, I wonder what it is he sees in me. Not that I don't think I'm pretty, or anything like that. Just that, I'm not like the other women here.

"You're not wearing your glasses," Tracker says, cutting into my thoughts.

"I left them next to your bed."

He leans forward and brushes his lips against my cheek. "Your eyes are sexy. Big, brown, and soulful. Doe eyes. But you look cute with your glasses on too. Like a naughty librarian."

"I'm still here," Anna says in a dry tone.

"Ignore her," Tracker whispers. "Maybe she will go away."

Anna slaps him on his shoulder, then grabs the ladle to flip the omelet.

"Are weekend mornings always like this here?" I ask, my tone filled with humor.

"No," Tracker says, kissing my cheek and then looking behind me. "It's usually like that."

I turn to look at where he is pointing. Rake is walking into the kitchen, each arm around a woman. Both are average height and would be attractive if they were cleaned up. As it is, their hair is messy and the dresses they wore, presumably from last night, were trashy and crumpled. "'Mornin'," he rumbles. "Fuck yeah, breakfast."

Anna narrows her eyes. "Get one of your groupies to cook for you, you burger-stealing fiend."

Rake looks to me.

I throw up my hands. "She asked where it was. What was I supposed to do, lie?"

"That's exactly what you were supposed to do," Rake tells me with a smirk, removing his arms from the women and going to hug his sister. "Don't worry, Anna, I'll buy you sushi."

I roll my eyes, then look at Tracker, who is watching me with a curious look on his face. "Hope you don't have any plans today."

I have a book to finish, but I guess I can catch up on that tonight.

"Why?"

"'Cause I'm finally gonna get you on the back of my bike."

"Hmm, that depends," I challenge.

"On what?" he asks, a determined look taking over his expression.

"On how good your breakfast is."

He laughs.

"And what do I do with my car?"

"I'll get one of the prospects to drop it off later," he says.

I nod.

The omelet was crap.

But I let him take me for a ride anyway.

Arms wrapped around Tracker, his back pressed against my front, I have one thought on my mind.

I could get used to this.

Being on his bike is exhilarating.

Sharing this with him is amazing, like he's giving me a part of him. Not only is this my first ride ever, but it's my first with Tracker, and I can tell how much he loves to ride. How proud he feels. He loves his life in the MC.

Yes, I was scared shitless at first, but after the first fifteen minutes I calmed down and started to enjoy it. Clinging to Tracker for dear life, my fingers pressing into his ripped abs, I was sitting a little stiffly but still appreciated the feeling of being on a motorcycle.

Or is it just the feeling of being on *his* motorcycle?

I'd taken a shower and borrowed some of Anna's clothes—jeans that were a little loose on me and a black Harley T-shirt. Because I can't exactly wear house slippers on the bike, I'm also wearing her boots. I don't really look like me right now, but I feel like me.

I feel free.

The wind on my face, my arms around Tracker's body, and the speed. Every time we come to a stop he rubs my thigh. His earthy scent fills my nose. It feels right. Blocking everything out except the ride, I feel like we are the only people in the world.

Nothing else exists and nothing else matters.

Just him.

Me.

And the open road.

We ride for an hour, then stop at a scenic view overlooking the city. The view is amazing, the company even better. Tracker is attentive and a good listener. He surprises me at every turn. I keep looking to find something I don't like about him, something to put me off him, but keep coming up empty. I keep waiting for the other shoe to drop, because he seems almost too good to be true.

"I stop here when I need to think," he says, taking my hand in his. "It's quiet, and the view is nice. Kind of like you."

I laugh at that. "Flattery will get you everywhere."

He continues to watch me, an intense look on his face. "I've never brought anyone up here before."

"Ever?"

He shakes his head. "Never."

I look out over the city. "Then why did you bring me here?"

He absently rubs his chest, right over his heart. "I don't know. It felt right, I guess. Like you should be here too."

I don't know how to reply to that, so I squeeze his hand, which he threads with his own and continue to stare out at blue sky.

Suddenly he says, "I don't think I've ever just enjoyed silence with a woman."

I glance at him from the corner of my eye. "Maybe you should learn when to stay silent too?"

He grins, his eyes twinkling. "What I mean is, most women are chatty as hell. Sometimes comfortable silence is the best. When the woman is just enjoying, not angry or plotting."

I laugh. "Plotting? What kind of women have you been dating, Tracker?"

He gives me a *Don't act like you don't know* look. "Most times a silent woman is an angry one."

"Some of us are just quiet," I defend. "And tend to overthink things. Doesn't necessarily mean plotting."

"I'll keep that in mind," he says. "I need to take notes when it comes to you."

"I'm simple enough," I reply shyly.

"For some reason, I doubt that very much," he says, smiling. "Do you want to head back?"

I close my eyes, enjoying the feel of the breeze. "A few more minutes."

When I open them, he's watching me. He leans closer to me, and tilts his head to the side. "You're beautiful, Lana."

I don't look away this time. "Thank you."

We ride back and come to a stop at my house. Tracker helps me off the bike, his hands lingering on my waist.

"You liked it," are the first words that come out of his mouth, a grin playing on his mouth.

I smile shakily. "I did."

"I knew you would."

Leaning down, he rubs my cheek with his, his stubble tickling me. Pressing a kiss to my jawline first, he then moves to my mouth, giving me a sweet, gentle kiss, making me yearn for more.

"You fit," he says simply.

My brows furrow at his statement. "Tracker—"

"I'll see you Monday morning," he says, cupping my cheek, then nodding to my door. "Go. I'll wait for you to get inside."

I open my mouth to ask him what he meant when he said I fit. But for some reason I don't think he wants to be pressed right now.

"Thanks for the ride," I tell him before walking to my door.

He straddles his bike and starts his engine, but waits for me to be safely inside before he rides off.

I look at him disappear down the street through my window, afraid he's taken my heart with him.

EIGHT

O N Monday morning, I walk into the clubhouse, feeling exuberant. Looking forward to seeing Tracker, I even put in a little effort into my appearance again, wearing a black maxi dress and cute sandals. Hearing noise from the living room, I head there and find Rake watching cartoons with Clover.

"'Morning, Rake," I say, leaning down to kiss Clover on top of her head. "Where's Faye?"

"She had to go to work earlier this morning, so I've been keeping the princess company. Haven't I, Clover? I even fed her breakfast."

He sounds proud.

"What did you feed her?" I ask in suspicion.

"Food."

"Food from where?"

"McDonald's drive-through," he admits, shrugging sheepishly. "And I'd do it again. It was good."

"Me too!" Clover chirps in, a grin on her face. I grin back and sit down next to him. "Where's Tracker?"

Rake leans back on the couch, turning to me. "He didn't tell you? He went to meet up with Sin and the others. They needed him for something."

I refrain from asking what they needed him for.

"Oh."

Rake nudges my shoulder. "First Anna, now you. You two used to be such good girls." He sighs wistfully. "You with your glasses and braces. Anna with her fat little face."

I smirk. "I remember you before you were a man-whore. Those *were* good days."

He grabs me and gets me in a headlock, messing my hair. "See? The old Lana wouldn't be mouthing off like this. Tracker's already a bad influence on you."

"Uncle Rake leave Lana alone!" Clover calls out. "You're both missing the show!"

Rake lets me go and we both glance at Clover, who has narrowed her eyes at us in disapproval.

"That's enough TV, don't you think? Why don't we go to the park?" I ask her. She, like me, is on school break, so I have to think of things to amuse her every day. The pools, park, and animal farm are her favorite places. Pretty sure the kid is a better swimmer than me too.

"Which park?" she asks suspiciously.

I hide my grin. "Whichever park you want."

"Okay," she quickly agrees. I know which park she likes, it's the one farthest away.

I turn to Rake. "Is her car seat in your four-wheel drive?"

He nods. "Do you want me to put it in your car?"

"That would be great, thanks, Rake."

I get Clover changed and put her in the car. Rake must have

let her choose her own outfit, because she was wearing mismatched clothes.

"You ready for a day of fun?" I ask her, turning to look at her in the backseat.

"Sure am," she replies. "I'm the princess of fun."

I drive her to the park with a smile on my face.

Since Clover is napping, I decide to start dinner so Faye won't have to when she gets home. The chicken-and-broccoli pasta is done and I'm just pulling the garlic bread out of the oven when Tracker walks in, looking tired. His hair is disheveled, his clothes rumpled. He slides off his cut and places it on the back of one of the dining table chairs.

"Fuck, Lana, something smells good," he says with a small smile. Just as I put the garlic bread down, he pulls me into his arms, holding me close. "Could get used to coming home to this."

Such a caveman.

"I cooked for Faye, not you," I tease, closing my eyes and resting my head on his chest. "Where's everyone else?"

"Outside," he says. "I knew you'd be here so . . ."

So he ran inside ahead of them? He really can be a sweetheart sometimes.

"I didn't want to miss you before you left," he continues, while I try and process his sweetness. "I know sometimes Faye finishes early."

I pull back from him just as the others start piling through the kitchen door.

"Hey, Lana," Sin greets, nodding his head at me.

"Hey, Sin." I smile. "Clover is sleeping, and Faye is on her way home."

He nods. "Something smells good."

My mouth twitches. "Help yourself; I cooked plenty. I knew Faye would be tired after work."

Sin walks past me and kisses my cheek, then grabs a plate and starts piling.

"Leave some for me, asshole," Tracker tells his president, grabbing a plate and pushing him out of the way.

"Lana," Arrow says, wrapping an arm around me. "Anna here?"

I shake my head. "She's still out with Talon." Anna only met her stepbrother a few months ago. He's from a rival MC, so Arrow doesn't like him, but he tolerates Talon for Anna's sake.

A muscle works in his jaw, but he just nods his head at me.

Trace, Irish, Ronan, and Vinnie walk in, all mumbling a greeting, then going to eat. Luckily I cooked enough for a small army.

"Can I go, or do you want me to stay?" I ask Sin.

"Stay," Tracker says, the same time Sin says, "You can go, Lana."

I arch a brow at the two of them. Sin raises his arms in mock protest.

"Just sayin' you can go; you're more than welcome to stay. You're off babysitting duty." I smile in thanks.

"Did you eat?" Tracker asks.

I shake my head. "Whenever I cook something, I don't feel like eating it, I don't know why."

The men look down at their plates, unsure looks on their faces.

"There's nothing wrong with the food," I say quickly. "I'm a good cook."

"It's delicious, baby," Tracker says, grinning. "The best."

I ignore the curious looks I get from the other men after hearing his endearment.

"I'll see you all tomorrow," I say, waving awkwardly and walking out of the kitchen. I go into the living room to grab my handbag, and turn around to see Tracker standing there, plate in his hand.

"If you think I'm letting you go right now after me being gone for two fuckin' days, you don't know me at all," he says casually. "So we can do this the easy way or the hard way. Your choice. The hard way sounds tempting though."

I put my handbag down, and sit down on the couch.

"Good girl," Tracker murmurs, sitting down next to me. He takes a bite of his food, swallows, then asks, "What did I miss?"

"Nothing much," I say. "Usual stuff. How about you?"

He glances at me, then back at his food. "Had club business to handle. Handled it, came home."

And would it have killed him to send me a message saying he was going? I know I'm not his girlfriend, so I don't have the right to ask him that out loud, but it would have been nice to hear it from him that he was leaving.

"You look tired," I say instead.

"I am." He sighs. "I need a shower, then you in my bed, so I can sleep."

"Tracker—"

"Why don't you leave some clothes here? Just a few things. Makes sense, right?" he continues, finishing up his food, then resting the plate on the couch. He lifts his arms, waiting for me to move closer to him.

Sliding over, I rest my head on his chest and sigh. My body relaxes immediately and I feel at peace. "What are we doing here, Tracker?"

"I'm taking what I want," he says, nuzzling my head. "And you, you're taking a chance."

That really does sum it all up.

"Do I get a kiss?" he asks quietly. "Because I really fuckin' want one, Lana."

I squint an eye at him, raising a brow, as though I'm weighing my options.

"Lana . . ." he growls playfully, making me smile.

Shyly, I lift my head up, giving him access.

With a hand on either side of my face, he leans down, his lips gently touching mine at first, then becoming deeper. With a swipe of his tongue, I open my mouth, letting him inside. Tilting his head, he takes control of the kiss, his body pushing me back into the cold leather of the couch. When he finally pulls away, he kisses my lips once more before studying me through heavy-lidded eyes.

"After that kiss, are you still gonna try telling me you aren't mine?" he rasps, lips quirking at the corners. "Because you felt like mine, melting for me like that."

It frustrates me that he always has to make me face everything when I'm happy to just pretend I don't have feelings for him and this is just a casual thing. Having to face reality means I have to make a proper decision, and I just don't feel ready. I'm so afraid.

I make a soft sound of frustration. "You want me to admit it? Fine. I'm crazy about you. Inescapably, obsessively—"

He cuts off my embarrassing rant with his mouth.

I don't complain.

He then lifts me in his arms and carries me to his room, placing me gently in the center of the bed.

"Don't move," he softly commands.

Wide-eyed, I sit there and watch as he disappears into the bathroom. The shower turns on, and soon I can see steam trying to escape from the door. My body fills with anticipation. When he walks out in nothing but a towel—and drops the towel on the floor—I can only imagine the expression on my face.

Shock. Lust. Want.

Drool?

His cock is thick, pierced, and beautiful. That's how I would have described it if I were writing about it. He's huge. And apparently not shy.

"Ummm."

"I like to sleep naked," he says, grinning wolfishly. "Since you admitted how you felt, I get to show you me without having to worry about you running scared. Don't worry, I'll take it slow with you."

"Wait, what?" I mumble, still staring at his penis.

"My eyes are up here," he says huskily. "Unless you want to fuck now? Because I'd be okay with that."

My eyes narrow. "Think I'll pass."

I'm not ready just yet. I don't know why, but I feel like I need to know Tracker a little more before we sleep together. "That's what I thought," he replies, sounding amused. "I need to sleep."

"It's only six p.m."

He slides in next to me and wraps me in his arms. "Been riding all day, baby, and didn't sleep much last night."

I run my hands through his hair. "Go to sleep, then."

He sighs contently as I play with his hair, which by the way, is nicer than mine.

When I know for sure he's asleep, I slowly get off the bed, grab my handbag, and leave his room, closing the door softly. I hear laughter as I walk by the game room, so I curiously peek my head in to see Rake and Irish playing pool. There are two women standing next to them, dressed in short shorts and their bras.

"I guess Faye and Clover must have left," I say when Rake notices me.

He laughs. "Yeah, they're gone. You wanna play some pool?"

"It's strip pool," Irish adds, winking at me. "Sure as fuck hope you're a bad player."

Rake laughs again, slapping Irish on his arm. "You want to die, man? She's Tracker's. And no offense, Lana, but you're like family, so I don't wanna see that shit."

I roll my eyes at that.

Irish nods. "Tracker claim her?"

"In the process," Rake adds, sitting down on one of the stools. One of the women drops in his lap, wrapping her arm around him possessively.

"Yeah, I'm just gonna go now," I say, waving 'bye and making a quick exit.

I'm at my car door when I hear her voice.

"He's going to get sick of you," Allie says in a calm tone. "It's not you he wants."

"And I suppose he wants you, then?" I ask in a dry tone.

She smiles sadly. "Actually, no. But it's not me who's going to end up hurt."

"You need to move on, Allie," I tell her.

She raises her eyebrow. "I remember you, you know. Took me a while to place you. But yeah, I remember you." She laughs, a cold sound. "William, now Tracker. Have a thing for my sloppy seconds, do you? This isn't high school, Lana. Taking Tracker is going to have a completely different consequence than taking William did."

So she finally remembered me from school.

My mind flashes back to the first time I met Allie, which was eight years ago.

Is he smiling at me?

I look around me, behind me, but no one else is there.

He is smiling at me.

Fidgeting nervously, I push my long black hair back behind my ear and smile tentatively. I've been waiting what feels like forever for William to notice me. I've had a crush on him since I first saw him, our freshman year of high school. Four years later and this is the first time he's smiled at me.

I'm not usually a girl who gets noticed. I'm not popular and I never put myself out there, so people tend to just walk by me without a second glance. I know William was dating the head cheerleader, but I heard a rumor that they broke up. Maybe it's true? My best friend, Anna, always says that William isn't worth my time. But Anna isn't here now—she moved away and left me to get through senior year without her. It sucks, big-time. I don't find it easy to make new friends—most people mistake my shyness for something else. They think I'm a snob. But I'm not. I just find it hard to con-

nect with other people. Maybe it's because I'm shy—or maybe it runs deeper.

Oh my god. He's walking toward me. My heart is beating so fast I worry he can hear it.

"Hey, Lana," *William says, sitting down next to me. I am all alone in the library, working on a creative-writing assignment for my English class.*

"Hi," *I squeak, clearing my throat and risking a glance at him.*

He smiles, something flashing in his eyes. "You look pretty today."

My eyes widen. That isn't something I ever expected to hear out of his mouth. While I know I'm not unattractive, I'm also nothing exceptional. Especially compared to the stunning, curvy, blue-eyed blondes he usually goes for. "Oh. Umm. Thank you."

He leans forward, and I don't stop him.

This is like a fantasy come true.

His lips graze my cheek before he whispers in my ear. "Do you want to come for a drive with me?"

"Wh-where to?" *I ask, swallowing hard.*

He pulls back, shrugging as he runs his hand through his messy brown hair. "I was thinking of going to the beach. Weather is good."

"Oh, umm," *I look down at my assignment, which really needs to be done, but this is the William Dean.* "Okay."

I collect my things and stand up. When he wraps an arm around my waist and pulls me to him, a thought occurs to me. "Wait, what about your girlfriend?"

He suddenly looks amused. "Old news, babe. We broke up. Now are we going or what?"

I nod and let him take my hand in his.

Anna isn't going to believe this!

*   *   *

The next morning, with a huge smile on my face, I walk to my locker with an extra spring in my step. Yesterday, William had kissed me. He'd tried to go a little further, but I told him I wasn't ready yet. He seemed frustrated but agreed, stopping his wandering hands and concentrated on just kissing me.

It was my first real kiss. Games and dares don't count.

Today, he is going to take me out again.

Stopping at my locker, I drop my bag to the floor.

What the hell?

Someone has written the word whore in black marker. Underneath it, the words home wrecker are written. I am confused. And hurt. I double-check that this is indeed my locker. I mean, I'm a virgin with no dating record. How the hell can I be a whore? I am pretty sure I was one of the last few virgins in the whole damn school.

A throat clears behind me, an impatient noise.

"Thought you could steal my boyfriend away, did you?"

I turn to face William's ex-girlfriend, flanked by two of her friends. Does she still think she is his? He'd told me in detail yesterday about how they weren't together anymore, how he was single and interested in me.

"He said you two b-broke up," I whisper.

What is she going to do to me? It isn't my fault that they had broken up; she can't hold it against me.

"We didn't. We're practically engaged," she sneers, flashing me a plain, cheap-looking ring. "And you knew it. Everyone knew it. We usually ignore you because we think you're a loser, but now, Lana, I'm going to make sure the rest of your life is a living hell."

With that parting shot, she storms off, her two friends trailing behind her like loyal servants.

They are still together.

He lied to me.

He thought I'd be easy. He thought I'd sleep with him on that beach, and he liked the idea of being able to tell everyone he'd had sex with a virgin, but I had refused him.

And I know she'll keep her word. She will make my life a living hell. I can see exactly how it will play out. No one will want to cross her, so everyone will ignore me, not wanting to replace me as her number one enemy.

In that moment, as I watch her and her friends strutting down the hall, I know I'm doomed to spend my senior year alone, lost in my books, my studies and writing. William won't care that he made me a social outcast. He'll just go back to ignoring my existence.

I wish Anna would come back. She is strong. If I had her, I wouldn't need anyone else.

I have learned many important lessons in such a short amount of time.

Number one. Men can't be trusted.

Number two. Sometimes you have to learn to enjoy your own company.

And number three. I will never be vulnerable again. I won't let people make me feel insecure and like less of a person because of their own cruelty and small-mindedness.

In that moment, the soft, nervous girl I was just minutes before developed a core of steel.

Sure, people will still call me a nerd.

But I'm more like Supergirl, because underneath these glasses is a woman no one wants to mess with.

I shake my head, staring at Allie, coming back to the present.

"Don't threaten me, Allie," I snap. "You're right, this isn't high school. I'm not that girl anymore, but it looks like you are. You still think you're the queen bitch and nothing can touch you. I let you bully me before, but I'm not fucking scared of you now. And it's not me who takes your men. William came to me, and Tracker and you aren't even together. If they really wanted you in the first place they wouldn't have left."

I hide my trembling hands, hating myself for the nasty words, but I want her to see I'm not weak anymore. I'm not going to let her or anyone else walk all over me.

She smirks. "Grew a backbone, did you? Don't say I didn't warn you about Tracker."

"Yes, I grew a backbone," I fire back. "I'm not scared of you, Allie. I can handle whatever you try to throw at me. Hell, I'll even catch it and return it tenfold."

Her face contorts. "We'll see who has the last laugh in the end."

She walks inside, and I drive home wondering what she's talking about.

NINE

YOU left me," Tracker says in annoyance when I open my door the next morning.

"Ummm, Tracker can we do this later?" I lower my voice. "My mom is here!"

"Good," he says. "I can finally meet her."

I shake my head frantically. "No, no, no—"

"Lana?" my mom calls out, walking to the door. "You must be Tracker."

He holds out his hand. "Nice to meet you, ma'am. I can see where Lana gets her beauty from."

I roll my eyes. Yes, my mom is beautiful, but that is the oldest line in the book.

"Come in, Tracker," she says, then turns to me. "Where are your manners, Lana? Invite him inside."

"Thank you," Tracker says politely, then flashes me a smirk. "So you've been talking about me, have you?"

Mom laughs softly. "She's mentioned you a few times, yes. Can I get you something to drink? My name is Nicole, by the way."

"Lovely name," Tracker replies. "I'd love some water, if you don't mind."

"No problem, have a seat."

Grabbing my hand, he leads me to the couch where we sat last time.

"Your mom is a babe," he whispers. "Now I know how you're gonna look when you're older."

I purse my lips. "She's going to annoy me and ask me about you every day now!"

He kisses my palm. "Good, then you'll never forget me."

I expel a sigh. "You're something else, you know that?"

His mouth twitches. "Saturday night we're having a party. Men from the other Wind Dragon chapters will be coming, their old ladies. That sort of thing. Do you wanna come?"

I shift in my seat. "Ummm. Will Anna be there?"

He nods. "Yeah, they'll all be there."

"All right then, I'll come."

"Good," he replies.

My mom returns with water and iced tea, then sits down with us and starts to ask Tracker questions.

"So what do you do for a living, Tracker?"

I look at him and wait for his answer.

"I'm a part owner of a bar called Rift. You might have heard of it. I also part own a motorcycle repair shop."

He clears his throat. "And a few other businesses."

Yeah, like Toxic, the local strip club.

"What other businesses?" I ask innocently, keeping a straight face.

"Oh, you know, this and that," he replies vaguely, shooting me a look that clearly says *Be quiet.*

"That's wonderful," my mom beams. "Especially for some-one so young. You're in your midtwenties right? Same as Lana."

Tracker nods. "Yes, I am."

"How lovely," my mom says, taking a sip of her tea. "Lana never brings boys to the house. In fact, you're the first one, so you must be someone special."

I cringe.

Did she have to let that one slip?

"I didn't exactly bring him here," I point out.

My mom waves her hand. "Semantics. Well, I have to get to the hospital for my shift. You two have fun."

She kisses my cheek, then does the same to Tracker before leaving.

Leaning back on the couch, he grins. "She loves me."

"At least someone does," I mutter, making him laugh. "You never talk about your parents. Do you have siblings?"

"My dad died a couple years back. My mom's remarried and lives overseas," he says. "No brothers or sisters."

"Sorry to hear about your dad," I say.

"What about your dad?" he asks, eyes steady on me.

I shrug, looking away. "I don't have a father."

Okay, I *have* a father; I just don't have any contact with him. Seeing as he's absent, I feel no need to give him any significance. Or even admit his existence.

"I mean, we don't talk," I add. "He's never been in my life."

"His loss," Tracker says quickly. "Your mom did an amazing job raising you on your own."

I duck my head. "Thanks."

"You wanna change out of yet another fuckin' cute pair of pajamas and spend the day with me?"

I look down at my pink shorts and matching top. They were covered in red cherries. "I have work, remember?"

He flashes me a slow spreading smile. "You have the day off. Jess is watching Clover."

"You got me the day off?" I ask, surprised.

"Yep," he says, smirking. "Faye loves me. She said it's no problem."

The sneaky man. "What did you have in mind?"

"A long ride. Lunch. A swim at the beach," he suggests. "Who fuckin' knows where we'll end up?"

I smile. "All right."

"Good," he says in a gentler tone. "Now give me a kiss and go get ready."

I do as the man says.

"So are you and Tracker dating?" Anna asks as she paints her toenails black. "I don't want to see you get hurt, Lana."

"I know," I whisper, looking down at my own red toenails. "I didn't want to give him the chance to hurt me but, he's . . . you know."

"Tracker?"

I grin. "I can't seem to say no to him. It's something I obviously need to work on."

Anna smirks. "You sleep with him yet?"

I shake my head. "Not yet."

"Good plan. Make him work for it," Anna says, wiggling her toes. "He's too charming for his own good sometimes."

"He invited me here on Saturday," I tell her. "What do I wear?"

Anna smirks. "Most of the women wear as close to nothing as they can get. But just wear whatever you're comfortable in. I usually wear tight jeans and a top. You can wear a dress if you want. Anything goes."

"I'll bet."

"For the record, the two of you look cute together," she continues. "I love him, but if he hurts you, I'm gonna cut off his dick and choke him with it."

My eyes widen at her description. "No need, Anna. I'm going into this knowing that I'm probably going to get hurt in the end. You don't need to ruin your friendships over it."

She makes a noise of frustration.

"Besides, if you cut if off, two heads will probably grow back."

She laughs, holding her stomach. "You're probably right. Has Allie been giving you any shit?"

"Not really. A few comments here and there. She's nothing I can't handle."

"Hmmm. Don't underestimate her, Lana. Not everyone is as nice as you."

"Noted," I tell my best friend. "Can you tell me something though? What's the deal with her and Tracker? I can't pretend it doesn't bother me; I mean, they were together for ages." I didn't want to bring it up, but I need to know.

"'Together' is a stretch," Anna says. "They hooked up a lot, but they never went on dates or out anywhere really. I don't know what Tracker wanted from her, but she took it pretty seriously. Anyway, they haven't hooked up in months, if not longer. Not since he started getting hooked on you." She smiles knowingly at me. I change the subject, satisfied with her answer.

"So how long until your house is ready?"

Anna and Arrow were building their own house to live in.

"Six months to go," she says, smiling. "It's gorgeous. There's plenty of room for you if you ever want to stay with me."

"I'm sure Arrow will love that."

"He's a little stingy with me, isn't he?" She sighs, glancing up at me. "But too bad, because you're always welcome wherever I am. I know it's selfish of me, but I really do hope you and Tracker work out. Then you're going to be stuck with me and the MC forever."

I grin. "You're stuck with me anyway, whether I'm with him or not."

"I know," she says quickly. "But you wouldn't be going to the Saturday night party, for example."

"That's true."

"Everyone here loves you, you know that?" she adds. "Everyone has a soft spot for you. I know you aren't exactly a crazy, wild biker bitch, but you still fit in here. . . . Do you know what I mean? You don't have to change to be with Tracker, or fit in with the MC, because everyone loves you how you are. You're gentle and sweet, yet with the backbone of a warrior princess."

I smile widely at her description of me. "I think you're a little biased."

"Probably," she replies, eyes sparkling. "But Tracker obviously sees it too. And Rake adores you."

"I think you're getting a little ahead of yourself," I say, wincing. "Tracker will get bored and move on eventually."

"I think you're wrong," Anna states simply. "I know Tracker, and when he looks at you there's something there I recognize, because Arrow looks at me the same way. He can't hide it."

"Weren't you just saying you didn't want to see me get hurt?"

She shrugs her slender shoulder. "He's a man."

And men always fuck up. Wasn't that the cold, hard truth?

I scrub my hand down my face. "I tried to stay away from him. I tried."

I could have tried harder though—but deep down inside I didn't want to.

I'm so out of my element.

"Just see how it goes," Anna says gently. "Find out what you both want. Make sure you're happy. You deserve it. And we all know you've had a thing for Tracker since you first laid eyes on him."

Like I need that reminder.

I hear a rumble of motorcycles.

"Looks like our men are back," she says, standing up.

I do the same.

I haven't seen Tracker since we spent the whole day together the day before. We'd had lunch, gone for an hour ride, then changed into bathing suits and swam at the beach. After that we'd dried in the sun, lying in the sand, before riding back home.

Anna and I walk out front to where the men are parking their bikes. When I see Allie sliding off the back of Tracker's bike, my chest tightens. I look to Anna, whose lips are pursed. Yeah, she notices it too. I don't get him. He had made me think it was a really big deal to ride on the back of someone's bike. Why would he let her ride with him? He's been trying to prove to me over and over that she's nothing to him, that their relationship is in the past, and he's never going back to her. But when I see them like this, what else am I meant to think? I feel betrayed. Stupid, even.

And yes—I'm jealous.

When I first met Tracker I had to watch them together. He wasn't mine then, and I never thought he would be, but I still liked him, so it hurt, although I kept my feelings to myself because I'd never go after a man who was taken.

Tracker, glancing up and seeing me, smiles widely. Rushing to me, he sees my face and slows his pace. "What's wrong?"

He couldn't be that stupid, could he?

"Nothing," I say. "I'm just leaving."

He looks back to Allie, then winces. "We went out. She needed a ride. It doesn't mean anything, Lana."

Any of the other men could have given her a ride.

Any.

But no, he had to.

I turn to Anna and kiss her cheek. "I'll see you."

"You want me to come home with you?" she asks, brow furrowing.

"No go spend time with your man," I reply, forcing a smile. Ignoring Allie's smug look, I walk to my car, Tracker following behind me.

"Lana," he says patiently. "You're overreacting."

Unlocking my door, I open it, then look at him. "So if I ride with any of the other men that's okay with you?"

His nostrils flair. "Fuck no. And they'd know better than to let you."

"Exactly," I snap. "She's your ex, you were with her for years and she's still acting like she's yours. I didn't want to get involved with you, Tracker, not because I didn't want you but because I want you so much. So don't fuck with my feelings. Either you want me and only me, or you don't. I think you need to decide—

because it kind of looks like you liked the chase, but now that you have me, you aren't sure what to do with me."

"I have you?" he repeats, scowling. "We haven't even slept together."

Wow, okay.

"So no sex means what? We aren't anything? Okay, good to know."

"That isn't what I meant," he says, sounding frustrated, reaching his arm out.

"It sounds like it's exactly what you meant," I snap. "I knew something like this would happen, but even I didn't think it would be this soon."

"Lana—"

"What, Tracker? Tired of the chase already? Well, let me make it easy for you. I'm done playing this game."

I get in my car and lock the doors just before he tries to open them. I start my engine and watch as he steps back.

I drive off, and he lets me.

When I get home, I lose myself in my book. I write about a man who can be amazing one second, a complete jerk the next. I write about perfect kisses, swimming in the ocean, and slutty ex-girlfriends. I write about the complications of romance.

And of unsure endings.

TEN

HE problem with working for Faye is that I can't avoid Tracker. I shat where I ate, and now I'm going to have to face him. I'm not at all surprised to see him standing there, arms crossed over his bare chest, when I walk into the clubhouse the next morning.

"You're in trouble," he rumbles, taking me by the upper arm and pulling me to his room. Closing the door he points to the bed. "Sit."

I don't sit.

He sighs and sits down, then pulls me onto his lap. "You can be stubborn, you know that?"

"Pretty sure you're meant to be apologizing right now," I grumble, moving my face away when he tries to kiss my cheek.

"I should be. But so should you," he says, gripping my chin and moving my face to his. "I won't let her on my bike again. I fucked up, yes, but you didn't handle the situation properly. Number one, our shit stays private—don't be turning your back on me in front of my brothers. You wait until we're alone, then if you need to, you can give me hell. What you don't do is give me the cold shoulder in front of my MC."

I never even thought of it that way. "I was upset, and I just reacted. I wasn't thinking about how you looked in front of your brothers. In that moment, I didn't really care. I was hurt, Tracker. It might seem like something small to you, but Allie isn't someone I want to see you with. You know she was one of the reasons I didn't want to be with you. History shows that eventually you'll be back with her."

"I know," he whispers. "I know she's a sore spot for you, Lana, but fuck, when I see her, I feel nothing. She's just someone I used to know and fuck, all right? You've clouded my mind, Lana, I don't see anyone else. You have no reason to be jealous."

"Still," I grumble. "I didn't like it."

"I know you didn't. It won't happen again, but neither will your tantrum in front of the others. Deal?"

"Fine," I reply ungraciously, still upset. "What you said about us not having sex . . ."

His eyes soften. "I was pissed and said stupid shit too. I didn't mean it. You don't wanna rush into sex? Then I'll walk around with a fuckin' hard-on until you decide to let me in you."

"Really?" I ask dryly. "You sure you aren't getting action whenever I leave here?"

Another worry. Can Tracker be faithful to me? I didn't want to sleep with him just because I was worried he would sleep with someone else. That isn't a valid reason to sleep with someone. Did I want to have sex with him?

Yes.

Did I think that giving him that piece of me would also be giving him everything else?

Hell yes.

This was my last defense against him.

If I give him that, then . . . I'm done for.

Sighing, I lift my mouth to his, initiating a kiss for the first time. He allows me to take control of the kiss, groaning when our tongues meet.

"So sweet," he moans, lifting me up and pushing me back on the bed, then reclaiming my lips. Threading my fingers through his loose hair, I pull gently on the ends, urging him on. His lips trail down my neck, sucking on a spot, making my toes curl.

"Tracker," I rasp.

He lifts his head and looks down at me. "We should stop."

I lick my lips and stare him in the eye. Then I remember that I'm here for a reason. "Fuck," I almost yell, sitting up. "Faye hasn't left yet, has she? I'm the worst nanny ever."

He chuckles, taking my arm and pulling me off the bed. I stand up and practically run to the door, Tracker's laughter chasing behind me. When I enter the kitchen I see Clover sitting there with Anna.

"I'm so sorry!" I exclaim. Anna looks amused as hell.

She covers Clover's ears with her hands. "Is he that quick? I was thinking he'd be another hour at least."

"Anna," Tracker frowns, coming to stand behind me. "Those are fighting words."

She smirks. "I better get to work."

Anna worked part-time at the zoo. She used to work at Knox's Tavern, a popular local bar, but Arrow kept coming in and starting fights, so Reid Knox fired her. We all give her shit about that.

"Say hi to the tortoise for me," I say, referring to Anna's favorite animal.

"Will do," she says, slapping my ass as she walks past me.

"Hey that's my a—," he stops himself, careful not to swear in front of Clover. "Ah, my bottom. Mine."

She just smiles at him. "You wish."

"I do," he grumbles, walking to the fridge. "Want me to cook for you again, Lana?"

"No!" I almost yell, then soften my tone. "I mean, no, thanks. I want to cook for you instead."

"Okay," he beams, sitting down next to Clover and asking her what she wanted to do today, making me feel as though I'd just been played.

I fry some bacon with scrambled eggs and sautéed mushrooms. Clover has a little, calling it her second breakfast for the day.

"I can hang out with you guys for a few hours, then I have to go to work," Tracker says after he helps clean up the kitchen.

"Sounds good, what do you want to do?"

"Ladies' choice," he says, looking to Clover. "What do you want to do today, princess?"

"I want to ride a motorcycle," she announces, looking proud.

I glance at Tracker, amused. "Good luck with that."

He looks thoughtful. "I think you should ask your dad that, Clover."

She nods. "Okay. We could go to the movies."

"What do you want to watch?"

"Something about princesses."

Tracker sighs unhappily.

I grin, amused.

We get ready to take Clover to see a movie about a princess.

I look at my reflection in the mirror, turning to each side, taking in my outfit. I'm wearing tight white jeans, a white tank top, layers and layers of silver chains, and red pumps. I don't know if I'll fit in with what others will wear, but I don't care. I feel good, and comfortable with my choice. Spraying a little perfume, I press together my red lips and touch up my hair. Black locks fall down my shoulders and back in waves. I leave on my glasses. Jumping when I hear a knock at the door, I rush to open it. Tracker stands there looking delicious. I lift my hand up to brush his stubbled cheek.

"You look . . . fuck, Lana," he grits out, checking me out from head to toe. Taking my hand from his cheek, he lowers it to his groin. "Feel how hard I am. That's how amazing you look. Fuck. I'm gonna have to beat the shit out of one of my brothers tonight, I know it."

I blush, touching his hardness, then removing my hand. "You look good too, Tracker. Sexiest man I've ever seen."

He groans and takes my mouth in a punishing kiss, his hands gripping my ass cheeks and squeezing. "Love this ass," he growls as he pulls back. "In fact I've yet to find anything I don't like about you, Lana."

"There's still time," I reply shakily, his kiss leaving me breathless.

"Give me a second to calm down, then we'll go," he says, eyes on my chest. "Fuck. You can wear my leather jacket so you're not cold."

He takes off his jacket, leaving him in a black T-shirt.

"You smell good."

"So do you," he replies, pressing his nose against my neck. "So fuckin' good."

As he helps me into his jacket, I'm aware of the tension between us. His fingers brush my neck, and I feel like I'm going to jump out of my skin. His touch is electric. I want him, badly. Who am I kidding? In my mind, I'm already his. If he breaks my heart . . . that's a chance I'm going to have to take.

"Tracker," I whisper, looking up at him. He's tall, around six foot two, so I have to lift my chin.

"Yes," he replies, just as soft.

"Tonight," I say.

His eyes widen. He knows what I mean. Tonight.

I want him tonight.

I'm ready to give myself to him.

"Are you sure?" he asks, taking my hand and kissing it. "I don't want you to regret anything. I know you're different from . . . what I'm used to."

My lip twitches at that. "I don't think I'm different at all. But yes, I'm sure. Now let's get back to the clubhouse. I'm interested to see what happens at these parties."

He grins. "Fuck the party. I'm gonna throw you over my shoulder and take you straight to my room."

I laugh.

"Baby, I'm dead serious," he says. "I have no fuckin' clue why you're laughing."

I shake my head and climb up behind him on the bike.

I'm so writing this scene in one of my books.

ELEVEN

THE clubhouse is swarming with unfamiliar, scary-looking men and beautiful, hard women. Tracker stops every few seconds, greeting his friends from other Wind Dragon chapters. There are so many people; I don't know how he remembers everyone. Rake does a double take when he sees me, his eyes almost popping out of his head. Putting out his cigarette, he walks over and stands directly in front of me.

"This is like that scene from *Grease*," he says, smiling widely. "When Sandy walks out and everyone's all, where the fuck did she hide that body? Shit, Lana, you look smoking."

"Stop staring at her like that," Tracker snaps, half serious, half joking.

Rake laughs. "You have it bad, you fucker." He then looks back to me. "Anna was looking for you."

Sin walks over to us, his eyes widening when he sees me. "Shit. Looking good, Lana."

"Thanks," I say, ducking my head shyly.

"Tracker, need to speak to you," Sin says, all business in his tone.

"Rake, stay with Lana for a sec," Tracker says, looking down at me. "Don't move, Lana."

I nod and watch as he disappears back outside with Sin.

"You want me to get you a drink?" he asks, scanning the crowd.

"No, thanks," I tell him. I want to be sober for my first time with Tracker. I have a feeling it's going to be a night I'm not gonna want to forget.

"We have water and soda too, you know," he adds in an amused tone. "We don't just drink straight from the bottles of alcohol."

I roll my eyes. "Really? Big, bad bikers need chasers with their drinks?"

He laughs, eyes crinkling. "I don't. But some do."

"Uh-huh," I mutter, sharing a smile with him. "Thanks for making me feel so welcome here, even though I'm completely out of my element."

"You're good people, Lana," he says quietly. "In fact, you're probably way too good for the likes of us, just like Anna is, but if you want to be here, we'll always have your back. Tracker's a goner when it comes to you. It's good though. He deserves someone like you."

I shift on my feet, then admit, "I hope it works out, but we're still getting to know each other, I guess."

What if we aren't compatible sexually?

He's experienced, I'm not. I've been with two men, both once each. I'm so nervous about not matching up to his other sexual partners.

Screw it, for what I lack in experience I'll make up for in desire for him. I don't think a woman has ever wanted him as much as I do, and I don't just mean his body.

"Lucky bastard," Rake mutters, shaking his head. "I saw that look on your face."

I clear my throat. "Maybe I will have a soda after all."

Grinning, he wraps his arm around me and takes me to the kitchen, where I find Anna.

"Lana!" she yells, smiling widely. "Holy shit, you look beautiful. I'm so fuckin' happy you made it."

"I haven't run scared . . . yet," I tease, pulling her in for a quick hug. "Hey, Arrow."

"Lana," he says, lifting his chin. "You look different."

Anna elbows him. "Real smooth, Arrow."

He shrugs and takes a sip from his beer, his other arm wrapping around her. She tugs playfully on his beard, then kisses his mouth.

"Want to dance, Lana?" she asks, still looking at Arrow.

"I'll dance with her," Rake says, handing me a cup.

Anna looks at her brother. "Rake, I didn't recognize you without a woman hanging from your arm."

"I have one," he replies, nodding at me.

"Where's Tracker?" Anna asks, frowning.

"Talking with Sin."

Arrow suddenly looks alert, his head lifting. "Everything all right?"

Rake nods. "All good, brother."

Anna grabs my arm. "We're dancing."

"Tracker said not to let her out of my sight," Rake says. "So I'm coming."

"Then come," Anna says. "Show us your moves, bro."

With Anna and me on each of his arms, Rake walks us to the game room, where the music is coming from. We dance to two songs before I find myself back in Tracker's arms.

"You're a good dancer," he whispers into my ear. "I'm ready to have you all to myself now."

"Aren't you going to dance with me?" I say loudly so he can hear.

"I am," he replies, "Between the sheets."

I squeal as he picks me up and throws me over his shoulder just like he said he would. I ignore the whistles and catcalls as he takes me straight to his room, ignoring anyone who tries to talk to him. He turns on the lights and slams the door shut with a kick of his foot, closing us in. He then throws me on the bed, staring down at me like a hunter looking at his prey. I swallow hard as he pulls off his T-shirt, revealing his powerful body. My heart is in my chest as he unbuckles his belt, undoes his button and zipper, and lets his jeans fall to the ground. He kicks them away, then pulls down his boxer briefs, exposing himself to me fully. Looking down at me, he puffs out a breath and rubs the back of his head.

"Fuck, maybe I should take a cold shower before I come to you," he mutters. "I can't remember the last time I went without sex for this long . . . and it's *you*. I don't wanna fuckin' scare you."

"I can handle anything you want to give," I say in a voice that doesn't sound like my own.

It sounds strong.

Sultry.

A woman who knows what she wants and is going to get it.

I allow my gaze to lower to his cock, which is jutting out,

strong and proud. I linger on the piercing, wondering what it was going to feel like.

"Fuck," he grits out. "With you looking at me like that . . ."

Sliding to the end of the bed, I slide off my pumps and jewelry and then stand up. "Undress me," I tell him in a soft command.

Licking his lips, he reaches out and pulls my top off, staring at my white lace bra before undoing my jeans and sliding them off. When they don't come off easily— they're so damn tight—I giggle. He groans, "How did you get into these? Christ, Lana, they're like a second skin."

"Are you complaining?" I ask breathlessly as he makes me lie back down on the bed so he can pull them off.

"Right now I am," he says, kissing my stomach after he finally gets them off, leaving me in my panties and bra.

"Beautiful."

I shiver at the reverence in his tone.

Kissing my belly button, he trails his mouth lower, kissing over my lace panties until he reaches my center. Then, with his thumbs, he pulls the scrap of cloth down, his face right in front of my pussy. Without hesitation, his mouth is on me, his tongue working magic, licking and sucking with purpose. I look down at his blond hair, threading my fingers through it and pulling. Lifting my hips, I silently beg for more, and he gives it to me, his tongue flicking on my clit.

It hits me with no warning.

My back arching, I grit my teeth to stop myself screaming as I come.

He's merciless with me, gripping my thighs to spread them farther, his whole face all over me.

"Tracker," I whimper as I come back to myself, the feeling getting too sensitive. He sits back on his knees and wipes his mouth with the back of his hand.

"Perfect," he rasps. "But next time I wanna hear you scream, Lana, don't try to be quiet. I want to hear you."

"I've never come that hard," I rasp.

Tracker grins, a satisfied look on his face. "Baby, this is just the beginning."

Getting on the bed, he straddles me, a knee on each side of my hips, his cock resting on my stomach.

"Are you okay?" he asks softly, sliding down the straps of my bra, then pulling down the cups. "Been greedy with you, haven't I? I haven't even tasted these yet, rushed straight to your sweet pussy."

I really didn't mind.

Lowering his head, he sucks a nipple into his mouth, then pulls back to taste the other. Plumping my breasts together, he licks the space between them. "Even better than I imagined."

"Tracker." I sigh.

"Are you on the pill?" he asks, reaching a hand down between us to position himself.

"Yeah."

"I wanna fuck you raw," he says kissing my lips. "Been tested while I was waiting for you. Let me have you, Lana."

Not thinking, just feeling, I nod. "Okay."

"Thank fuck," he growls, sliding into me, slowly. I can tell he's using all his restraint not to slide home in one thrust.

"Tracker," I whisper. "I can take it."

He slides the rest of the way, cursing. "You feel so good Lana. So fuckin' worth the wait."

I lift my hips in time with his thrusts. I soon realize the extra sensations I can feel are because of his piercing, something which I plan to explore further. His mouth stays on mine, our lips never losing contact. I can tell that he's a man who loves kissing, and I couldn't be more thrilled. The way he kisses is perfect, so sensual and erotic, especially the way he slides his tongue over mine and nibbles on my bottom lip. When he starts kissing my neck, I feel my orgasm building.

"Come with me, baby," he whispers against my mouth, before returning to kissing me. Raising my arms over my head with our fingers threaded together, he pushes me into the mattress, taking what he needs and giving me the same in return.

His thrusts become deeper, and faster, and I can't help the moan that spills from my lips. Everything is so intense, including my physical and emotional response to him.

"Lana," he whispers, his mouth returning to mine, kissing me like this is the last time he'll ever taste my lips.

He waits for me to come a second time before he joins me, spurting his hot come inside me. Resting his forehead against mine, his eyes tightly closed, he vows, "I would do anything to protect you Lana, to protect this."

It was in this moment I lost my heart to him.

I'm his, solely.

And I know, the depth of my love will be the depth of my pain if I lose him.

TWELVE

IME to face reality.

I'm going to have to do a walk of shame.

Dressing in last night's clothes—which don't look so great this morning—with my red shoes in my hand, I kiss Tracker's cheek before making my exit. When I smell bacon, I stop by the kitchen to investigate. Two women I don't know are in there, making themselves at home. Not wanting to intrude, I walk by Anna's room, almost choking when I hear her voice.

"Put that baby maker inside me and fuck me, Arrow!"

Baby maker?

I can't help it.

I lose it.

With my mouth covering my hand, I start cracking up.

"Lana, is that you?" I hear her call out.

I can't speak over my laughing.

Then I hear her laughing too.

And Arrow growling.

Still giggling, I walk outside and to my car. As I'm driving off, I see Allie being dropped off by a random man. I can't really see him, but she's wearing what are presumably last night's clothes with her heels in her hands. She bends down to kiss him good-bye through the window. I feel relieved, happy to see her moving on. Even though I know Tracker wants nothing to do with her, it's good to know she may be over him too. I don't need or want that drama.

Ignoring her, I look straight ahead and drive home. After making love to Tracker last night—and he can say what he wants but that was making love—I'm suddenly inspired to write the sex scenes of all sex scenes. Just thinking about him, about last night, makes me smile. Who would think a man in a biker club could be so damn sweet? Sure, he talks dirty, but I like that. No, I love that.

Last night was . . . swoon. I can't think of another word for it.

We stayed in the room the whole night, getting to know each other's bodies. I don't know how he did it, but he made me feel comfortable, brought me out of my shell. I felt . . . beautiful. It was the way he looked at me, like it was *me* who was perfect. Not him, me. Nothing is off bounds with him. Nothing is judged.

We just *felt*.

He's insatiable. An animal.

A man in his finest form.

And somehow . . . he's mine.

"So," I start. "Are you and Arrow trying to have a baby?"

Anna's eyes widen. "What makes you ask that?"

I shrug nonchalantly. "It might have been the whole 'put your baby maker' line I heard the other day."

She covers her face with her hands. "Oh. Right. That. I knew that was you laughing!"

I smirk. "I can't remember the last time I laughed so hard."

Anna removes her hands and grins. "Yeah, we're trying. Arrow is loving the trying."

"I can imagine," I reply, picking up my coffee and taking a sip. "How come Allie's never around anymore?"

Anna nods. "I know, right? She doesn't wanna see you with Tracker, I think. She comes by every few days; I think she's found another man to terrorize."

I nod, sighing. "At least she's not terrorizing me. She did mention something once though. Something about it's not her Tracker wants, or me. Any idea what she was talking about?"

She studies me for a few long seconds. "I may have heard something, but I have a feeling you'll make it a bigger deal than it is."

"What?" I ask, sitting up straighter.

She sighs. "When Faye came into the house, apparently—I say apparently because I wasn't here so I don't know the truth—but I heard Tracker had a thing for Faye. He wanted her, obviously he couldn't have her, so he hooked up with Allie instead."

"He wanted Faye?" I ask in a broken whisper. Faye? That freaking supermodel of a woman?

Great, just great. I can't stop the hurt that slowly fills my body.

"Lana," Anna growls. "Number one, this was years ago. They're just friends now. And Tracker is crazy about you. Arrow said he hasn't seen him pay this much attention to a woman in . . . forever."

When I stay silent, she continues. "Look, I'll be the first to admit I actually warned Tracker away from you a few times. I thought it was a bad idea. He's . . . him, and I didn't want to see you get hurt. But, and I can't believe I'm going to say this, I was wrong. He's so good to you. I haven't seen him even look at another woman, and you're happy, I can see it. I know you're also unsure, and scared of getting hurt, but I think the two of you have something great going. If you think you can handle him and his lifestyle, I think he will make you a happy and lucky woman."

"You're right," I admit. "If it's in the past then . . . as long as he's not secretly pining away for her."

Anna laughs. "No. They're friends, just like he and I are."

Then why did Allie try and throw it in my face? Or maybe it was her issue, considering she was his second choice. Pushing it to the back of my mind, I change the topic.

"There's something I have to tell you. I didn't really need the nannying job. I took it because I needed something different in my life, a change, and because I knew Faye needed the help."

I want to tell Anna everything. I don't want to keep everything inside anymore, I want to try and be open, and there's no one I trust more than Anna, besides my mom.

"I'm glad you took it. Faye can't stop raving about how amazing you are with Clover," Anna says. "But if you don't need the job, just give Faye a little warning so she can find someone new. She'll have to find someone else when you go back to school anyway."

She's missing the point here.

"Yeah, I know, but what I'm trying to tell you is—"

"Lana!" Tracker calls out from the front door.

"In here!" I call back, turning to Anna with an apologetic glance. "This conversation is to be continued."

She nods, grinning slyly. "I thought he was working all day."

"Me too."

He walks into the living room, gaze searching for me. His eyes brighten when they land on me. "Want to come for a ride?"

"Clover?"

He looks to Anna. "Can you watch Clover for the rest of the day?"

Anna nods. "Sure. When she wakes up I can take her to the zoo with me."

Tracker grins. "Thanks, Anna. Lana, get your shoes on."

I get ready, then follow him outside. As he puts his helmet on me, I ask, "Where are we going?"

"I have to get back to work."

"Oh. Then why am I coming?" I ask, frowning.

"'Cause I missed you, and I want you there with me," he says, kissing me.

"Oh."

"Yes, oh," he replies with a chuckle.

"Well, let's go then," I say, smiling shyly.

Another kiss, this one longer, and then we're off.

I keep thinking about my conversation with Anna and realize she's right. I need to judge Tracker on who he is now, who he is for me, rather than who he was or what he could do. I need to put the past behind me and take a chance.

* * *

Standing outside of Toxic, a strip club, I scowl. "This isn't what I had in mind when I said I'd spend the day with you Tracker."

He grins and cups my chin. "Just a stopover, sheathe those claws."

Pursing my lips, I let him lead me inside. The place is what you'd imagine a strip club to be, except there are no girls dancing.

"Is it closed?" I ask, as we head to the bar where a man is cleaning glasses.

"Yeah, it opens in an hour or two," Tracker says, smirking down at me. "Why? Disappointed?"

I shrug. "I've never been to a strip club before. I might as well get the full experience."

I can almost feel a new plot coming on.

"I'll bring you back another time then," he murmurs, shaking his head in amusement. "You never react how I expect you to."

"I don't like the idea of you coming here," I admit.

"Why?" he asks. "None of the women here have shit on you."

I blush. "Tracker—"

He brings his lips to my ear. "You're the most beautiful woman in the world to me. And my opinion is the only one that fuckin' matters, baby."

I look directly into his eyes and see that he believes what he says.

"You're not going to stop until you own every inch of me, are you?" I whisper.

"I'm not going to stop until you want me to," he replies, kissing my forehead. "I need you to need me as much as I want you."

I'm already there.

"Sit here for a sec, all right? I gotta go out back and handle something. Anyone comes near you, tell them you're mine and they'll back off if they have any brains."

I nod and sit down. No one is around anyway.

"You want me to get you a drink?"

"A soda would be good."

He heads over to the bar and gets a can of soda for me. Placing it down, he kisses my temple, then disappears behind one of the backroom doors. Opening the drink, I take a sip and look around the club. There are a few different stages and podiums, and I wonder what it looks like when everything is in full swing. The door opens, and two pretty women walk in.

"I saw his bike out there," one says. "Do I look okay?"

The other nods. "As always."

One sees me and gives me an odd look. "Are you a new dancer?"

I see her giving me a once-over, as if I were competition, then smiling when she finds me lacking. "You don't look like the usual dancers they hire here."

"That's because I'm not one," I reply, pushing my glasses up on my face.

"Oh. Are you a cleaner here or something then?" one, the blonde, asks seriously.

I grit my teeth. "No."

Not that there's anything wrong with being a cleaner, but why was that her first assumption?

Tracker walks out in that moment, his eyes widening as he sees me cornered by these two women. Eyes on me, he comes straight over to me. "You okay?"

"Tracker!" The blonde beams. "I knew it was your bike I saw."

She puts her hand on his chest.

I see red.

I stand up. "I'd rather you didn't do that."

She turns to me. "What?"

I ignore her and walk up to Tracker, moving her out of the way. I thread my hand through his hair and pull him down to me, kissing him hard. When I pull away, he's out of breath and his eyes are alight with passion.

"God, Lana," is all he manages to say. I smile up at him, proud of my own nerve. I nod toward the women, who look pissed off and confused, and he takes the hint.

"Ladies," Tracker says, turning toward them but keeping his eyes on me. "I'm off the market. This is my old lady, and if I were you I'd stay the hell away from her. Now, baby," he says to me, "let's get going."

When we walk outside, he turns to me, "Christ, that was the hottest thing you've ever done. I'm so fucking hard right now."

I shrug, feeling my cheeks heat. "You're mine. I wanted to let them know."

My man studies me. "I think you fit in with us fine, Lana."

My lips twitch. "Only because you make it that way."

THIRTEEN

AFTER spending the rest of the day with Tracker, stopping by Rift and their bike shop, he takes me out for a bite to eat and then drops me off at home. When walking me to my door, he grumbles, "Why don't you just move into the clubhouse? I don't like you not being there."

"I'm actually going to look for a place of my own," I tell him, pausing. "You know, you can stay here tonight. My mom will be working."

He tilts his head to the side. "You want me to stay?"

I nod. "Yeah, I do."

He smiles slowly. "You getting as addicted to me as I am to you?"

I bite my lower lip. "Is that what you want?"

He swallows, his throat working. "You know it's all I want right now. I don't want you to see something you don't like and want to run. I need you tied to me. Bound. In deep."

I shake my head. "You want me to be tied to you so when the realities of your world hit me, I won't run scared?"

He nods, then scrubs a hand down his face. "Sounds fucked-up but it's the truth."

"At least you're honest," I reply in a dry tone.

"I'll always be honest with you, Lana," he replies in a serious tone. "I don't lie. The truth hurts, but lies cause even more shit."

Yes, they do.

I tilt my head to the side. "Okay then, I have a question for you. Let's go inside first."

I open the door and the two of us head straight to my bedroom. We sit comfortably on the bed, facing each other.

"What did you want to ask me?"

"Did you used to have feelings for Faye?" I blurt out.

He frowns. "Where did you hear that?"

Not about to drop names, I ignore his question. "Is it true?"

He sits down next to me. "When Faye first came to the clubhouse, confused, lost, and pregnant, we became friends. Just like I did with Anna. Yeah, I felt something for Faye. I thought I wanted her. If Sin didn't want her, yeah, I would have had her. But more than that, I think I wanted what they had. Faye was a good woman. She won't cheat, lie, or backstab. She can be trusted. She takes care of not only her man, but the other men in the MC too. A true old lady. That's what I really wanted."

"Then why did you choose Allie?" I grumble.

He chuckles. "She was there; she wanted me. I was lonely, I guess. Arrow and Sin seemed so happy after finding their women, and I guess I wanted that. Looking back, I know I didn't have real feelings for Faye. Or Allie. Do you know how I know this?"

"How?" I ask.

"Because what I felt for them is nothing like what I feel for you. It pales in comparison. It's fuckin' nonexistent. Do you understand? *You* are what I was searching for. Waiting for. Not them. I can't even understand it. I saw you, I wanted you, and I knew you were it for me. I resisted for a while because Anna kept threatening me away, but nothing can keep me from you now."

"That simple, huh?" I say, barely a whisper.

"Getting you wasn't simple," he replies, amusement lacing his tone. "You put up a good fight, babe."

"I tried anyway," I tease.

"Aren't you glad you gave in though?" he asks, pulling me onto his lap. "I'm going to take such good care of you."

"I don't need to be taken care of," I tell him honestly. "But I am glad. Otherwise I wouldn't be able to do this."

I kiss him.

"Or this."

I bite his neck.

Then I whisper in his ear, "Have your way with me, Tracker."

"Fuck, Lana," he groans. "Only you make me this fuckin' crazy. Strip down and lie back for me. You're going to be a good girl and do exactly as I ask, aren't you?"

I nod.

Within reason, of course.

"Good," he grits out, stripping down himself, watching me through heavy-lidded eyes as I do the same. I lie back, fully naked. "Now spread your legs."

I spread.

"You want my mouth or my cock?" he asks, stroking himself, eyes connected with mine.

"Both," I reply, making him smile seductively.

"My greedy woman," he says. "I think I'm going to take from you first, before I give you everything you want. Open that pretty mouth for me."

I open my mouth and let him gently slide himself inside. I start slow, moving my mouth on and off his cock. I run my tongue over his piercing, and hearing his groan, I do it again, grabbing the base of his cock with my hand, making an *okay* sign with my hand. Then I speed up, and he starts thrusting slightly, gently, as though afraid he'll hurt me. My hands go to his ass, using it to push him deeper into my mouth, silently giving him permission to thrust harder. I feel his body spasm and he fills my mouth.

After he comes, he keeps his word and makes me come with his mouth and his cock.

Twice.

I wake up to my mom making Tracker breakfast in the kitchen. You'd think she'd be opposed to my relationship with a huge, tattooed biker, but no, my mom just goes with the flow. I suppose she had a thing for bad boys too, considering who my dad is.

"I hope you're hungry," I hear her tell him, sliding him a plate piled high with a mountain of bacon. She's busy in the kitchen while Tracker sits at the breakfast bar.

He looks down with wide eyes. "Thank you, Nicole."

"'Morning," I say, glancing from Mom to Tracker.

"'Morning, baby," Tracker says with a smile, standing up and coming to me, giving me a hug. "Help me eat all this food, please."

I smile into his chest. "As if you can't finish it."

"I'm gonna go to bed," my mom says, "Just got in. Take care of my daughter, Tracker."

"Always," Tracker replies, looking at me when he says it. "Thanks for breakfast."

"No problem," she calls out as she makes her way to her bedroom.

I look up at him. "Ever had a girl's mother make you breakfast before?"

He grins. "No, this is a first. Your mom is a nice lady. Can see why you're so sweet. She's also the first mom ever to actually like me."

I laugh. "She doesn't judge people. If I'm happy, so is she."

"I better make sure I always keep you happy then," he murmurs, leaning down and sucking on my lower lip.

"Mmmm," I sigh. I'm loving the normality of our behavior, the way he looks at me and touches me. "Let's eat and get to the clubhouse before Faye has to go to work."

"Okay," he says. "Better get to work on this pile of bacon."

"You don't have to eat all of it." I laugh.

"I know. But . . . it's bacon."

"Greedy."

"Cute."

We get to the clubhouse just in time.

Later that evening, as we lie in his bed, Tracker announces, "I'm gonna be gone for a couple of days."

"Where are you going?" I ask quietly. I don't want him to go.

"On a run with the men. Club shit, babe," he says, tracing a pattern over my bare shoulder with his finger. I want to ask where he's going and what he's doing, but I know he won't answer. *Can't* answer. Can I get used to this lifestyle? "One of the prospects will pick you up and take you anywhere you want to go."

"That's not necessary—"

"You being with me means people can try to hurt the club by hurting you," he interrupts, kissing my collarbone. "Just humor me, all right? For my damn piece of mind, just let me make sure you're safe."

"I don't know any of the prospects," I protest. "It will be awkward."

"You've met Blade," he says gently. "He'll be the one dropping and picking you up. I trust him. And if anything happens, just call me, okay?"

I have met Blade. He's younger than me, around twenty-one, and a pretty good-looking guy.

"Okay," I concede. I remember what happened with Anna when she tried to leave the clubhouse without an escort. She was kidnapped. Yeah, I didn't want that. With Tracker gone, at least I could get some writing done, even if I would miss him like crazy. He's become such a huge part of my life so quickly. It's amazing but terrifying.

"*Okay?*" he asks warily, pulling down the blanket and licking my nipple. "You're not gonna give me shit? Just . . . *okay?*"

I nod, now concentrating on what he's doing with his tongue. "Yeah."

"Fuck, you're so good to me," he says, now sucking my nipple into his mouth.

"Pretty sure it's you being good to me right now," I rasp, closing my eyes, my hands fisting the sheets.

He blows on one and then the other, teasing me. "You're mine, Lana. I'll always take care of what's mine."

Freeing his hair from its bun, I run my fingers through it, cradling the back of his head as he worships me. Tracker loves making love, but he also likes playing, just like this, with lazy strokes and slow seduction. He's not always in a rush to make us both come. Like right now, sometimes he just enjoys being with me, drawing out my pleasure. One of his fingers slowly touches me intimately, the softest of caresses. He's going to kill me. Death by pleasure, I'm sure it's a thing. If it's not, then it should be.

"You gonna miss me?" he asks, licking down my stomach.

"No," I reply, earning me a nibble just under my belly button.

"You sure?" he asks again, pressing openmouthed kisses down my inner thigh.

"I'm sure," I say in a husky tone. "I won't miss you one bit."

He flips me over in one quick motion and spanks my ass.

"Don't lie to me, Lana," he says, sounding amused. "You're gonna miss me like fuckin' crazy. Get up on all fours."

I slide up on my knees, spreading my legs.

"Good girl," he croons. "Now tell me."

He licks me once, right on my sweet spot, spreading my thighs with the hard grip of his hands. "Tell me what I want to hear."

I need his tongue, so I say, "I'm going to miss you."

He slaps my ass again. I love it.

"What was that for?" I snap.

"That one," he chuckles, "was just for fun."

Jerk.

Then he puts his mouth on me and I don't think he's a jerk anymore.

FOURTEEN

T HE next morning, Tracker leaves with Rake, Irish, Arrow, Trace, Ronan, and Sin. Vinnie is staying behind, currently peering over my shoulder as I make breakfast. His usually shaved head actually has a little hair on it for once.

"Be patient," I tease.

"Uncle Vinnie is hungry," Clover calls out from where she is drawing on the dining table. "We need to feed him or he gets grumpy."

"I can see that." I look at Vinnie, who is grinning at Clover affectionately. "Clover has more patience than you."

He stares at the waffles longingly, then glances up at me. "They smell so fucking good."

Clover gasps. "That's a bad word. I won't tell Mommy though. I'm not a snitch. I heard Daddy tell Uncle Arrow no one likes a snitch."

Vinnie and I share a glance, then start laughing. The things this kid remembers!

When the waffles are ready, I let Vinnie and Clover eat first, then make a huge pile of them for anyone else who wants them. When Blade steps into the kitchen, I point to the pile and he grins.

"Can we keep you?"

I laugh. "I'm here every weekday until I start school again."

"You need a ride anywhere today?" he asks as he eats.

I look to Clover. "Where do you want to go today, Clo?"

She thinks it over. "Can we go to the animal farm?"

I nod. "Sure. Are you going to come with us, Blade? We can have some lunch too."

He shifts on his seat, suddenly looking uncomfortable. His dark eyes stay on mine as he says, "Sorry, Lana, I can only drop you off and pick you up." I squint my eyes at him, wondering if that is Tracker's doing or if there is something else he needed to do. He runs a hand over his short dark hair, waiting for me to say something.

"Oh," I say. "Okay, if you don't mind."

"That's what I'm here for."

Clover and I get ready and Blade drives us in a black four-wheel drive. When we get there, he double-checks that my phone is charged and that I have his number before he drives away. We have lunch first, then see all the animals. A few hours later we get picked up and head back to the clubhouse. Faye is waiting for us when we get there, having gotten home early from work.

"Mom! I had so much fun today," Clover says after she hugs Faye. "I fed a horse!"

"Sounds like you had a ball," Faye says, kissing her head. Clover runs off, and Faye looks at me. "You're so good with her,

Lana. I know that every time I leave she's going out to explore and have fun, not just sit here and watch TV all day."

I shrug a little shyly. "She's a great kid."

"That she is," Faye replies, grinning. "Do you wanna stay and chat for a bit, or do you have to leave?"

I think of all the work I have waiting for me at home. "Love to stay, but I better go."

She nods. "No problem. See you tomorrow."

"'Bye, Faye," I say, smiling, then walking to the front door. I look around for Blade but don't find him. When I spot Vinnie I ask him if he can give me a ride home instead.

"Of course I can," he replies. "But I need to go somewhere else after so we're taking my bike."

I've never been on anyone else's bike.

"Ummm," I mutter, not knowing if this is okay.

Vinnie laughs. "It's just a ride. I'll deal with Tracker."

It's not like Vinnie is an ex, like the situation with Allie. And Tracker is the one who made me promise I wouldn't go anywhere alone. Shrugging, I get on the back of his bike, not pressing my body to his like I usually do with Tracker. When we get to my place, I thank him, then walk to my front door while searching for my house keys in my small handbag. When I find them, I unlock the door, waving to Vinnie. Once I'm safely inside, I hear the rumble of his bike as he rides off. Closing the front door, I turn the lock. I'm about to spin around when something hits me on the back of my head, pushing me against the door.

My vision flashes.

I hear a voice. Female.

And another. Male.

Another hit.

Laughter.

And another.

I slide down the door, falling to the floor.

I fight to stay conscious.

I don't want to leave Tracker. I just got him.

"Tracker," I mouth, but no sound comes out.

All I feel is pain, all I see is darkness.

I wake up, my whole body hurting.

Every inch of me is in pain. My ribs are throbbing. My legs feel numb. My jaw is swollen.

My right eye is swelled shut, but my left manages to open.

"Lana?" I hear my mom call my name. "Thank god."

I feel her hand in mine. I squeeze back.

Then I fall asleep again.

"Lana?" I hear his voice. "Fuck. Lana, can you hear me?"

I open my left eye and look at him. He looks like hell. His eyes are red and his face pale. "Tracker?"

My voice is weak.

Broken.

"What happened?" I ask him.

"You're hurt," he whispers. "Christ, Lana, whoever did this to you is going to wish they were dead."

I shiver at the intensity of his voice.

"You were hit on the back of your head. Doctor thinks you

passed out on impact. You're mainly bruised. A few broken ribs. You were kicked."

Who would want to hurt me? I didn't do anything to anyone.

"How long have I been here?" I ask him.

He takes my hand in his, kissing my knuckles. "This is your second night here. They gave you pain medicine and you've been in and out of it. I rode back as soon as Faye called me. Your mom found you and called her to tell her what happened and that you wouldn't be in to take care of Clover."

I lick my dry lips and he instantly brings me some water with a straw. "Drink, baby."

I drink greedily until he pulls it away. "Not so fast."

Even swallowing hurts.

"Can I get you anything?" he asks.

"No," I whisper. "Just stay here with me."

"I haven't left your side," he says. "It fuckin' hurts to see you like this, but I'm trying not to be selfish, since you're the one in pain, not me. Trust me, if I could take the pain away for you I would in an instant."

"Tracker," I whisper. "I love you."

His fingers tighten on my hand. "I love you too, Lana. 'Bout time you realized it though."

I fall asleep feeling safe.

"I'm fine," I tell a fussing Anna, who won't leave me the hell alone.

"You are not fine," she snaps, her eyes starting to water.

"Anna," I say softly. "I'm fine. Banged up, but fine. Whoever beat me must hit like a girl."

Her head suddenly snaps to me, like the chick from *The Exorcist*. "A girl?"

"What?" I ask at the look on her face.

"Nothing," she says instantly, softening her expression. "Let me fuss over my best friend, would you? It's either that or I lose my shit."

"Fine." I give in. I spent two nights in the hospital and now I'm in the clubhouse, because Tracker won't let me go home. To be honest, I'm fine. Ribs hurt, yes, face is swollen and bruised, yes, but it could have been a lot worse. I'm on pain medication and catching up on some reading. Nothing was stolen from my house, so I don't know why it happened, but it happened. Vinnie felt awful. Tracker told me he had refused to sleep until I woke up. I reassured Vinnie that it was okay and he wasn't at all to blame. I feel safe in the clubhouse, and I'm surrounded with people who care about me. Tracker has been amazing.

"Do you want to watch a movie?" Anna asks.

I nod. "Sure."

We're halfway through my favorite part of the movie when Tracker storms into the room, giving my forehead a quick kiss before looking at Anna. "Need to talk to you."

I sit up. "What's going on?"

He glances my way, eyes softening. "Nothing for you to worry about, baby. You relax. Faye will be in in a sec to keep you company."

Anna stands and follows Tracker out.

What the hell is going on?

Faye walks in a few minutes later, redirecting or straight out ignoring my prying questions.

"Whatever you want to know, you ask Tracker," she says. "I don't know anything."

She so did.

"How's Clover?" I ask. "I miss her."

"She's good," Faye replies. "I took the week off work."

Shit.

"I'm sorry," I mumble.

She gives me a stern look. "You have nothing to be sorry about. You're family now, Lana. Family takes care of each other. If what happened was because of your affiliation with the club, Tracker is going to handle it. Even if it wasn't, Tracker is going to handle it."

"I don't want him to get hurt."

Or end up in jail.

Faye laughs. "You know why they call him Tracker, right? He can find anyone. Anyone. Whoever did this to you will pay."

She says it like a vow.

In this moment, I see Faye, the president's wife.

She is kind of scary.

"Remind me never to mess with you."

She grins. "You wouldn't. You're a nice girl, Lana, and you make Tracker happy. That's all I want: all the men happy."

"And out of jail," I add.

She smiles sadly. "And out of jail. As their lawyer, I try and make that happen too."

"Must be a full-time job," I joke.

"You have no idea." She laughs, her eyes sparkling. "But I've found them to be the biggest contradictions. They have a dangerous side. Arrow for one—but see how he is with Anna?

He'd never let anyone hurt her. Not everything is black-and-white."

I nod. "I had preconceived notions of what the men here would be like, but they weren't anything like it. Most of them were welcoming."

Faye smirks. "That's because you were already one of us. If you were a random woman it would have been a whole different situation. Tracker warned them to be on their best behavior if they wanted to live." She clears her throat. "I believe he said, 'If you want to live to fuck another pussy.'"

I almost choke, making Faye laugh harder. "Not all of them are good, but you, you got a good one, Lana."

I smile. "He's been good to me."

"He better if he wants to keep you," she adds. "He's smart; he knows what he has."

"You're kind of awesome," I blurt out.

"Right back at you," she says, eyes flashing amusement and kindness. "You rest up. Call out if you need anything."

"I will," I tell her. "Thanks, Faye."

"That's what family is for," she says, walking to the door. "You know who else is awesome? Your mom."

I grin. "She is, isn't she?"

FIFTEEN

I T'S my last few days with Clover.

My body is mostly healed from the beating. Ribs are still sore and a few bruises linger, but for the most part I'm back to my normal self. Clover and I have spent the day reading books, coloring, and getting her ready for the rest of the year back in school.

When Tracker walks into the clubhouse as I'm just about to leave, he's not alone. There's a group of men with him, and one of them instantly catches my eye. I let my gaze linger on him for a moment, before returning my attention to Tracker. Forcing a smile, I wrap my arms around him.

"Just going home," I say into his chest.

"No, you're not," he replies casually, nuzzling my head. "Haven't seen you all day."

"Gimme a sec," he tells the men, walking me to his room. As soon as he closes the door he's on me, kissing me, his hands wandering over my body.

"Stay the night," he demands. "I'll have a few drinks with

the men, then spend the rest of the night with you. Making you scream."

"I have to go home, Tracker," I reply. I need to write. If I don't write daily, I feel like I'll go insane. I want to tell Tracker about my career, but I think I'm going to do it in a fun way. Maybe I'll make him read one of my books and ask what he thinks. I'm sure he'll have a few pointers for the sex scenes.

"Stay."

"I have some work to do on my laptop and I didn't bring mine—"

"Use mine," he says, cutting me off, sliding his hand down my panties. "Hmmm. Wet. But I'm gonna get you even wetter."

His finger presses gently inside me, while I remove my cotton shorts and panties, giving him access since he clearly couldn't wait. When he pushes me back against the wall and lowers to his knees, my breath hitches. Lifting my right leg over his shoulder, his hand holding my thigh, he goes down on me like a starving man.

"Oh my god," I say between clenched teeth.

"Love this pussy," he groans, nipping at my inner thigh before returning to my clit, sucking it in his mouth.

He's clearly trying to kill me.

A knock at the door has me gripping his head so he doesn't move.

"Tracker! We have church, bro," I hear Vinnie call out.

Church? I'm confused for a moment, then I realize they must be talking about a club meeting. I'd never heard it called that before. "Coming!" Tracker calls out, then grips my ass with both hands, lifts me to his mouth, my back pressing into the wall.

So. Damn. Sexy.

I come whispering his name, wave after wave of pleasure making me almost want to weep with its force. He puts me down, but my legs are shaky, so he swoops me in his arms and carries me to the bed.

"I have to go, baby, but when I get back, I want those pretty lips wrapped around my cock," he says, sweetly kissing my brow. "I want you, but I have club business to deal with. I'll be back. I want you naked and ready for me, baby."

He leaves the room, leaving me to wonder what the important club meeting was about.

Shrugging, I fall into his sheets, sleepy and sated.

I wake up to Ed Sheeran singing "Afire Love."

My ringtone.

"Hello?" I rasp, lifting my head to look at Tracker, who is fast asleep next to me and hogging all the blankets.

It's my mom, complaining about my not letting her know when I'm not coming home. She got worried. I really do need a place of my own.

"I'll be home soon, Mom," I tell her. We say 'bye and hang up.

Glancing at Tracker, his messy bun, his stubble and long brown lashes, I decide to wake him up in the best way possible. Lifting the sheets, I scoot down the bed, staring at his naked body.

No man should be so perfectly created.

Taking him in my hand, I lick up his length, then suck him into my mouth, feeling him instantly harden.

"Allie," he rasps in a voice thick with sleep, making me stop, his cock still in my mouth.

Allie?

My chest suddenly burns.

Removing my mouth with a pop, I glare at him. When he doesn't stir or say anything, I realize he's still asleep.

But it doesn't really change anything, does it? He's thinking of her. Dreaming of her. It stirs up all my doubt.

I get dressed and get the hell out of the clubhouse.

Tracker calls me.

I ignore it, putting my phone on silent. I'm not ready to talk to him. I'm upset and don't know what I want to do.

So I pull out my laptop and descend into a different world.

The next morning when I arrive at the clubhouse, Tracker isn't there. Neither is Anna or Arrow. Rake and Irish are the only ones around.

"Where's your sister?" I ask Rake, who is standing half-naked in the kitchen, scratching his chest with one hand, a piece of cold pizza in the other.

"She went somewhere with Tracker and Arrow," he replies. "Said they'll be back in the evening."

Okaaaaay then.

My rage fuels. They're all just going out for a fun day or something?

"Did they say where they went?"

Rake studies me, a little too intently for my liking. "They had some club shit to take care of."

"Then why is Anna with them?" I ask. Rake shrugs, focusing all too hard on his pizza.

Feeling frustrated and confused, I nod my head and pretend like everything is fine. I must have failed, because Rake walks past me and kisses my cheek. "It's fine, Lana."

"I don't even know what's going on," I grumble.

He grins. "You know your man. You know Anna. Trust them. Maybe you should have answered your phone last night. Tracker was raging."

I cringe. He's right, I should have.

Rake chuckles. "He was fuckin' pacing up and down. Never seen him like that before."

"Don't you have somewhere to be?" I ask, annoyed.

His lips twitch. "Nope. Tracker asked me to stay here and keep an eye on you and Clover."

I eye him warily. "Why do I have to have an eye kept on me?"

"Well, you just got the shit beat out of you, so it's probably a good idea," he says bluntly. I say nothing but figure he's right.

He shrugs and grabs another slice of pizza from the fridge. "Want some?"

"No, thanks," I say. "I hate cold pizza."

He mumbles something about me being high-maintenance, then looks up at me. "You should make some waffles."

"I will if you tell me some information."

"Blackmail?" he asks, brows rising. "You've been around us too long, Lana. We've corrupted you."

"Rake—"

"Tracker is my brother, Lana," he says quietly. "Anything to do with anything, you have to hear it from him, not me, you know? Don't put me in the middle."

He's right.

I sigh. "Okay. I'll make you waffles."

"Thank you." He grins. "I'll go watch TV with Clover. I've gotten her to like all the cool cartoons now, like *Transformers*."

I've finished cooking when Irish walks in. I notice his knuckles are busted up and look extremely painful.

"Irish, what happened?" I ask, gasping.

He gives me a look that says I should know better than to ask but then grumbles, "You should see the other guy."

"I can imagine," I reply dryly. "Stay here, I'm going to get the first-aid kit."

"Not necessary, Lana," he replies in his sexy accented voice. "It's just a scratch."

Scratch, my ass.

"Well, then you won't mind if I get the first-aid kit and put some antiseptic on it," I say. "Then you can have some waffles."

"Fuckin' hell," he grumbles. "Fine. Fuss over me and waste your time."

Taking that as a yes, I run to the bathroom and get the kit, then come back and apply some lotion on his knuckles so they won't get infected.

"There," I say, feeling proud. "Now you can eat."

I look up to see Rake staring at me, leaning against the door-frame, one arm raised.

"Love the man, love the club," he says, eyes soft and gentle on me.

So much meaning in those six words.

I do love Tracker.

And I do love the men in his club, because they are a part of him.

His family.

And now mine. The club is my family. The MC lifestyle is for me, because they're a part of it. I'll do anything for my family.

And whatever Tracker's up to right now, I'll deal with it.

After I kick his ass for saying another woman's name.

It's evening by the time they return. I'm reading in Tracker's bed, waiting for him, when the bedroom door finally opens. I'm determined. It feels so good to know what I want, to know that Tracker is all I want.

"Lana," he says. "You're here. Thank fuck."

Sliding next to me on the bed, he pulls me into his arms and kisses me.

"Where were you today?" I ask as he tries to distract me by kissing my neck.

"Lana, can we fuck, then talk? You ran out on me yesterday and I'm not fuckin' happy about it, but right now I just need to be inside of you."

Something about the anxious look in his eyes has me nodding.

He blows out a breath, relieved, then continues to kiss his way down to my breasts, pulling my top up. I'm not wearing a bra. He gets rid of my shorts and panties next, then slides into me without warning.

"Fuck yes," he grits out, mouth returning to mine with frantic kisses; his thrusts becoming harder, faster, more desperate. My hips rise to meet his, my arms wrapping around his back, my nails digging into his shoulder blades. The way he fits me so perfectly kind of pisses me off in this moment, because I know after this, I'm going to start a fight.

SIXTEEN

H E slides out of me and rests his forehead against mine. "We need to talk."

"Yes, we do," I agree, my tone angry.

He lifts his head, eyes narrowing. "What are you so angry about?"

I clench my teeth. "How long do you have?"

"Lana—"

"Oh, so you *do* know my name," I snap.

"What the hell are you talking about? You'd think I fucked the angry out of you, but you're still fired up."

I grit my teeth.

"Why don't we start with yesterday? You were sleeping, so I decided to wake you up with my mouth wrapped around your dick."

His blue eyes widen. "What do you—"

I cut him off. Now is my time to talk. "I had you in my mouth when you moaned. Do you know what you moaned, Tracker?"

"What?" he asks warily.

"*Allie's* fucking name! I had your dick in my mouth, nice and hard, and you said her name. How the hell do you think that makes me feel?"

"Lana, wait a second—"

"*You* wait a second, you asshole! Imagine if you were going down on me and I said some other man's name! You would have lost your shit. There's nothing you can say to get you out of this one!"

"Of course I was thinking about Allie," he growls. "I've been thinking about her for the last fuckin' few weeks."

My jaw drops.

I can actually feel my heart cracking and my temper breaking free at the same time.

I lift my hand and slap him, right across his too-handsome-for-his-own-damn-good face.

Fuck. Him.

"Go and be with her then, Tracker, because I'm done," I yell. "Fuck you! I can't believe you'd say that to me!"

"Calm down," Tracker snarls. "Let me finish."

"Fuck you."

"Been there and done that."

"Bastard!"

"Wildcat, calm the fuck down," he says, grabbing me and pushing me underneath him. Holding my hands above my head, he pins me to the bed, while I try to control my breathing.

"Calm down," he whispers. "That's it, take deep breaths."

I exhale slowly.

"Good girl," he praises, nuzzling my cheek. "Now listen before you lose your temper at me again. Are you listening?"

I nod.

"We found out it was Allie who broke into your house and beat the shit out of you, so of course the bitch was on my mind. I was so damn angry, Lana. I still am, and I don't think I've ever been this angry before. Haven't you wondered why she hasn't been around? After she did that to you, she took off. I had to search for her, and today we finally found her. If she was on my mind, it was because I was probably murdering her with my bare hands in a dream. I hate the bitch."

She really must hate me, is my first thought.

I knew she was a bitch, but I didn't think she was capable of something like this.

"I'm sorry," Tracker murmurs, barely a whisper. "This was all my fault. She was jealous and . . . fuck, Lana. How am I supposed to live with the fact that this happened to you because of me?"

"You're not the one who did it, Tracker, so no, it isn't your fault."

He scoffs. "It's because of me that she did it though, my actions. Domino effect, or whatever. My mistakes landed you in the hospital." I see the grief in his eyes and feel bad. I haven't even thought about how he'd be feeling. Of course he'd feel responsible. I want to reassure him. It isn't his fault, he doesn't control other people's actions.

"Tracker—"

"I don't know how the others watch the women they love get in to all this dangerous shit," he says quietly, not listening to a word I'm saying. "Shit, Lana. And this is only the start. It will always be like this."

I didn't like where this was going.

"I'm strong enough," I say slowly, enunciating each word. "To be your woman, Tracker. Don't ever say otherwise. If Faye and Anna get to be here, then so do I."

"Lana." He sighs, peppering kisses all over my shoulder. "I want to kill her."

"What did happen to her?" I ask warily.

"Told her not to step foot in the clubhouse again," he says, face darkening in anger. "She was a brother's daughter, so we told her we can hook her up with some money, but she isn't coming back. Oh, and Anna punched her in the nose."

"She did?" I ask, lifting my head.

He grins wolfishly, all straight, sharp white teeth. "Decked her. Bitch deserved it. She's lucky I don't hit women. If she were a man, she'd be dead."

I scowl. "Why didn't you two tell me? This is bullshit. I should have been the first person to know what was going on. It should have been me who confronted her. I'm the one she hurt and I should have been the one to put her in her place. Now it looks like I'm weak and can't defend myself."

"Baby," he soothes. "I don't even want you near her. I didn't want you to worry, all right? I'm your man, and I took care of it. End of story."

"Anna—"

"Anna wouldn't take no for an answer. She was more than pissed. Arrow had to pull her away from Allie so she didn't do more damage."

I cringe, imagining Anna's wrath.

"Exactly," Tracker adds. "Anna's a damn good fighter. Pretty sure she broke her nose."

Anna grew up fighting a lot; she's tough as nails. I didn't want to make this a big deal, or whine, but I'm not a baby. I feel like they decided they should handle everything for me. They should have told me it was Allie, told me what happened. I should have been able to confront her. I glance up at Tracker, grateful he cares about me, even if he can be controlling and overbearing.

"And I wasn't awake when you were sucking my dick," he continues. "I don't even remember it, but I'm sure it felt fuckin' good. I was in a deep sleep, babe. You can show me again now though, and I promise I won't be thinking about anyone but you. I never do. She was only on my mind 'cause I was planning all the ways I wanted to end her."

"I watched you with her, you know," I say. "When we first met. It hurt, but I knew you weren't mine, so I tried to forget."

He smiles sadly. "I couldn't leave you alone. Saw you and, fuck, did I want you. Anna warned me off. Rake warned me off. But fuck them. Tried to leave you alone but I couldn't. And I don't regret it; do you know why?"

"Why?" I ask.

"Because you're the best thing that's happened to me and I'm man enough to admit that."

My heart soars with his words. Could I really be that lucky?

"We haven't even been together that long," I point out. Things this good usually don't last long. Sad but honest truth.

He just smiles. "Don't give a fuck. That doesn't change anything. I'm not playing any games with you Lana. Don't question it; it is what it is."

I roll my eyes at his casualness. I still don't forgive him for saying Allie's name. I want to, but it still hurts.

*   *   *

"I'm sorry," she says for the third time. "But you're my best friend and no one messes with you!"

"You guys treat me like a baby," I mutter. "I don't need you to stand up for me, Anna."

"I know," she says, holding her hands up. "But you're too nice and forgiving. She needed a little more physical punishment to teach her a lesson. And I don't regret it. I'd hit her again right now if she were here. I might throw in a throat punch as well."

I hate that my lip twitches, laughter threatening. "You need anger management."

"Coming from you!" she yells, then starts laughing herself.

"I'm not bad. So I snap now and again, big deal. Your anger is always there, simmering under the surface, looking for a chance to get out."

"I'm not angry. I'm bitchy—there's a difference."

I roll my eyes. "You're not a bitch."

"Yes, I am," she replies, sounding amused. She pushes her hair back behind her ears, her lips quirking up at the sides.

"Fine, you're my bitch then," I tell her, winking at her.

She glances at me with wide eyes. "Pretty sure I'm Arrow's bitch."

I shake my head. "Such a feminist, Anna."

She laughs. "It's the honest truth. I'm his old lady. Same shit, right? Potato, potato."

"That's not the saying at all," I deadpan. "What's the point of saying potato the same way twice?"

Anna tilts her head. "Are you grumpy? Tracker not giving you his giant cock?"

My mouth drops. "I can't believe you just asked me that."

"Evading, interesting."

"Nosy!"

"Prude."

"Sex-starved!"

"Psycho woman who goes around beating people up," I say, rushing the words out so I don't lose the effect.

"Come on," Anna says, nudging my shoulder and dropping our previous argument. "Fuck her. She let jealousy turn her into a crazy bitch; she got what she deserved. She's lucky I only got to hit her once."

I scrub my hand down my face. "This feels like high school all over again."

Except this time it's Allie getting shit, not me.

"And you," I say, pointing to my best friend who now wore an innocent expression on her face. "Miss 'I'm trying to have a baby'—no more fighting."

She flips her hair. "I'm a biker bitch. No one messes with me or mine."

I feel a headache coming on. "I need a drink. Like tequila."

She comes closer and wraps her arm around me. "You were hurt, Lana. I never want to see you hurt again."

Her voice breaks on the last two words.

I hug her back. "I'm fine. Shit happens, right?"

"Tracker must be a beast in bed for her to go apeshit over losing him," she says with wide eyes.

"It's the piercing," I tease.

Anna shakes her head at me. "You know you can talk to me about anything, right?"

I nod, even though there's so much I haven't told her, or anyone else. I've kept everything bottled inside.

Swallowing hard, I say, "Remember how you asked how come I never kept in touch with anyone from school or had many friends? Well after you left, I kind of became a social outcast."

Her eyes widen. "What happened?"

"Remember William Dean?"

She nods. "Yeah, preppy bastard you had a thing for."

"Well, he happened," I say with a cringe, then explain the story to her.

"Anyone who would sit with me, they would start getting bullied as well, so everyone avoided me like the plague. Boys who asked me out were blacklisted, so to speak. I mean, looking back on it now, it doesn't seem so bad. I could go through it and be fine, but back then fitting in at school was everything, so it really got to me, you know? I kind of learned to manage on my own and only rely on myself."

"Fuck them," she growls. "Now I wish I hadn't left."

I smile sadly. "It was in the past. I guess I just wanted to share it with you because I tend to keep everything to myself. I do trust you, Anna, with my life, but I guess I'm not real good at sharing. I didn't want you to feel guilty or anything either."

"Still," she says. "It hurts me to think of you going through that. Especially since when I was at school with you we always stuck together, so we didn't really branch out and make other friends because we didn't need them. All we needed was each other."

"That's true." I grin. "Who needed anyone else right? One true friend is more than what most people get these days."

"I never thought . . ." Anna sounds defeated.

"Anna, its fine. I'm stronger because of it, and you can't protect me from everything. I need to look after myself. Looking back, I feel stupid. It was just high school. I should have punched that girl in the face, not let her intimidate and bully me."

"Bitches," she scowls. "They were probably just jealous of you."

I laugh. "I seriously doubt that."

Anna shrugs. "When Clover gets to high school, I'm going to make sure no one even breathes in her direction."

"Poor Clo," I say. "She is going to be the most overprotected girl in the history of overprotected girls."

Anna nods her head. "All the MC princesses are."

"There's one more thing," I tell her, watching her face closely for her reaction.

"What?" she asks, leaning closer to me.

"The cheerleader, William's girlfriend . . ."

"Yes?" she prompts.

"It was Allie," I blurt.

"Fuck," she gasps. "No way! Tell me everything."

I start from the beginning and tell her every little detail.

SEVENTEEN

NSTEAD of going to class, I make a detour. After thinking it over, I realize that Tracker and Anna should have let me deal with Allie. Feeling pissed I didn't get to confront her, I decide to take matters into my own hands. I know the two of them want to protect me, baby me even, because of my petite size and usually gentle demeanor, but if I want to survive by Tracker's side, I need to make a stand. I need to let people know that I'm not an easy target, that I have a backbone, and that I'm someone who should be respected. After asking around, I find Allie outside a local bar and walk right up to her.

Her eyes widen as she sees me, and then she looks behind me, as if wondering who I came with.

"Why did you do it, Allie?" I ask, straight out. No games.

"Why do you think?" she snarls. "Tracker was mine; the club was mine. You took everything. Now just fucking leave, because I told them I wouldn't come near you again."

I step to her, getting in her face. "You hit me from behind. Unexpectedly. Next time you want a fight, don't be a pussy and a coward. Step up to me like a grown woman and we can handle it."

She laughs. "All right then, Lana. How about right now? It's a long time coming, don't you think?"

I nod. "Definitely."

Allie rears back to slap me, but I block her hand and use a move Faye taught me. Bringing my leg up to her stomach with all my might, I grab her by her hair and then smash her face into my knee. She curses, then falls back, holding her face. "You fucking bitch!"

I bring my hand up again but she raises her arms, and I see blood dripping down her chin from a cut lip.

I look around. People are watching, but no one is doing anything.

Good.

Let them see.

There's a new biker bitch in town.

"You did what?" Anna yells, looking a mixture of surprised and impressed.

I look at Tracker, who is sitting next to me on the couch, a speculative look on his face.

"How did you even find out?" I ask him, curious about what his reaction was going to be.

"You went to a biker bar, Lana," he says in a dry tone. "Everyone knows you're my old lady. Why do you think no one stopped you? They called me the second you left."

"And you called Anna?" I ask, then mutter, "Tattletale."

He shakes his head. "Anna was with me and Arrow when I

got the call. Fuck, Lana. We've been protecting you and fuckin' babying you, but you don't need us to, do you?"

I shake my head. "I can hold my own."

Anna throws her head back and laughs while Tracker's lip twitches in amusement. "Will you at least tell me next time you go on a fuckin' mission? Shit could have turned bad, Lana. What if Allie had a group of girls with her who had her back?"

"So next time I should bring backup just in case?" I ask, then look to Anna with a raised eyebrow. A silent invitation.

Anna laughs again. "You're fuckin' crazy, you know that? 'Course I have your back. Always."

"Christ." Tracker sighs, rubbing his forehead.

"You should be thrilled," Anna says. "Looks like you found someone to match you perfectly after all."

Tracker looks at me, his eyes softening. "I already knew that."

Swoon.

The man Tracker was with, the man I recognize, is back at the clubhouse.

And he doesn't recognize me back.

He smiles at me, in a friendly way, with respect in his eyes, because he knows I'm Tracker's woman.

But not that I'm his daughter.

And it makes me see red.

"What's wrong?" Tracker asks, speaking so no one else can hear.

"Nothing," I reply sullenly, staring daggers at Quinn Rhodes. I didn't want to get into everything right now. I'd tell Tracker when Quinn was gone, so there wouldn't be a scene.

"You recognize him, don't you?" Tracker says, making me freeze. "He used to be in that rock band."

I sigh in relief. "Yeah, I know."

My dad is a famous musician. Well, was, I guess, considering the band broke up. I heard he sings solo now, at local clubs and bars. And he's such a bastard that he doesn't know what his own daughter looks like. Even though he isn't in my life, he did teach me one very valuable lesson.

No matter what, men leave.

"Why is he here?" I ask, trying to keep the bite out of my tone.

Tracker gives me an odd look, his brows furrowing. "He used to be friends with Jim, our old president before Sin took over."

"Oh, okay," I say, forcing a smile. Just my luck, he is a friend of the club.

"If you want to go to bed, just let me know," he whispers in my ear. "Much rather be inside you than looking at their ugly mugs."

My lips kick up at the corners as I show him my drink. "Let's have a few drinks first. We haven't had drunk sex yet."

Tracker runs his free hand down my back and smiles lavishly. "You want me wilder?"

"I want you however you are," I reply. "Whatever you have to give, I'll take. And you'll do the same with me."

"Christ," he mutters. "Temptress."

I smile into my drink, "Only for you."

"Damn straight."

My mind returns to my sperm donor. I am a mixture of him and my mom—how the hell did he not know his own blood when he looked her in the face? I realize I've been staring when

Tracker tilts my chin in his grip, bringing my eyes to him. His own are narrowed. "I don't like you looking at other men."

"I'm not."

He's not a man; he's an asshole.

"Lana," Tracker growls. "Talk."

Am I just going to drop it on him like this? I look around, scanning the room, looking for a distraction.

"Can I tell you later? In private?" I whisper, pleading with my eyes.

I avoid looking back at the first man who ever let me down. I know my lack of a relationship with my father fueled my mistrust, the reason I tend to keep everything to myself, bottled up tight. I didn't need a shrink to tell me that. If my own father could leave me and not care if I was alive or dead, how could other people be trusted? I'd watched my mother hurting, still in love with him after he left us, working hard to get by while he made it big. We saw him on TV, and she would cry. Still, she never sold her story or asked for a handout. My mom was and is a damn strong woman, and if I'm half the woman she is, I'll be satisfied with that. It hurts that my own father didn't care about me. Still doesn't. I knew it had nothing to do with me—all to do with him—but it still hurt like a bitch.

And to see him sitting here, nursing a drink, not a care in the world . . . I kind of want to throw something at him. I want to yell. Scream. Demand answers. Instead, I cut off my emotions as best I can and pretend my chest isn't hurting, that my mind isn't racing with old memories, old pain.

From the look in Tracker's eyes, I know he wants to know what's going on with me right *now*. When he stands and takes my hand in his, pulling me in the direction of his room, I know

I'm right. Dreading telling him the truth, I lag behind him, allowing myself to be gently pulled. I know I have to open up to him about it, and I want to, it just isn't my favorite subject to discuss. I've tried not to even think about my dad over the years and the lack of relationship we had, and had spent most of my life pretending I didn't care about it. When we enter the room, I put my glass down on his chest of drawers, then sit down on the very edge of the bed. Tracker, on the other hand, stands there with his arms crossed, drink still held tightly in his hand, expression brooding. Did he think I found Quinn good-looking or something?

So very awkward.

"Why were you staring at him like that?" he asks in a low tone, studying me intensely.

"Tracker, I—"

He starts to pace.

"Remember I told you I had nothing to do with my dad?" I start, rushing the words out. "Quinn Rhodes is my dad. And he hasn't seen me in so long he doesn't even recognize me. So yeah, I was staring at him."

I growl the last line.

He stops, expression softening, then hardening again. "That motherfucker. I'll kill him."

I stand up and grab his forearm. "You will do no such thing."

"He hurt you. He still hurts you, I can see it on your face," he says, downing his drink, then placing the glass down next to mine.

I shrug, playing it off. "So? He's still my father. You can't hurt him, Tracker; just let him be. And remember that the way you handle this will determine how much I tell you in the future."

His jaw clenches. "You want me to go out there and sit with him, have a fuckin' drink with him, acting like everything is okay?"

"No," I say quickly. "I just don't want you to go out there and punch his face in."

"The things I do for you," he says, capturing my lips in a quick, punishing kiss. "You want to go back out? I'd rather just fuck you, because if I go back out there you know what's going to happen."

I slide my dress down, and it falls to the floor. "Is this answer enough?"

He licks his bottom lip. "So many things I want to do with you. Hmmmmm."

I shiver at the husky tone of his voice. "Where shall we start?"

"At the top," he says, staring at my mouth. "Then we will work our way to the bottom." He stares at my lace panties. "I'm suddenly feeling a little hungry."

I swallow.

"Then I'm going to bend you over and fuck you until you pass out."

How I love his dirty mouth.

"So are you going to just talk or are you going to fuck me?" I taunt, feeling bold.

"Baby." He grins. "You should know better."

In a flash, he has me on the bed, panties down, face buried.

Every woman needs a Tracker.

"What the hell is this?" I growl two days later, slamming the magazine down on the table.

Tracker glances at it innocently and sips his coffee. "A gossip magazine."

"It says Quinn Rhodes got beaten up outside his apartment. They suspect a random act of violence, since nothing was stolen."

He raises an eyebrow. "You shouldn't believe everything you read."

I point. "There's a picture of him with a black eye."

"Lana, are you going somewhere with this?" he asks, then takes another sip.

I growl in frustration. "Did you or did you not beat the shit out him?"

"I can honestly say that I didn't. Babe, I told you *I* wouldn't."

My eyes narrow. "Did you get someone else to?"

"I can't talk about club business," he says with a serious expression on his face.

I throw my hands up in the air. "You're unbelievable, Tracker."

He slides his mug away and pulls me down to sit on his lap. "And you're unbelievably beautiful."

He kisses my neck.

I pinch his biceps.

"This is why I didn't want to tell you, and you reacted just how I suspected. You get angry when I don't open up and keep things to myself, but then you don't listen to what I tell you. I said I didn't want you to touch him, Tracker."

He stills. "Fuck, I'm sorry. I couldn't just let him get away with hurting you. Lana, he doesn't deserve to breathe the same air as you, okay? He knew he deserved what he got. We went easy on him. I'll try to be good when you ask something of me like this, but fuck! How can I sit back and do nothing when someone who hurt the woman I love is right in front of me?"

"Well, crap." I deflate, my anger lessening. "Just listen to my wishes next time, Tracker. Or don't blame me when I don't want to tell you everything."

"Okay," he says instantly, kissing my lips.

"I really dislike you right now," I say, trying not to melt into him but failing.

"Can you dislike me later? You have class soon and I have to get to Rift."

Anna walks in, Arrow next to her. "Lana, do you want to get something to eat before you start class?"

I nod. "Sushi?"

She beams. "And this is why you're my best friend."

I kiss Tracker. "I'll see you later."

"Let Blade drive the two of you," he suggests, glancing at Arrow, who nods.

Anna glances at me. "We don't need Blade. We're fine."

"We weren't asking," Arrow says, heading to the fridge.

"Fine," I say, not wanting to be late. "Blade can take us. Come on, Anna."

She says 'bye to her man, and then asks Blade to drop us off at the Japanese place near my school.

We order, then Anna starts in on the questions. "Quinn Rhodes is your dad? Why did you never say anything?"

"I never told anyone," I admit. "Mom told me not to. We didn't want people to know, for the media to find me, et cetera. Plus I was embarrassed, to be honest. My dad was famous and we could hardly make ends meet."

"You had no reason to be embarrassed," she growls. "He's the bastard; you guys did nothing wrong."

"Does the whole club know now?" I grumble, crumpling a napkin in my hand. "He's more of a sperm donor. Yes, I know he's my father, but he's never been in my life. He didn't even recognize me when he saw me. I don't know if he just doesn't care or what."

Anna's face hardens. "Your dad is a famous, rich musician, and you and your mom struggled to make ends meet your whole lives? I remember when you had to waitress to help pay the bills. What an asshole. I'm glad he got his face smashed in."

"So bloodthirsty," I quip.

She flashes me a sheepish smile. "I spend all my time with Arrow, what do you expect?"

I laugh at that. "Rubbing off on you, is he?"

"Why does that sound dirty?"

"Because you're dirty," I retort.

"So are you," she says, smirking. "Like we can't hear your screams echoing through the clubhouse."

I gasp, my face heating. "You so cannot!"

"Can too."

"Not."

The food arrives, interrupting our immature discussion.

"Any luck finding a place?" Anna asks after a few bites.

I nod. "Saw two listings I like. I'm going to see them this week."

"You know Tracker wants you to move into the clubhouse," Anna says, looking amused. "You should. I'm there; it'll be fun."

"I don't know. Isn't it a little too soon to be moving in with him? And you'll be moving out soon anyway!"

"There aren't any right or wrong rules, Lana," she says. "Just do whatever feels right. Fuck what people think. Besides, you're pretty much there every day anyway."

All valid points.

"Still. There's so many people coming in and out of there. There's no privacy unless you stay in your room."

"That's true," she admits. "But it's fun too. There's always something going on."

"How do you get any work done?" Anna is completing her master's program while working at the zoo.

"If I go in my room I'm left alone," she says, chewing and swallowing thoughtfully. "That's private space, you know? No one will just come in. They knock and wait."

I know that. Okay, I can't think of any other excuses.

"If you're not ready to live with him, that's a different story. I know you like your own space. There are some cute apartments near the school."

"Remember I said I had to tell you something?"

She nods, giving me her full attention.

"Have you ever heard of Zada Ryan?" I ask, feeling nervous.

"That romance author Faye talks about?" she asks, eyes flaring. "Yeah, apparently she writes good sex. Why?"

I widen my eyes at her, then smile sheepishly, waiting for her to get it.

"Get the fuck out of here!" she yells when she has the lightbulb moment. "You . . . What . . . Holy shit, Lana!"

She asks questions, and I answer everything, telling her how it came about from the very start.

EIGHTEEN

I CAN'T believe my father actually has the balls to come back to the clubhouse. I overhear him talking to Sin.

"Jim wouldn't have allowed any of his men to lay a finger on me," I hear him say.

"Jim's not here," Sin replies dryly. "But I am. From what Tracker told me, he was standing up for his old lady."

"So he sent Rake to beat the shit out of me?" he growls.

Rake's the one who did it?

"Lana didn't want you hurt. Trust me. Tracker wanted to come himself but kept his word to her to not lay a finger on you."

"So he got someone else to," my dad says in a dry tone.

"Yeah," Sin says, sounding amused. "Pretty genius."

"I want to see her," he says in a low tone. "I haven't seen my daughter in years, of course I didn't recognize her when I saw her."

"Speak with Tracker," Sin says. "His old lady, his rules on how to deal with this."

"She's my daughter—"

"Doesn't look that way," Sin snaps, then sighs. "We consider you a friend of the club. Jim respected you, I know this. Talk with Tracker and we can go from there, all right? Just know my brothers will always come before someone who is just a friend of the club. You aren't the club. So remember that before you try and piss off Tracker with any bullshit. One word from him and we will cut all ties."

I hear him leave and only then do I walk out into the game room, where Sin is sitting alone, a glass of Scotch in his hands. He lifts his gaze to me as I walk in.

"Sorry about all the drama," I tell the Wind Dragons president. "You must hate me."

He chuckles. "Sweetie, you wouldn't be an old lady if you didn't cause any trouble. All of them do."

I allow myself a small smile. "But still. I guess I'll talk to him and sort this mess out."

His eyes cut to me. "After you talk to Tracker, right?"

I nod. "Right."

"Good girl," he comments. "You're good for him. He's usually restless. Never seen him this grounded before and I've known him for years."

"He was pretty angry," I say, shifting my weight on my feet. "I should have hidden my reaction and told him everything afterward. Maybe it would have gone better."

Sin chuckles. "Lana you should have told him about this before. Why the fuck didn't you? If you don't mind me asking," he adds quickly.

"Ummmm. I tend to suffer in silence and keep everything to myself. My problems, my issues. I don't know. I've always been like this," I try and explain.

"You need to open up to Tracker or you're gonna drive the man insane."

"I'm working on it," I say, smiling. "I'm going to head to class."

"Tracker said Blade has to take you," Sin says, sipping on his drink. "He's out front."

"I know," I say, turning and rolling my eyes.

"Oh, and Lana?" he calls. I stop and turn around.

"Yes?"

He cringes. "Clover made me promise to say . . . Hello, Lana Bear."

I grin. "I miss her. How is she liking being back at school?"

"She loves it," he replies, eyes softening. "She misses spending so much time with you though."

"I'll come see her after class," I say. "Will she be here or at your house?"

I noticed that she doesn't come here much anymore.

Sin smirks. "My house. She only came here while you were looking after her because Tracker made that happen."

My eyes widen. "No shit?"

"No shit," he replies. "You think Faye wanted her kid around here all day?"

I laugh at that. "To be honest, I don't think she minds."

He says nothing to that, so I make my way outside.

Dancing to the music with my eyes closed, I put my hands above my head and shake what my mama gave me. Rift is packed tonight, but I'm glad Anna and I decided to come. Tracker and Arrow are at the bar, keeping an eye on us and handling business at the same time, whatever their business here is. Rake is in the VIP lounge, and Irish is somewhere around here as well.

"I love this song!" Anna says to me, swiveling her hips. She looks stunning in black jeans, a white lace top, and her hair curled. I'm also in jeans, mine distressed and matched with a black top that shows off some of my stomach. My hair is down and dead straight, framing my face. Anna cheers when she sees Faye walking up to us.

"Who's looking after Clover?" she asks Faye.

"Dex is," Faye replies. "I deserve a night out."

We cheer.

Faye dances with us, and I notice everyone giving us a wide berth, male and female. I also notice Tracker and Arrow keeping a close eye on Faye, as well as on Anna and me. Faye and Anna sandwich me, one in front and one behind. We're having the time of our lives when Tracker cuts in, pulling me to his side.

"Give me a kiss," he demands.

On my tiptoes, I kiss his lips while his hands find my ass. With a possessive squeeze, he says, "Stay with Anna and Faye. I'll be out back for a bit, all right? Arrow is at the bar, keeping an eye."

I nod, and he presses a kiss to my forehead before disappearing. Rejoining the girls, we start busting out our moves again. Several songs later, we head to the bar for drinks. Anna joins Arrow, and he quickly wraps his arm around her and whispers in her ear. Rake wanders out, smiling when he sees us.

"So this is where they're hiding all the pretty ladies tonight."

Anna rolls her eyes at her brother's charm.

"Already been through every woman here, Rake?" Faye teases.

Rake brings her closer to him. "Not every woman."

Arrow chuckles. "Sin is probably on his way to kill you right now."

Rake grins and scans the dance floor, probably looking for his next victim. When he sees someone who catches his interest, we lose him in the crowd. Glancing around myself, I still when I see a familiar face. "Is that . . . ?"

I nudge Anna and point.

"Shit," she says quietly when she spots him. Talon is on the dance floor. As the president of the Wild Men MC, he is a complete badass. He is also Rake and Anna's stepbrother. Their father was the last Wild Men president. The one Arrow killed. Talon seems like a good man, and he's friends with Anna. Arrow didn't like it much, but he dealt with it to make Anna happy. I see his arms tighten around Anna almost mechanically. I'm not even sure he realizes he does it. Talon makes his way over to us. I notice he's not wearing his cut, just leathers and a black T-shirt. He's good-looking, with shaggy white blond hair, green eyes, and a lean build. He too is covered in tattoos, and they look good on him.

"Anna," he says warmly, then nods at Arrow.

"Hey, Talon," Anna says, smiling at him. "How've you been?"

"Good, good," he replies, then smiles down at me. "Lana."

"Hey, Talon." I smile.

"No one told me he's this hot," Faye says, arching her eyebrow. "I'm Faye. I don't believe we've met."

Talon smiles. "The queen of the Wind Dragons."

Faye laughs. "In the flesh."

"What brings you here?" Arrow asks in his gravelly voice. "You knew we'd be here."

"Want to talk to you," Talon says. "In private."

Arrow nods. "Stick together," he tells Anna, then kisses her before walking away and expecting Talon to follow.

Anna and I share a glance, then shrug. Who knows what that was about.

"Tequila?" Faye asks.

"Why not," I reply at the same time Anna says, "Fuck yeah."

We order a round, then do another one. Yeah, it was going to get a little messy.

Irish joins us at the bar, winking at us. He's obviously our new babysitter.

Back on the dance floor, my eyes widen when I see another familiar face. "Is that Bailey?"

Anna snaps her head to the dance floor, staring at Rake's old high school sweetheart.

"Holy shit, it is," she says, smiling in amazement.

We both loved Bailey but haven't seen her in years. We rush over to her, Faye staying behind with Irish. Anna says hello first, Bailey's expression one of shock and happiness.

"Anna Ward? Oh my god!" she beams, then looks to me. "Lana Brown I should have known the two of you would still be friends. Do you want to go outside so we don't have to talk over the music?"

Anna nods, and we all walk out the front. The bouncer eyes us warily until Anna says, "We won't leave this spot."

We all start speaking at once.

"How have you been?" I ask her. It's been years since we've seen her.

"Good," she replies. "Just got out of a relationship, getting back into the dating scene."

"How's that going for you?" Anna asks with a cheeky grin.

Bailey winces. "I feel like I've been thrown back into the dating pool with no floaties."

We all laugh at that.

"I can be your float," Anna jokes.

"You're not single," I remind her.

"Oh," she says. "Is that a rule? Do I have to be single to guide her in the right direction?"

I giggle. "No, but you have to know what you're talking about."

Anna scowls while Bailey and I laugh.

"I got Arrow, didn't I?" Anna says defensively, hands on her hips. "And trust me, it wasn't easy."

Bailey asks for details, and Anna shares the basics.

After about ten minutes, Tracker storms out of the club, coming to a halt when he sees us standing there.

"Christ, Lana. Pretty sure I told you to stay where you were," he growls, looking at Anna, then Bailey. "Who are you?"

I roll my eyes at his rudeness. "Tracker, this is Bailey, an old friend of ours. Bailey, this is Tracker."

Tracker smiles, his natural charm taking over. "Nice to meet you."

"You too," Bailey replies, glancing at me with wide eyes.

Yes, I know. I did well.

My eyes crinkling at the corners, I turn back to Tracker, "We came out here to catch up."

"I can see that," he murmurs. "Do you guys want to go into the VIP room? It's much quieter and safer than standing out here where any man who drives past can see. Rake's in there, but you can just ignore him."

Anna and I share a glance. Bailey obviously doesn't know Rake as Rake; she would know him as Adam. I didn't think it was fair for us to drag her in there in case she didn't want to see her ex-boyfriend, which she probably didn't.

"Can you give us a second?" I ask Tracker, eyes pleading with his.

He nods, says something to the bouncer, then heads back inside.

"You're dating a biker?" she asks me as soon as Tracker disappears.

"I am," I say slowly. "So is Anna."

Bailey turns to Anna. "No shit? What does your brother think of that?"

I look at Anna, who says, "He didn't like it at first, but now he's okay with it."

Bailey looks like she wants to ask more but doesn't. "Let's go check out this VIP room," she says excitedly, heading back inside. Anna and I quickly follow behind her.

"Bailey, wait," I say. "Before we go to the VIP room—"

A man accidentally bumps me.

"Sorry," he says, hand sliding down my waist.

I step back, "That's okay."

It's an accident after all. When I turn to move around him however, he stops me, blocking my body with his. "How about a dance?"

"No, thanks," I quickly say, not wanting to start a fight with the man. "I'm here with my boyfriend."

He looks behind me, then around. "I don't see a boyfriend."

Calling Tracker my boyfriend felt so . . . underrated.

"Sorry, I really have to go," I say once more.

"How about we—"

"The lady said no," I hear Arrow growl from my right side. "Now fuck off before her man sees you, 'cause he's not going to be as nice as I am."

The man takes one look at Arrow's cut and flees.

"Thanks," I tell him, looking around for Anna and Bailey, both of them lost in the crowd. "Where's Anna?"

"They're waiting for you in front of the VIP room. Said I'd find you. Come on, Lana."

I walk up to them, about to tell Bailey about Rake, when the man himself walks out, zipping up his jeans, woman by his side.

Well, fuck.

Had Anna warned her at least?

From the look on Bailey's face, no, Anna didn't tell her yet.

"Adam?" she gasps, taking in Rake's appearance.

"Bailey?" Rake whispers, his eyes widening and his jaw going slack.

Bailey looks to the woman next to her ex-boyfriend. "I see some things don't change."

The tension around us spikes, the air thickening, the awkwardness for us watching them palpable.

"Should we go into—"

Rake cuts me off. "Anna, you and Lana go inside. Bailey and I need to talk."

He can't take his eyes off her. Does he still care for her?

"What about me?" the woman next to him snaps. "I just had your dick in my mouth and now you want to talk to this bitch?"

Pure. Class.

I look down at the floor and wish it would swallow me whole.

So. Damn. Awkward.

Anna grabs my arm. "Let's give them some privacy."

We quickly enter the room and get far away from the two of them, who look like they want to kill each other and tear each other's clothes off simultaneously. When I see Tracker with a beautiful woman next to him, my eyes narrow. She has dark hair, a killer smile, and a body that even I wouldn't mind seeing naked. Is this the type of woman he has being thrown at him on a daily basis? Tracker laughs at something she says but turns to look at me, finding me watching him. He says something else to the woman and then heads toward me. What would he have done if I wasn't here? Would he have left with her? I know he didn't do anything, but why do I feel like damage has been done anyway?

NINETEEN

WE end up at Toxic. Don't ask me how it came about, because I don't know.

"Your boobs are really huge," Faye was telling one of the strippers. "Like, massive."

"They're natural," the dancer beams.

"I'm pretty sure you could lick your own nipples," Faye says, nodding her head. "I always wondered if other women could lick their own boobs."

Safe to say, Faye is drunk.

And hilarious.

Arrow, who's been watching Faye throughout her conversation with the stripper, plucks the drink from her hand. "Think you've had enough."

Faye huffs. "I hardly ever go out, let me live a little, would you?"

She tries to reclaim her drink.

"Should we take her home?" I ask Tracker quietly, who slides me farther up his lap so I'm sitting on his groin.

"She's okay, let her be. No harm in talking to strippers about their tits," he says into my ear.

I look around the strip club. "Have you slept with any of these women?"

"No," he says, nibbling on my earlobe. "Fucked a few. We did no sleeping."

I slap his arm. "You're such an asshole."

I scan the club, wondering which women he's been with, jealousy seeping through my pores.

"Baby," he whispers, turning my face back to him. "I'm sorry you have to see women I've fucked, but that's all they were to me. I've never felt what I've got with you before. You need to put the past behind us, all right?"

"All right," I grumble. Can I really trust him? I can't deny the doubt I feel at the back of my mind. Men don't stick around. He'll move on when he's done with me, and I'll be left to pick up the pieces.

"You wanted to come here, remember?" he says. "Try something new. I'm happy to experience new things with you like this, but at the end of the day it's you and me."

I lay my head on his chest, pushing away all other thoughts. "You can be so sweet sometimes."

"Only for you."

"Good. I like it that way."

"No, Faye, you can't get onstage," I hear Anna growl. "Unless you want us all dead."

"Next time Sin is coming out," Arrow says, shaking his head in amusement. "Faye is too much work."

"What did Talon want?"

Tracker gives me a quick kiss. "Apparently there's a new MC in the area, starting shit. Wanted to talk to us about it."

My eyes widen. I didn't actually expect him to answer. "Did you just give me a little bit of club information? I think I'm going to die of shock."

"Smart-ass," he teases. "I'll tell you what I can tell you, no more no less."

"I can deal with that."

He kisses me again, this one deeper, hungrier. Suddenly he stands with me still in his arms, and takes me through a door to an office.

"Here?" I ask, glancing around the room.

"Here," he growls. "Pull those jeans down and bend over the table."

I call Tracker, excitement racing through me. "I found a place!"

"Where is it?" he says. "Close to the clubhouse?"

"About ten minutes away," I say. "The rent is a good price and it's stunning."

"Want me to come have a look?"

"Would you mind?" I say, clutching the phone.

"Not at all," he says. "Text me the address, I'll be there in five."

We hang up.

"I said ten minutes, and he says he'll be here in five," I mutter to myself as I text him the address.

He arrives on his bike, like he said, in five minutes. We both take a look around, as I talk him through every room.

"I don't like it," he announces, crossing his arms over his chest.

"Wh-what? What do you mean you don't like it? It's perfect," I argue, my head snapping to him.

He glances around. "No it's not. You can find something better."

"Tracker . . ."

"I don't see why you don't move in with me," he says, a muscle ticking in his jaw. "You practically live there anyway."

"Don't you think it's a little too soon?" I ask, wringing my hands together.

"No, no I fuckin' don't," he says, a stubborn, determined look taking over his expression. "I don't like the thought of you here alone. At least at your mom's, she's there some of the time. Here you're all by yourself, while I'm ten minutes away. It makes no sense. If you're here, I'm just gonna come here anyway, so we might as well just live together."

Scrubbing a hand down my face, I say 'bye to the real estate agent, telling her I'll be in touch. Tracker doesn't take us back to the clubhouse. Instead, he takes us to the beach.

"Why are we here?" I ask.

"Just wanted to spend some quiet time with you," he says, sitting down on the sand, and pulling me to sit between his legs. The fresh breeze is nice. With my head against his warm chest, we sit there watching the sun go down.

"This is kind of romantic," I tell Tracker.

He nuzzles my neck, kissing behind my ear. "I can be romantic."

"So you really want me to move in with you? You're that sure we'll work out?"

"'Course I am," he says a little gruffly. "Why, you planning on leaving? 'Cause I'll track you down and bring you back. It's what I do."

"I'm not going anywhere," I say. "As long as you treat me right and you're faithful to me, I'll be right by your side."

For as long as he wants me.

"Where you belong," he adds.

I sigh in contentment. "Where I belong."

When I see my dad sitting on the stairs in front of my mom's house the next day, I stop in my tracks.

"What are you doing here?" I ask.

"Wanted to talk to you."

I know this conversation is long overdue, but I still don't want to have it. There's nothing this man can say to fix the situation.

He didn't want me.

It is what it is, there's no point sugarcoating it.

He wasn't there on the Father's Day lunches we held at school. I'd stand there alone, watching everyone else interact with their fathers, figuring out what I was missing. He wasn't there on my birthdays, and he wasn't there to see me grow up into a successful young woman.

He wasn't there to fix my broken heart when William screwed me over.

My heart was already broken because of him, the one man in this world I should have been able to count on but couldn't.

"What's there to say?" I ask, putting my bag down at my feet and looking at him.

He puts his head in his hands. "The band was just making it when you were born. Your mother and I tried to make it work, but it was hard. I was on the road a lot and was dealing with the fame. Looking back it was stupid, but then and there it was a different situation. I struggled with many things, with what I wanted in life, with money. With my ego. At times it felt like I had to choose between my family or my dream, and then I'd feel resentful over that."

"You could have tried to do both. I'm sure lots of musicians do," I say, already tired of his excuses. I try to see it from his point of view, but at the end of the day there was me, an innocent child in the mix, and even if he wasn't there all the time he could have still made an appearance, put in an effort. I was his daughter, and I didn't get asked to be brought into this world. If he had such an issue with it, he should have worn a fucking condom.

He nods. "That's what I should have done, yes. Instead, I blamed your mother for trying to weigh me down, ruining my career. I got lost in that world, Lana. It became everything to me. Fame. Money. Women. I thought it was all that mattered. I stopped confiding in your mother. Kept things from her. I remember, once, she learned I was going overseas for a long tour from a magazine, I hadn't even bothered telling her." He pauses. "I didn't consider her my equal anymore I guess, as fucked-up as that sounds. I saw you whenever I could, but then each time became longer apart, until I just didn't come by at all."

"What was the final straw that ended things between you?" I find myself asking.

He breathes out through his nose, his nostrils flaring. "Pictures came out."

He says no more, and I can only imagine what pictures. Probably him with another woman. Did he even tell Mom he didn't want to be with her anymore? Or did he just keep her on the sidelines? I'm not sure I want to know.

"I knew you were busy, and I get it, but you mustn't have cared at all if you couldn't see me even once a year on my birthday, or just to pick up the phone. Did you even think of me?" I ask, letting my vulnerability show. "Because we thought about you all the time. I know Mom did."

"Of course I thought about you. Both of you," he whispers, voice catching. "I guess I thought I didn't deserve you both after leaving you."

"Then what makes you think you deserve to be in my life now?" I ask.

He shrugs. "You're my only child. All I have is a life full of regrets. It's now or never to try and make things as right as I can."

I exhale slowly, thinking about everything I've just learned. I didn't know what to say. I'd made myself numb toward anything to do with him, because that was the only way I could deal with it, by making myself pretend I didn't really care where he was or whether he cared about me. The unfortunate truth is that he's my father, so I always cared, I always hurt just beneath the surface, wondering why I wasn't good enough, something Anna and I had in common. Why other kids had loving fathers but we didn't. What was it about us? Of course now I know it had nothing to do with me, it was all to do with him, but as a child I obviously didn't see it like that.

"What do you want me to say?" I ask quietly. Then I admit, "I'm sorry Rake hit you. I didn't want that to happen."

"We all know I deserved it," he says, smiling sadly. "I deserve much more. And luckily it was Rake, not Tracker. I'd probably be in the hospital if it was."

I don't bother denying it.

"Still," I say.

No point sinking to his level.

"You're a beautiful woman, Lana," he says, a proud glint entering his eyes. "Tracker is a lucky man. I know it's much too late, but if you ever want to talk, or . . . anything. I will never turn you away again if you need me."

"Thanks," I whisper, not knowing what to say. Memories resurface. Mom crying at night, sobbing into her pillow. Me hugging her and not understanding why she was so sad. Me standing outside my school waiting for Mom to pick me up. Watching other dads with their kids. Feeling lost. Empty. Us not having electricity one week when we were struggling and behind on bills. All while my dad had a shitload of money but didn't care to send us any.

"But I made it through my whole life without you, so I think I'll be okay," I say, steel in my tone.

How could I let him in my life again? It won't change the past, will it? Could I ever forgive him completely? And do I even want to? Who is the forgiveness for, me or him? I don't know how I feel. I need to process everything.

His face drops, but he nods. "Right. Of course, I understand. 'Bye, Lana."

I laugh without humor. "You know, because of you, I have trust issues? I can't trust anything anyone says to me, especially a man. I'm waiting for Tracker to turn his back on me, because men don't stick around, right? All they do is leave destruction behind when they move on to the next best thing."

He swallows hard, his throat working. "Good men do stick around." As he walks away, the picture of a defeated man, I hurt for him.

I don't want to hurt him, but it would hurt me to have him in my life at this moment in time. I know I need to let go, to be able to forgive and move on, but I guess I don't see that happening right now. He made his decision, and now he has to live with it. He didn't need to cut me out of his life. He made the conscious decision to do so.

I had no say in it.

I was just part of the wreckage left behind.

Still, I watch him as he disappears from my sight, regret tethering us together.

One thought runs through my head.

Tracker is a good man.

"What happened with Bailey the other night?" I nosily ask Rake, who scowls as the mere mention of her name.

"We had words. She left. That pretty much sums it up."

"She still looks smoking hot. Even hotter than I remember," I prod.

Rake stabs his fork into his food harder than necessary. "Really? I didn't notice."

I'm waiting at the clubhouse for Tracker to get back. Rake's keeping me company. He's eating his dinner on the couch, while I make him watch some talk show.

"What did she mean when she said some things never change?" I ask. Did he cheat on her?

Rake throws me a look.

"Fine," I grumble. "Not my business."

He finally cracks a smile. "You hear about my birthday?"

"What about it?" I ask.

"It's next week," he says. "Everyone is throwing me a party here, it's gonna be wild."

"Am I invited?" I ask, raising my eyebrows.

He smirks. "Ask Tracker, that's his call. When I say wild, I mean wild. Are you gonna get shitty and run off, giving him hell?"

"No," I reply. "He'd be with me. What would I get angry over?"

Rake plays with his lip ring. "Naked women. Public sex. Take your pick."

I wince. "Is Anna going to be here?"

"Fuck no," he replies, chuckling. "She's taking me out to dinner the night before."

"Good call," I say.

"I know. Nothing screams cock-block more than your little sister showing up."

"So you don't mind if I see . . . whatever," I ask, my face heating in embarrassment.

"If you wanna see, all you have to do is ask, Lana."

I throw a pillow at him, which just misses his plate.

"Oops," I say insincerely. "My bad."

"You're a pain in the ass."

I rub my eyes. "I'm sleepy. I'm gonna go nap until Tracker gets back."

"Okay," Rake says. "I'll tell him you're waiting for him in his bed." He pauses. "Naked."

I ignore him and make my way to Tracker's bedroom.

TWENTY

WAKE up alone.

Hearing voices, I search for Tracker, finding him shirtless in the gym. He and Arrow are in the middle of a ring, fighting. My heart in my throat, I watch as the two powerful men fight for dominance, each hitting the other with brutal force. Why are they doing this? Ever since I've been here, I haven't seen Tracker get in the ring. And here he is now, in the middle of the night? I gasp when Arrow clocks him on the side of the face, but Tracker simply spits out blood on the floor and continues to fight back. When it's finally over, the two of them sit down on the floor. Arrow pulls something out of his pocket, and the two of them light up and smoke it. Is that . . . weed? I didn't even know Tracker smoked.

"Really needed that," I hear Tracker say. I know I shouldn't be eavesdropping, but I can't seem to make my feet carry me away.

"What's up with you?" Arrow asks. "Things okay with Lana?"

Yes, I definitely wasn't going to move.

"She's amazing," Tracker replies. "Just fuckin' hard some-times. I'm always trying to keep her away from things, the dark side of me, I guess. I don't want her to run, you know? But in the process I'm losing some of me. I love to fight, and I haven't been in this ring for ages, just 'cause I don't want her to worry."

"You live like that, you're gonna be miserable," Arrow replies quietly. "You have to do you, Tracker; I'm sure Lana will take you any way you come. If not, then she's not the one for you."

Arrow is off my Christmas list.

"She's the one," Tracker says quickly. "Feel it in my gut. She's my old lady. She's mine."

"She's stronger than you think," Arrow says, taking a deep draw from the joint. "She's small, but her mind isn't."

"I didn't want her to know, the blood I have on my hands. She knows nothing. I thought that was best, but now it feels like she doesn't really know all of me. I need her to accept all of me," Tracker admits, lying down on his back, staring at the ceiling. "I'm not a good man, I don't think. But I'm not a bad man. I've hurt people. Never a woman or a kid. But men, yes."

"You're a good man," Arrow says gruffly. "And fuck you for thinking otherwise. We all have our demons, Tracker, some worse than others. When I see Lana, the way she looks at you. Fuck, man, just be up front with her. Pretty sure that girl will follow you straight to hell and back."

"Hopefully that won't be required," Tracker replies in a dry tone, then admits in a whisper, "I'd kill for her. I just want to protect her."

"And you do," Arrow says. "But when shit gets tough, as it usually does at some point around here, you need to have her ready, not left in the dark."

I step away and head back to the room, thinking about what I'd heard, feeling glad I'd heard it and guilty over hearing it at the same time. I had no idea he felt that way, that he was still trying to be what he thought I wanted him to be, not who he was.

Censoring himself.

I don't want him to feel as though he has to. I've accepted him, who he is, what he belongs to. He wants me in deep, and I'm so deep that I can't stand. Now, I just need to prove it to him.

The next time I wake up, he's spooning me.

Much better.

I decide to wake him up with my mouth on him, trying not to be put off over what happened last time.

And when he comes, it's my name he growls in pleasure.

"Lana, wait," Anna calls, grabbing my arm. "Slow down."

"What is it?" I ask, glancing around. We'd just had lunch together and I was about to start my first class for the day. Following her line of sight, I see four men on their bikes watching us. They aren't Wind Dragons, nor are they Wild Men.

"Who are they?" I ask, trying to not make it obvious we're talking about them.

"No idea, but I don't like the way they're watching us," she says quietly, pulling me in the other direction. We get in my car and drive to the clubhouse first, then get Blade to drive me to school. Anna doesn't want me to be alone, just in case. Class is boring and drags on. Instead of paying attention, I find myself writing out an outline for a new book. When it's over, I'm surprised to see Tracker waiting for me instead of Blade.

"What a nice surprise," I say, practically jumping into his arms.

"You and Anna did well today, coming back to the clubhouse instead of going off on your own," he says, giving me a quick, sweet kiss.

"I know," I say. "I think Anna is maturing. Did you find out who those men were?"

"Kind of," he evades. "We're going on a run tonight."

"How long will you be gone for?" I ask, tilting my head to the side.

"Two nights," he replies.

"Okay," I say, trying not to show my disappointment. "Who's staying behind this time?"

"Arrow," he says. "And you're going to stay in the clubhouse while I'm gone so I don't have to worry about your ass."

I puff out a breath. "Okay, yeah, I can do that."

"That's my girl," he says, taking my bag from me. "Come on, let's get out of here. I wanna spend time with you before we have to ride out."

"Okay," I say, then take a deep breath. "There's something I want to talk to you about."

"What?" he asks, opening my car door for me. I look around. "How did you even get here?"

"Got dropped off by Rake," he says. "Blade left with him. So what do you want to talk to me about?"

We get into the car and he waits patiently, looking at me expectantly. "I woke up last night and you weren't in bed, so I went to find you. You were in the gym talking with Arrow and I kind of heard everything."

Because I was trying to.

I leave out that part.

Tracker studies me in silence. "Just how much of it did you stay for?"

Yeah, he's angry.

"I don't know," I say in a quiet, remorseful tone. "More than I should have. But it was about me, so obviously I listened. If it was about something else, then I wouldn't have."

I think.

He runs a hand through his hair, which is loose around his shoulders. "Fuckin' hell, Lana—"

"I just want to be honest, so that's why I'm telling you," I say shyly. "I also want to tell you that I'm a writer. I kept that to myself too. I don't know why. It was just mine, but I want it to be ours."

He looks at me like I'm crazy, which I probably am. This isn't exactly the time to bring up the whole writer thing.

"What did you think," he asks. "About what you heard? I don't want you to think that you don't know me, because you do. You just don't know that side of me, and it's my fault because I've been hiding it from you."

"Tracker," I say, swallowing hard. "I do know you. I know you'd never hurt me; I know that you take care of me. You're good to those you care about. I can handle every side of you. That's what I'm trying to say. I'm not going to run, I promise."

He glances out the window, before returning his gaze to me. "I don't think you know what you're saying."

"Tracker—"

"What if I end up in prison, or something like that? How are you going to handle that? What if you were kidnapped like Anna was, or if men broke into the clubhouse with guns in the middle of the night? That happened to Faye. I'm not saying I don't think you're a strong woman, because you are, but the thought of something like that happening to you makes me crazy. I'm stuck between wanting to protect you, every inch of you, and the love for my club. I will never leave the Wind Dragons, they're my family, but if you were hurt or something because of my lifestyle, I wouldn't fuckin' handle that well either."

"Well you should have thought of all this before you made me fall head over fucking heels in love with you!" I snap. "I'm trying here, Tracker. I'm telling you that no matter what, I know your soul and I will never turn my back on you. Why can't you do the same for me?"

His eyes widen, as if he never thought of it that way.

"Come here," he demands.

"Come where?" I ask.

His mouth twitches. "My lap."

I straddle him, my palms on his cheeks. "Now what?"

"Now kiss me, Lana," he says. "Wanna be inside you but that will have to wait until we get back to the clubhouse."

I kiss him like it's the last kiss we'll ever have.

TWENTY-ONE

LISTENING to "Live Without It" by Killing Heidi, I browse through my clothes looking for something to wear to Rake's birthday. When there's a knock at the door, I open it to see Faye standing there. I'm not sure how she knows where my house is, but I don't bother asking.

"Hey," I say in surprise.

"Get in the car, we're going shopping."

We share knowing smiles.

An hour later, I'm watching Faye try on outfits. When she walks out in an extremely low-cut black number, my eyes widen. "Holy shit."

"Just the reaction I was going for," she says in approval.

"I can almost see your nipples," I decide to point out, blinking slowly.

She looks down. "So you can."

Thinking that meant she wasn't going to get it, I'm surprised when she says, "It's perfect."

"But . . ."

"There are going to be strippers there," she says. "No matter what we wear we're still going to be wearing more."

"Ummm, Faye—"

"Ohhh, you should try this on!" she says excitedly, grabbing a cute royal-blue dress. "This color will look gorgeous on you."

She then proceeds to grab a few other dresses for me to try.

"Unless . . ." she says to herself, glancing at me thoughtfully. "Can I give you a biker-chick makeover?"

She laughs at whatever expression she sees on my face. "You should have seen me when I first came here. I was so conservative because I was brought up that way. Now I just wear whatever I like, professional for work, but for parties like this you get to play up a little and go as daring as you want to."

"How daring are we talking here?" I ask in a voice full of skepticism.

I get a slow spreading smile in response. "Let's see what we can come up with."

I gulp.

Tight leather pants.

A black crop top—which looks more like a bra than a shirt if you ask me—and heels higher than I've ever worn.

Yet . . .

I feel strangely sexy. Empowered. The epitome of an old lady.

I suddenly realize that the tables have turned, and now it's me wanting him to be in deep. I could see that he was considering us breaking up, for my own good or whatever, but I wasn't about to let that happen.

"You look amazing," Faye gasps. "Tracker is going to die. His penis is going to explode."

"Okay, I hope neither of those things happen," I tell her, giving her a wide-eyed look.

She grins and goes back to applying her makeup. "So who organized this whole deal for Rake?"

"I helped," she admits. "He told me what he wanted. I believe his exact words were 'I want to turn the clubhouse into a sex club.'"

"Only he would say that," I grumble, applying some bloodred lipstick and some mascara. Teasing my hair a little, I stare at my reflection, then glance at Faye from the corner of my eye.

"I'm ready to make tonight my bitch."

She laughs, poking her eye with mascara. "Dammit!"

I laugh harder. "Shit."

"Great, now I'm going to have one red eye," she complains, pointing the mascara tube at me. "Your fault."

"I'm sure one of the men has some Clear Eyes," I joke.

"Are you drinking tonight?" she asks. "We should make some cocktails or something."

"I'll have a drink or two," I say, then turn to her iPod as the song changes. "You like One Direction?"

Her eyes narrow. "Don't judge me."

My lip twitches. "No judgment here."

Amusement fills her pretty eyes. "I like you, Lana."

"I like you too."

"We should have a threesome."

I drop my phone on the floor.

"You should see your face!" she calls out, hooting.

I'm beginning to think there are two sides to Faye. One, the scary biker wife who can kick ass, and two, the immature girl who was never going to grow up. I found myself liking both of them.

"What's going on in there?" Tracker calls out, hovering by the door, which we'd locked from the inside.

Faye rolls her eyes. "Loosen the reins a little, Tracker, Jesus. What could I possibly be doing to her in here that you have to worry about?"

"I'm not worried," he says, then pauses. "Maybe I just want to see."

"There's nothing to see here, you pervert! Except your woman looking hotter than any woman you've ever seen in your life."

Silence.

Then banging.

"Lana, open the door!"

"I can't," I call back. "I'm naked."

I hear him curse. "You two aren't spending any more time together."

Faye and I share a glance, then burst out laughing.

"Is Anna pissed she can't come tonight?" she asks once we calm down.

"Yes," I reply, shaking my head. "But who wants to see their brother do God knows what? I think she said she might drop by before everything gets too crazy, then leave with Arrow."

"That's a good idea," she says, pausing. "We could probably set up a safe area and sneak her in without Rake knowing."

"I approve of this plan."

"I'll message her and let her know," she says, pressing together her lips. "I like this."

"I do too. If Rake finds out, he's going to kill us though. I know he really doesn't want Anna to see whatever it is he has planned for tonight."

"Rake will be busy," Faye says, sliding her feet into her black strappy heels. "We have an hour, let's go make some drinks."

As soon as we unlock the door and step out, I see Tracker stalking toward me from where he was leaning against the wall, talking to Sin.

"Fuck," he mouths, his gaze roaming over every inch of me. He then adjusts himself, right there in front of everyone.

I hear Faye making explosion sounds.

Closing the space between us, he grips my chin in his hand and stares deeply into my eyes. "You're a fantasy, you know that? Now we're going back into the bedroom because I'm so hard I'm about to come in my pants."

More explosion sounds from Faye.

She and Sin whistle, and Tracker lifts me in the air, throws me over his shoulder, and drags me back into the room. He doesn't even bother to close the door, leaving it open as he lies me down on the bed, his mouth already on mine.

"Close the door," I growl.

"No," he replies. "No time."

"Tracker!"

"No one can see anything," he says, kissing my neck. "I'm covering your body. And if anyone walked in here I'd kill them. Okay?"

"Okay," I whisper back, trusting him.

He slides down my leather pants to my knees then pushes my

thighs apart as far as they can go. Pulling down his own pants, he pulls out his hard cock and rubs it against my entrance.

"This is going to be hard and fast, Lana," he grits out.

"Yes," I moan, so turned on right now that I can barely see straight. "Fuck me, Tracker."

He slowly pushes himself inside me until he is balls-deep, then pulls out and slams back in harder. Kissing me hungrily, his tongue mimics his cock, thrusting in and out in a sensual rhythm. My fingers digging into his scalp, I urge him on, not wanting him to hold back. It feels so good that I can turn him on like this with just one glance at me, that he wants me this much. A woman could get used to being this appreciated, giving this much attention.

"So good, baby," he moans. "You feel so damn perfect. You fit me like a fuckin' glove."

I squeeze myself around him, inciting another moan. "Harder."

"You get what you're given, Lana," he replies, biting down on my earlobe. "Don't think you're in charge just 'cause you come out looking like a wet dream."

I come screaming.

Tracker soon follows, his body jerking, his face contorting into a sexy mask of pleasure. Kissing my forehead, my cheeks, and my nose, he finally places a gentle, sweet kiss on my mouth.

"Party start without me?" I hear Rake call out through the open door.

"Get out of here if you want to live," Tracker yells back, with no heat in his tone. Instead, his eyes are locked with mine, full of a mixture of tenderness, possessiveness, and satisfaction.

"Lana," he says quietly.

"Yeah?"

"When you walk around tonight in these sexy-ass leather pants, and every man is watching you, picturing you just like this, except under them, just remember this moment. You're mine to sink into, mine to pleasure, to love, to fuck."

I roll my eyes and ask in a dry tone, "Why don't you just pee on me?"

"I put my come inside you instead," he says, winking at me, playful Tracker back. "That's going to have to do."

"Tracker?"

"Yes, baby?"

"Close the damn door."

TWENTY-TWO

RAKE is sitting on a chair, getting a lap dance from two naked, very flexible women. Anna made an appearance but left after an hour when she saw him making out with two women—different ones than the ones on his lap now. I would have done the same. I helped Faye set out some food and drinks and am now sitting on Tracker's lap, watching the craziness around us. Faye is dirty dancing with Sin, while the other men in the MC are enjoying the women and the alcohol.

"Are these Toxic girls?" I ask, looking around the room.

"I think some are," he says, rubbing his hand down my thigh. "Some of them I haven't seen before."

I choose to ignore that comment.

I don't know why Rake didn't want to just have his party at Toxic, because the clubhouse looked like a strip club right now anyway.

"Lana, come dance!" Faye calls out when she loses her dance partner. Getting off Tracker's lap, I dance with her for a few songs. When I turn back, Tracker has moved from his spot.

"He left with Irish," Faye says, nodding her chin at Sin. "He has my man keeping an eye on you."

When my gaze lands on Rake, I quickly turn away.

Holy shit.

One of the girls is on her knees, giving him a blow job.

In the middle of the room.

I look at Faye, too scared to look anywhere else. She starts laughing as my awkwardness over the situation increases. "Let's get a drink."

Lifesaver.

We walk arm in arm to the kitchen, even though there's a table of drinks outside as well. "Rake must be a freak in bed."

Faye laughs. "The stories I've heard"—she cringes—"and seen. But he's Rake. You gotta love the man."

"That's true," I say, pouring myself some orange juice with a dash of vodka.

Jess walks in with a few other women I've seen around the clubhouse at various stages. "Shit is getting crazy out there."

"I know," Faye says. "As long as Rake enjoys himself though."

"And as long as the women stay away from our men," Jess replies, smirking. "Saw a few of them eyeing our president."

Faye straightens. "Who would be stupid enough to dare? I'm going to find out."

She storms out, and I follow behind her. Before I can catch up to her, Tracker finds me and leads me outside, where Irish and Vinnie are sitting, smoking together. I say hello to both of them, sitting down next to Tracker.

"Not enjoying the show?" I ask.

"The night is young," Vinnie replies, winking at me. "I'll wait until you and Faye leave. Don't want to scar you for life."

I look at Tracker. "Are you staying here for that?"

He nods. "Yeah, Arrow is coming back too. We're gonna have some time with just the Wind Dragon members."

He studies me, waiting for my reaction. It's then I realize he thinks I'm going to get angry. I say, "Maybe Faye and I could do something together, instead of us being sent home."

His eyes narrow. "You guys aren't going out anywhere."

"We'll go to Faye's house or something."

"I'd rather you two both went to bed early," he grumbles. "Stay here in the clubhouse, but give us a little time to party with Rake."

He wants me to go to bed early? While he stays up to party without any of us around? I decide to stay quiet because two of his brothers are here with us, listening to our conversation. Instead, I sip my drink and enjoy the music flowing outside from the house. The men talk among themselves but I don't pay attention, I just snuggle up with Tracker. Needing to use the bathroom, I walk back inside to see that the party has gotten even wilder. People were literally having sex out in the open, naked and not one shit given. This isn't the kind of scene I ever thought I'd see with my own eyes, but at the same time, it is damn good research material. As I walk by two men with one woman, I even get inspired to write a threesome scene.

"Like to watch, do you?" Tracker says, pulling me back against his chest. "You always surprise me, Lana."

We sit down on the couch, and watch the sensual couples around us. I feel embarrassed. I feel curious. I don't know where to look. But here I am, and I'm going to make the most of . . . whatever this is. Tracker lazily strokes the curve of my breast as I see Rake lie back, one woman sucking him. The second woman sits on his face. My cheeks heat. Yeah, I need another drink. Something stronger. Tracker pulls me closer to him and starts kissing up my collarbone.

"You okay?" he asks. "We can go to our room if you like. Or you can stay and watch. No one will dare touch you, even if they wanted to."

I gulp. I don't know what I want. I'm frozen.

Tracker grins and lifts me onto his lap. "Kiss me."

His command snaps me out of my shock.

Giving him all my attention, I straddle him and kiss him. His hands cupping the cheeks of my ass, I grind on him gently when the kissing turns deeper, more erotic. His tongue sucks on mine, and then he nips at my bottom lip. I grip his cheeks in my hands, feeling the rough blond stubble on his face and wanting to feel it elsewhere. When he pulls down my top a little, exposing my breasts, I don't stop him. He moves me close so no one can see my nipples except him, his eyes glazing over in lust.

"Tell me to take you to the room, or I'm fucking you right here," he says in a ragged voice.

I say nothing.

"Lana," he growls. "Tell me, now."

He pulls my entire top off, baring me from the waist up.

My last warning.

"I'm not fuckin' around, Lana," he says. "Everyone is about to get a show, and I'm too turned on to care."

A Nine Inch Nails song plays in the background: "Closer."

Closer.

I still stay quiet.

"Need the words, Lana."

"Fuck me here," I demand. "Right now, I don't care either."

He lifts me up and lies me down on the couch.

He pulls down my pants and takes me.

Just like I asked him to.

The next morning, my mind clear, the atmosphere completely different, reality hits me.

Oh my god.

I had sex.

With Tracker.

In a room full of people.

Sure, they were doing the same, and probably not paying that much attention, but still.

I'm never going to be able to look anyone in the eye again.

I'll have to move.

To a different country.

I hear Tracker sigh from next to me. "How did I know you'd get up in the morning, overthink shit, and get pissed with me?"

"I need to pack," I whisper.

"What?" he asks, sitting up, the blanket falling down to reveal his sexy toned chest.

"I need to move. I'll never be able to face anyone. Ever. Again," I ramble. "Maybe I'll move to Ireland. I've heard Galway is really beautiful. A writer's paradise. Yes, I should move there."

"What you should do is calm down," Tracker says, looking on the verge of laughing now. "No one will say shit to you. Yeah, you might get a few knowing smiles, but who cares? Tell them to fuck off. They were all wishing they were me last night."

I exhale slowly.

Tracker continues, "And if you wanna go to fuckin' Ireland, I'll take you there. On a vacation. Now shut up and get back to sleep."

I scowl at him.

"You shut up," I mumble, closing my eyes.

I hear him chuckle as I fall back asleep.

I eat my cereal, avoiding Rake's gaze. "Had fun last night?" he asks in an innocent enough tone, but it still sets my nerves on fire.

I shrug. "I guess so."

"Heard you did."

"Well you would have seen for yourself if you didn't have a pussy on your face."

He chokes on his cereal, then starts cracking up laughing until he can't breathe. "Fuck me, did Lana just say *pussy*? Fuckin' classic. Tracker's corrupted you, hasn't he? Little innocent Lana is long gone."

If they knew the kind of things I wrote about daily, they would know my mind had never been innocent.

"I'm still the same," I grumble, stirring the milk in my bowl.

"I'm just teasing you," he says, chuckling some more. "As long as you were okay with what happened, so am I. No judgment here. Just giving you a hard time is all."

"Did everyone see?" I ask him on a whisper.

He shook his head. "No. I was there, but like you said, I was busy. I think Irish and Vinnie might have seen. And some members from other chapters who came to hang out for a bit. My friend Zach saw; he was saying how smoking hot you are."

I cover my face with my hands. "Someone just kill me. Right now. Shoot me, Rake, do it."

"Don't be so dramatic. Did you see all the shit going on here last night? You think everyone was concerned about some vanilla sex on the couch?"

Well. When he put it like that he made me sound self-centered.

"Okay," I say simply, still hoping that Anna won't hear about it, because she'll be giving me shit until she can't breathe.

Irish sits down, grinning at me. "Tracker is a lucky bastard. Faye or Anna wouldn't have done that. No way in hell."

"Oh my god. Shut up! Or I'm moving to your motherland," I tell Irish. "Galway, to be exact."

"Great place," he comments, a smirk on his handsome face.

"I'm going to my mom's house," I announce. "Until someone else does something notable we can all gossip about."

They all watch me in amusement as I bang my head against the table.

I ignore Faye's wide grin, stepping around her and grabbing my bag. "I'll be going now. And I'll be leaving my dignity behind."

She laughs, slapping her hand down on the counter. "You had fun. There's no shame in it, Lana. The guys think you're great."

"Yeah, but they're all pervy bastards," I say, shoulders sagging. "I better get home. I have a shitload of work to do."

"Where's Tracker?" she asks.

"He went back to sleep. Is Blade awake? If I leave alone, Tracker will be . . ."

I search for the right word.

"Up your butt?" Faye suggests.

I purse my lips. "No I was going to say angry. And that never happened last night." I pause. "Or ever."

Of course Rake has to walk into the room at that moment, hearing the last bit of the conversation. "So Lana isn't thaaaaaat much of a naughty girl, then."

I blink slowly. "I'm never coming here again."

"No, just on the couch," Rake quips.

He and Faye give each other a dorky high five.

And I find Blade and get the hell out of here.

"You did what?" Anna laughs, jaw going slack. "Holy shit. That sounds hot. Glad I didn't see you naked there though, getting pounded by Tracker."

She rubs her hand over her mouth. "You kinky little thing, you. Well, makes sense. Tracker was probably fucking Zada Ryan, not Lana Brown."

I pinch her arm. "Can you lower your voice?"

We both glance around the café. "No one heard me. Besides, only porn readers would recognize the name."

I scowl. "It's romance, not porn."

She shrugs. "Faye thinks it's porn. She says she and Sin have the best sex afterward because she's so turned on."

I sigh, resting my cheek on my palm. "There are no boundaries in that clubhouse, are there?"

Anna shakes her head ruefully. "No. But then again, most families are like that. Maybe not to the point of having sex in front of each other, but otherwise? No boundaries."

I slap her shoulder, but let the former part of her words sink in. She's right. "I should just move in with Tracker, shouldn't I?"

"If you think he's the one. It's up to you. I would though, if I were you," she admits, then arches her brow. "Plus I like the thought of having you there."

"I'm hardly ever home," I say. "I haven't seen my mom in what feels like days."

"How is she doing?" Anna asks, sitting back in the booth. "Any more news from your dad?"

"Mom is good. Busy working. Nothing from Quinn, no."

I didn't know how to feel about that, so I'm blocking it out.

"How's it going on the baby-making front?" I ask, changing the subject.

"Been two months and nothing yet, but I read for some people it takes a longer time. Unlike Faye who got knocked up in one night."

We make a few jokes about Sin's expert swimmers.

"I better head to class," I say, standing up. "Are you going to the zoo?"

She nods. "Yeah, then back to school."

"Students by day, old ladies by night."

"And porn writers," she adds cheekily.

"And baby makers."

We grin.

I don't tell Tracker I've decided to move in. Instead, I just move in. I bring a suitcase with everything I'll need for now and unpack my clothes in his drawers. When he walks in and sees me, the biggest smile takes over his face.

"'Bout time."

"You'll get sick of me soon enough."

"Never," he replies. "You want some help?"

"I'm good. I might need more space though."

"I'll make some for you," he says, removing his T-shirt and throwing it on the floor. His jeans come off next, and then his boxer briefs.

"Want some attention, do you?" I ask, taking him in from head to toe.

My own Adonis.

"Always," he replies, the gleam in his eyes telling me he wants me. Now.

I slam the closet door shut and stalk toward him.

Priorities.

TWENTY-THREE

TRACKER

MY woman has moved into the clubhouse.

Fuckin' finally.

Stubborn little thing she is. I smile as I watch her sleep on her stomach, the covers sitting on the curve of her round ass, showing off the cute dimples of her lower back. I want to trace the indentations with my tongue. I make a mental note to do so later.

She really is something. Fascinating. Infectious. Someone I just want to keep behind my body, protected from the realities of the world.

A treasure.

I've been with many beautiful women, had more than my share, and I enjoyed them all. I love women. Their smell, their gentleness. Softness. The sighs they make, the smell of their hair.

Every fuckin' thing.

But Lana, she is *my* woman, not just one in a crowd.

I've never felt so connected to a person before. I've never cared what someone thought so much before. I'd never given someone the ability to hurt me, but I've shared that with her. As Faye is to Sin, and Anna is to Arrow, Lana is to me. The woman born to be on the back of my bike, holding tight, living life with me to the fullest. I have a voracious appetite for life—I love to eat, fuck, ride, make jokes, and mess around with everyone. Make people around me laugh. I love my brothers, my club— and now that I have Lana to share my life with, I love her more than anything else.

I don't even know how it happened.

I've never been a possessive sort of man, but now I realize that's only because I've never cared so much. I didn't think I'd find anyone who fit me, which is why I usually just settled. Being with Lana isn't settling. It isn't easy, but it is right. I don't really know how someone who lives the kind of life I live could fit with someone like her. She's sweet, a little on the geeky side. Tiny little thing. Looks like a strong wind could blow her away. But she's tough on the inside. She fights with herself daily, I see it, and she fights to be stronger. To say what she feels, to not hold back. To try new things. To break out of her introverted shell. She loves my brothers as much as she loves me.

Love the man, love the club.

I can't even explain my obsession with her.

Her pussy is the best I've ever had, her lips the softest, her breath the sweetest.

Everything is better with her around.

It's like she was made for me, for my pleasure. For my happiness. Fuck, she has me twisted. And she wants me, just as much, maybe even more than I want her. She knows how to look after me; she has my back.

She's perfect.

She's wifey and mother material.

She's also old-lady material, which she proves to me over and over again.

I'm one lucky bastard, and I'm fuckin' thankful I fought for her.

I kiss her bare shoulder, then get dressed and leave our room, glancing over at her one last time before closing the door.

"There you are," Sin says as I walk into the clubroom. Only members are allowed in this room, unless invited, and never during church. It is a place where we speak about our private business, and where decisions are made.

"Everything okay?" I ask, watching him pace.

"Those fuckers are up to something," he growls. "We need them out of our town."

Talon had come to let us know about another MC around our territory. Kings of Hell MC are here for a reason, but none of us can figure out why. It is making all of us nervous as hell. We're wondering whether we should make the first move, or wait to see what their game plan is.

"Vinnie's keeping an eye on them, right?"

Sin nods. "Yeah. Looks like they're running drugs and guns. I don't know why they were watching Anna and Lana though. We're missing something, and I don't know what it is."

"The women are well protected," I assure him. "We aren't gonna lose one of them. Whoever tries will be gutted."

Sin scrubs a hand down his face, looking tired. "All right. The cops have been sniffing around here too. I think they know something is up, except this time it hasn't got anything to do with us. They're probably wondering what those assholes are doing here as well. Shit's about to hit the fan; that's all I know."

"See," I joke. "Even when we're good, we still get blamed for shit. We should just go fuck them up and kick them out of our town. Cops might thank us."

"Define *good*," Sin replies, scoffing. "And that can be our plan B."

I laugh at that. "Okay, not good. Let's go with better. Or improved. Hey, Arrow hasn't killed anyone lately. I call that a good thing."

Sin just grunts in response. "You can make a joke out of anything, can't you, asshole?"

I smirk. "You know me."

He shakes his head. "I do know you, brother. Know you have my back. We'll get this shit sorted; we always do."

"Sin," I say quietly.

"Yeah?"

"We'd all protect Clover with our lives," I say solemnly.

"I know," he says instantly. "Trust me brother, I know."

"Besides"—a faint smile plays on his mouth—"they'd have to get through my wife first."

"Tracker, long time no see," a familiar voice purrs.

Wincing, I turn to the woman, schooling my expression to passivity. "Leanne, what are you doing here?" I ask Jess's younger sister.

"Came to visit Jess," she says, smiling seductively. "Plus I missed you."

This time I don't bother to hide my grimace. "Sorry, sweetheart, I'm a taken man now."

She giggles, a noise that grates on my nerves. "Yeah, like you were with Allie?"

"Don't have to explain myself to you," I snap, then get my temper under control. "Fucked you a few times; won't be happening again. I'm sure Rake will be interested. Or one of the other men."

She places her hand on my chest, and I stare down at it in disgust. Why can't some women take no for an answer? They could be beautiful with a smoking body, like Leanne is, but that doesn't mean that I want them no matter what. I'm not about to lose Lana over a bit of easy pussy. Worst part is, Leanne is actually friends with Allie and still fucked me behind her friend's back. Women like this make me want to kiss Lana's feet, grateful that I found a woman who can be trusted. A loyal, honest-to-God good woman. More than I deserve, but no less than I'd settle for. Anna walks into the kitchen, taking in the scene before her.

"Get your hand off Tracker if you want to keep it attached to your skinny-ass body," Anna snaps, forever looking out for her best friend.

Leanne backs away. "Can't blame a girl for trying."

"Actually," Anna says. "I can. And I will."

"I'm gonna go find Jess," she mumbles, leaving the room.

"Anna Bell," I say, shaking my head. "You're becoming even scarier than Faye nowadays."

Her eyes stay narrowed. "Why was she touching you?"

"You kidding me right now? I told her I didn't want anything to do with her," I say, angry she jumped to that conclusion so quickly.

Her shoulders drop. "Okay."

"Christ, when did the women start running shit around here?" I ask, feeling like punching something.

"My thoughts exactly," Rake says, running a hand through his messy blond hair. "Soon they're gonna fuckin' take over."

Anna quickly leaves the room.

Smart woman.

"You wanna get in the ring with me?" I ask Rake. I really do want to hit something. Or someone.

"Yeah, give me an hour and I'll meet you in there," Rake replies. "Gonna fuck Leanne first just so she'll shut up."

I laugh at that. "Better you than me, brother."

Rake shrugs. "Any pussy is good pussy."

I grin. Rake has been going through even more women than usual, and I have to wonder what's up with him. I have a feeling it's something to do with his ex, Bailey.

Keeping my thoughts to myself, I slap his shoulder. "See you in an hour."

He better be ready, because I am in a bit of a mood.

Later that night, I return home from Rift, feeling tired and just wanting a good night's sleep with Lana in my arms. There was some drama at the bar, a few guys dealing meth who needed to be dealt with. We don't want drugs run out of our businesses, especially if it's not beneficial to us. We also don't want those drugged-up fuckheads frequenting the place. Our women go to Rift more often than not, and we want the place safe for them. Well, besides from us anyway. It's a biker bar, *our* biker bar, and one of the benefits is that we're in control of who enters the place.

I find Lana already passed out on the bed, her laptop resting on her stomach. Her glasses are still on her face, lopsided, and she's snoring lightly. A cute sound, unlike Anna's. I remove her glasses and set them on the side table. Kissing her relaxed mouth, I lift her laptop off the bed and the screen goes from black to a white document page, showing something Lana was working on. When the word *fuck* catches my eye, I grin and place the laptop on top of my drawers. What is she writing? I know she writes a lot—she's even mentioned that she wants to go to Ireland for inspiration. And she's casually stated in the past that she publishes some of her work, makes money from it, and once even made a joke about writing porn. When I see another word, *orgasm*, I begin to wonder if she was telling the truth.

My smile widens.

Curious, I read the first paragraph . . . then the second, and the third.

Sexy biker Rogue was having a birthday, but it wasn't like any other party I'd been to. With wide eyes I watched as people in the room openly touched each other, the clubhouse turning into a sex club for the night.

Sexy biker? Is she referring to Rake?

I see red.

I read all of it, from start to finish

Then, pissed off, I delete the whole thing.

She's writing about bikers? About shit she saw in the clubhouse? The club dynamics? Did she think that was okay?

How could she?

The club trusted her; I trusted her.

She's let all of us down.

*   *   *

When Lana wakes up the morning, I'm sitting on my chair in the corner of the room, watching her.

"'Morning," she says in her sleepy voice, a smile appearing on her lush mouth. "You're awake early."

I hadn't slept.

"I read what you wrote," I tell her, getting straight to the point. "I knew you wrote, but I didn't know that you wrote books. MC books. Is that why you're here? Research for your stupid fucking books?"

She sits up, frowning. "You can't seriously think that. It's just a little fiction, Tracker."

"Fiction based on the facts of our lives," I snap, anger clouding my judgment.

Pain spreads through my chest at the thought of Lana not being who I thought she was. Everything I've praised her for, loved her for, her loyalty, was bullshit.

"It isn't like that at all, Tracker. I'd never betray your trust like that. I told you, remember. I told you that I—"

"You said you wrote, yes, but you didn't tell me all the details, clearly," I snap. "You never mentioned it had anything to do with bikers. This is my fucking life, Lana! My club! If people find out who you are, what do you think they're going to think? They're going to know most of the shit you wrote is fact."

"The only thing that's fact is some of the sex scenes!" she yells back. "I never once wrote anything to do with the ins and outs of the club or anything that could be considered a betrayal. You're overreacting right now, Tracker."

But every scene I'd read had really happened. Rake's birthday, the way we fucked that night, to when we made love, every fuckin' detail of what we explored and shared together. She was documenting it.

Documenting our love life.

Christ.

I was living it, but she was remembering it so she could share it.

When we were fucking, was she making mental notes?

Christ, while I am so into her, in so deep I can barely remember my own name when I'm with her, her mind is racing. It's always the quiet ones, isn't it?

I feel betrayed.

And even worse, I feel like I don't know her. Have I put the club at risk? Has she written anything personal about us? Does she have information saved? Has she already published something?

Isn't this something you'd talk to your partner about in detail?

The whole thing is a clusterfuck.

And it's probably karma.

All the women I've hurt in the past, all the things I've done, have led to this moment.

The moment where a woman, a little slip of a thing, breaks my fucking heart with her lies and omissions. I finally fell in love with a woman, and now I feel exposed. Unsure. And fucking hurt.

I don't like it.

When did I give her the power to control my emotions? I don't think even I realized just how deep I was in, until now.

"Tracker, I would never write anything about—"

"Your time for explaining has long passed, Lana," I say in an ice-cold tone. "Get your shit and get out of here. I'm done."

I trusted her with everything. I gave her everything I had. I gave her my family, my protection, my love. I gave her myself. I changed for her.

And the whole time she was what, writing a book on my lifestyle?

This isn't a fuckin' story. This is my life.

I get up and leave, ignoring the sounds of her crying.

Leaving what's left of my mangled heart with her.

TWENTY-FOUR

LANA

I'S been a week. He won't talk to me, let me explain. And he deleted my work. All my hard work, lost because of his misguided anger. And now, we can't even talk about it because he won't see me. I haven't stepped back into the clubhouse since the day he told me to leave. I'm not going where I'm not wanted. I tried to call him, and send him a few messages, but there was no reply. Nothing. He cut me out of his life, just like that. At the very least, I deserve to be able to explain myself. I didn't do anything wrong, and he's not completely innocent either. He hurt me too by thinking the worst of me, by jumping to conclusions. I was right all along. All men leave. It's just inevitable.

I would never betray the club, and the only scenes I had written out, before Tracker deleted them, were sex scenes, the amazing moments Tracker has given me, now immortalized forever with the written word. How is that a bad thing? If he read the story like he said he did, he would know what I wrote. So why is he acting like this? I never used him. I love him, more than anything. Because I didn't tell him the whole story about my writing career, I'd now lost him. Over something trivial.

The love of my life.

I haven't typed a single word since.

Tracker wouldn't even let me make it better. Anna said he wouldn't listen to her either, leaving the room every time she tried to bring it up. He is done with me.

Done.

And I'm left a shell of a person.

I almost wish I could go back in time, before Tracker, so I could carry on with my life. So I didn't know what it felt like to live with a broken heart. So I didn't know what it felt like to be cared for and loved, because when you lose it, it hurts like a fucking bitch.

But life goes on.

The day after he kicked me out, I moved into that apartment I wanted, the one Tracker said he didn't like.

It feels lonely.

Sometimes I see Blade around, keeping an eye on me. I don't know if Tracker asked him to, or maybe it was Rake. Either way, I don't know if it is because they still care for me or that they no longer trust me.

That hurts, badly.

My writing is fiction. I'm not a journalist, trying to expose someone—I'm just a lover of romance.

Or at least, I was.

Anna visits me every day, but we stay off the topic of Tracker. I don't want to talk about him. I don't want to know who he's with now, or how much he hates me.

I want to erase every memory of him.

"Lana?" Anna calls out, walking into my bedroom. She sits down and stares at me. "Don't you have classes? I went by campus but you weren't there, so I came here. You didn't even answer your door. Lucky I brought my spare key."

"Sorry," I say, forcing a smile. "I'm not feeling too well, so I stayed home. And I was lost in thought."

She sighs. "I know you don't walk to talk about him, but I think the two of you need to stop being so stubborn and—"

"He doesn't want to hear what I have to say. We're both moving on with our lives. It's for the best."

She looks around my room. "How is this for the best? You barely leave this apartment. You don't see anyone. You're turning into a hermit."

"I'm dealing with everything the best way I can, and I'm going to be fine," I tell her, nodding my head. "Perfectly fucking fine."

"Yes, you sound it," she says dryly.

"Hearts get broken every day. I'm just another statistic."

"Would you listen to yourself?" she yells. "Get your ass up and into the shower right fucking now or I'm going to tell Rake and everyone to come here and deal with you. Decide, now."

"Fine," I grumble ungracefully. "I'll take a shower. You make something to eat."

"I'm on it," she says, leaving the room.

I get my ass in the shower, pushing Tracker and everything that goes with him to the very back of my mind.

A week later, I get a phone call from Arrow.

"Lana," he says gruffly. "Anna needs you."

I sit up. "What's wrong?"

"Just come to the clubhouse, please," he says, cutting the line.

Arrow said *please*?

Something isn't right.

I quickly throw on some shorts and put on a bra under my T-shirt, get in my car, and speed to the clubhouse. Walking inside, I ignore the looks from everyone—especially Tracker, who I can see out of the corner of my eye sitting on the couch.

He's not alone, and I didn't expect him to be.

A pretty blonde is sitting next to him.

I can't even look directly at them, the pain is so blinding.

I ignore the agony, which is so strong it feels physical, and demand, "Where is she?"

Rake steps out and grabs my arm, taking me to Anna and Arrow's room.

"She won't come out," he says, pain flashing in his eyes. "I can't save her from this, Lana. I don't know what to do."

I pull my arm from his hold and walk into the room without bothering to knock. Arrow is sitting there next to her. She has her knees to her chest, and she's sobbing into them.

"Arrow, can you give me a second?" I ask quietly.

He nods, kissing her forehead, then looking at me. His eyes plead with me.

Fix her, they say.

Make it better.

I nod at the door. I want to be alone with my best friend. As soon as he leaves, I climb into the bed with her, wrapping my arm around her shoulder.

"You want to tell me what this is about?" I ask quietly.

She lays her head on my collarbone, and I wrap her tightly in my arms. "I went to the doctor."

I stiffen, swallowing hard. "What did they say? Are you ill?"

She shakes her head, but says nothing.

"Goddammit, tell me, Anna!" I say, starting to panic.

"I just wanted to be sure . . . so I did some tests. . . . And . . ." She starts sobbing.

I want to shake her. "Tell me."

"I can't have children. They think I might have blocked fallopian tubes," she says, wiping her eyes with the sleeves of her T-shirt. "I might never be able to have kids. They want to run more tests, but . . . God, Lana. I can't even give Arrow kids."

I sigh in relief that she isn't sick, or dying, then rub her back soothingly. "Okay . . . first of all, do all the tests. You can still try IVF."

"I suppose," she whispers.

"You know what?" I tell her in a gentle tone. "You try the IVF, if that doesn't work, I swear to you, I will carry your baby for you. I'll be your surrogate. You want a kid, you're going to get one."

She looks me right in the eye. "You mean that?"

"I do. I promise. I'd do that for you in a heartbeat. My uterus is your uterus."

She laughs softly at that, some of the misery of her face clearing.

"Hard road ahead, Anna," I tell her. "But you will have a baby, all right? Might take a little more time than you wanted. But everything will work out."

We spend the next hour talking everything over.

"I better get going. You're going to be okay," I tell her, smiling. "Hey, I got invited to attend a book signing next week, about five hours from here. You want to come with me?"

"I'd love to," she says, smiling. "Finally get to meet some of your fangirls. Don't worry, Lana, I'll keep your ass humble."

My lip twitches. "Good to know."

She walks me to her door and opens it. Arrow is waiting on the other side. Did he just stand there the whole time? He enters the room, and exhales deeply, seeing her in a much better condition than she was in before.

"Thanks, Lana," he says. "I owe you. You ever need anything, you call me, all right?"

I give him a small smile. "What are friends for?"

I walk toward the front door, make sure not to look in the direction that I last saw Tracker.

"Lana!" Anna calls out just as I pass the living room.

"Yeah?" I ask, turning around.

"You're the best person I know."

"Right back at you," I say, waving, then I make my way to my car. I'm at my car door when I hear his voice from behind me.

"You gonna leave without even looking at me?"

I turn my head over my shoulder, keeping my face impassive. "Happy now?"

"No, I'm not fuckin' happy," he says, glancing over me. "You've lost weight."

"I'm not your problem anymore, Tracker," I say, unlocking my car door and opening it. "You've made that perfectly clear." I get in without another glance at him, although I can feel his gaze on me the entire time I pull out of the driveway.

I'd hate to pull him away from my replacement.

TWENTY-FIVE

TODAY is the day of my book signing.

My cover model, the sexy Wyatt Bruce, attends with me, along with Anna.

"He's hot," she says for the tenth time. "I think my fallopian tubes just unblocked themselves."

Well, it's a good sign if she's making jokes about it.

"Be quiet, he's going to hear you," I say with a grin as we figure out how to put up my banner.

"Need some help?" Wyatt asks.

"I think we might," I say, looking to Anna, who is holding a pole and scrunching up her face. The picture rail in this conference room is a good two feet higher than our upstretched hands.

"I got it," he says, chuckling.

He has the banner up in thirty seconds.

Anna starts stacking my books into neat little piles on the table, rambling about presentation, while I try and calm my nerves. What if no one wants a book signed? Most people probably don't even know who I am.

I'm a bestselling author, I remind myself. Now isn't the time to second-guess myself. My books have sold worldwide, and I was invited to the event. I've been invited to others before, but this is the first one I've accepted.

I'm nervous.

At least Wyatt is here. Surely women would want to see him.

The doors open, and the readers pile in.

When a line forms before me, I don't even know what to say. So I smile.

"I love your books!" a lovely lady with kind, warm eyes says. "I've read them all more than once."

"Thank you," I reply, feeling a little choked up.

"Would you mind signing all of them for me?"

"I'd love to," I reply honestly.

I sign anything and everything I'm given, from books to posters to photo books.

I chat with my readers; I take photos with them and thank them for buying my books.

At the end of the day, I'm exhausted, but my heart is so full I fall asleep with a smile on my face for the first time since Tracker kicked me out of his life.

The next week, Wyatt invites me for lunch. I say yes, not sure if it's for business or pleasure, but eager to get out of the house either way. It's time for me to try moving on with my life. I did have a missed call from Tracker the night of my book signing, but I didn't bother to call him back. He has a right to be mad at me, of course, but I don't understand why he won't let me explain myself. While I was with him, I didn't feel like I was only an author, I felt like I was *more*. I felt like I was a woman, like I was experiencing the things I write about in my books. I was no longer hiding behind my screen.

Instead of writing about life, I was living it.

For the first time ever. And I was the happiest I'd ever been.

He pulled me out of my head, and while I still loved writing and would write every day if I could, I was also experiencing more things on a day-to-day basis. If I wasn't with Tracker, I would have written a whole heap more than I did.

I meet Wyatt at the restaurant, dressed in jeans, white heels, and a white shirt.

"Hello," he says, smiling to reveal straight white teeth. "You look beautiful."

"Thank you," I say as he pulls my chair out for me.

A compliment. So this is a date?

Why did I have to be so awkward?

"So," I say, smiling a little shakily. "I've never eaten here before."

Note to self: work on my small-talk skills.

"Me either," he says, lifting the menu in his hands. "What do you feel like?"

I browse the menu and choose the least messy meal.

"So, are you going to do any more signings?" he asks. "It was great promotion for me. I've had a few other authors want to use my photos for their covers too."

"That's great," I say honestly. "I hope your modeling career becomes everything you dreamed it would."

When I see Anna, Rake, Arrow, and Tracker walk into the restaurant, I want to both die and kill Anna simultaneously. She knew I was having lunch here today with Wyatt. Why did I tell her? Tracker stops in his tracks when he sees me, his lips curving into a smile until he sees I'm not alone. He stares at Wyatt, his fists clenched and a scowl now etched where the smile used to be.

Anna walks over like she isn't seconds away from being stabbed with a fork. "Lana! Hello, Wyatt."

"Hey, Anna," Wyatt says, flashing her a friendly smile. "What a small world."

Small indeed. Too small.

"Anna, what are you doing here?" I ask her through clenched teeth. I mutter my hellos to the men, now standing right behind her. Arrow looks amused, Rake confused, and Tracker like he's about to murder Wyatt.

"We got hungry, so I suggested we go out for lunch," she says, smiling happily. "I had no idea you and Wyatt were having your date here!"

Could she be any more obvious?

"Really, well, we're about to order so . . ." I trail off, hoping they all get the hint.

They don't.

Tracker pulls out the chair next to me, and takes a seat. "You dating now?"

"I'm trying to," I say with a wince.

"We need to talk."

"Time for talking is over," I say, throwing his own words back in his face.

His lips tighten. "I'm not going to sit here and let you have a fuckin' date with another man. If you care about him at all, you will go outside with me. Otherwise my fist is going to be in his face in the next ten seconds."

Wyatt stares at me with wide eyes and says, "Maybe you should . . ."

I stand up, my chair pushing back. "You're such an asshole, Tracker."

I storm outside and stand next to his bike. I consider kicking it.

"Don't even think about it," he growls, grabbing my arm and turning me to face him. "You fucking him?"

"How's that any of your business?" I ask, crossing my arms over my chest. "You ended it. I don't belong to you."

"You will always belong to me," he snaps, then looks away.

"You've ignored me all this time. Now just because you see me with another man, you what? You want to talk? Why, you don't ever want to see me happy? Is that it? You want me pining after you for the rest of my life while you ignore me and fuck other women?"

I'm yelling at him by the end of my rant.

"Lana, you're a fuckin' famous author, and you didn't feel the need to tell me? When I saw what you were writing, I just lost it. I didn't know you wrote shit like that, because you never told me."

"I *did* tell you once, and you thought I was joking. And when you read it, you didn't even let me explain," I say. "Your first reaction was to assume I'd betray you. I might have not shared everything with you, but you should know by now that I'm not a bad person. The fact that you automatically thought the worst of me, what the hell am I supposed to do with that?"

"I don't know," he says, sarcasm lacing his angry tone. "Why don't you go write about it?"

I make a noise of frustration.

"Christ, my old lady is fuckin' Zada Ryan, and I didn't even know. How the hell do you think that makes me feel? What, you didn't trust me enough to share that information with me? Maybe you should be questioning why that is. Either you don't trust me, or . . . what? Why do you want it to be a secret?"

"I'd just kept it to myself for so long. No one knows about my writing except my mom, and then I told Anna. I was going to tell you, but whenever I tried, other shit was going on and I didn't feel like it was the right time. I don't know, Tracker." I sigh. "I don't want to fight, all right? I'm just going to go home. Tell Wyatt I'm sorry."

"I'm not saying anything to that fucker other than to stay away from what's mine if he wants to keep his pretty face," he declares, a muscle ticking in his strong jaw.

I open my mouth and then close it. "You're unbelievable."

"And you're delusional if you think I'm done with you," he states.

I throw my hands up in the air. "I've been so damn miserable and you didn't care. Now I'm trying to move on and here you are fucking it up for me."

"Bullshit I didn't care. I fuckin' care. I drove past your apartment at night just to check on things. I made Blade follow you to and from your classes, and why the hell should you be able to move on when I sure as fuck can't?" he practically yells at me, his chest heaving with each breath.

"Yeah, you looked heartbroken when I saw you sitting next to that blonde," I retort, sneering. "Must have been a real hardship for you."

"I was trying to get over you."

"Well maybe you should try harder," I say in a cold voice. "And leave me the hell alone."

He laughs without humor. "You forget that you're mine. No matter what you do or say, that will never change."

"I hate you."

"And I love you. I read your book. You're so fuckin' talented. It's a shame you didn't want to share that with me."

He turns and walks back into the restaurant, while I get in my car and get the hell out of there.

TWENTY-SIX

ANNA sends me five messages apologizing. I know she meant well—she thinks Tracker and I belong together—but now things are up in the air again and I have no idea what happened to Wyatt after I left. I know Anna made sure they didn't do anything to him. He messaged me and said he didn't think it was a good idea if we saw each other anymore. Tracker is cock-blocking me while he's able to get women any time he wants. Infuriating, but . . .

He read my book.

He hates reading.

It was a sweet gesture. And for him to say those kind words about my writing . . .

Damn him!

Pacing up and down my apartment, I'm about to go for a walk when there's a knock at the door. Opening it, I come face-to-face with Tracker.

"I don't like the thought of you alone here. In fact, I fuckin' hate it," he says in greeting.

"Well, too bad someone kicked me out of my last place," I say in a cold tone. My words hit their mark, going by the way he flinches.

"I still don't like it," he says in a much softer tone.

"Your feelings aren't high on my priority list anymore," I say, pushing my glasses up on the bridge of my nose.

He scowls, looking a mixture of angry and resigned. "I brought you something. A present. I know you like animals so . . ."

Looking down, I see that he has a basket in his hands. Inside is . . .

"Oh my god!" I say, taking the basket from him and peering down at the cute ball of black and gold fur.

"She's a purebred German shepherd," he says. "I thought maybe you might like to have someone in the apartment with you. I checked with your landlord, and you're allowed to have pets."

"She is perfect," I say, then glance up at Tracker. "Come in."

I walk into the kitchen and put the basket down, picking up the puppy and cradling her to my chest.

"She's so soft and fluffy," I whisper. "I love her so much!"

Tracker chuckles. "She's going to have long fur." He pauses. "It's nice to see you smile again too."

I kiss her head. "Thank you, Tracker; she's perfect."

"What are you going to call her?" he asks, watching the two of us together.

I think it over. "Evie. I'm going to call her Evie."

Tracker looks amused. "Isn't that what you wanted to name your daughter if you ever have one?"

I nod. "Who knows if or when I'll have kids. And she looks

like an Evie, don't you think? It's such a pretty name for a pretty little princess," I say in a baby voice.

"Christ," I hear him mutter. "I have a bed, food, and some toys for her in the car too."

"Glad you didn't bring her here on your bike," I tease, then look back down at Evie, stroking her fur.

"So," he says, looking around my apartment. "Are you going to offer me a drink?"

I purse my lips. "Is Evie a bribe?"

"Is it working?" he fires back, flashing me one of his charming, panty-dropping smiles.

I sigh heavily. "Maybe. Go bring her stuff in and I'll make some coffee."

He leans down and kisses my forehead. "Okay."

I watch his back as he leaves the room, then turn down to my new best friend.

"Sorry, Anna," I tell Evie with a grin. "You've just been replaced."

"You don't trust me, do you?" he asks, blowing on his coffee.

"I trust you more than any other man," I say slowly, trying to explain. "I love you, Tracker, but to be honest, I kind of expected you to hurt me at some point. And you did, but I guess it was because of my own doing. I guess my dad screwed me up, then the first guy I ever liked played me for a fool in high school. The two men I slept with afterward turned out to be jerks too. The first one played hot and cold, wanted me so much at the start but then just went silent after I slept with him. The second guy turned out to be an arrogant asshole. It's not that I'm making you pay for their mistakes—I guess I thought what we had was too good to be true. I was waiting for the other shoe to drop. I'm just not the girl who gets her perfect guy in the end." I look to Evie, who is sleeping in her bed. "I'm the recluse author who's going to turn into a crazy dog lady."

He cracks a smile at that. "No relationship is going to be perfect."

"I know that."

"But what you need to realize is, at the end of the day, I get pissed, we fight, but I'll still want you. It hurt that you didn't trust me. I felt betrayed. Like I didn't know you, I don't know. I fuckin' miss you, Lana. I wish that day never happened."

"Me too," I whisper. "Will you ever be able to trust me again?"

He tilts his head and studies me. "Will you forgive me for everything I did? Not listening to you? For being an idiot when I was pissed at you and we were apart?"

I suck in air. "How many women did you sleep with?"

It even hurt to say the words. I rub my chest with my palm, tears threatening to fall down my cheeks like raindrops.

"I didn't sleep with anyone, Lana," he says gently.

I raise my head. "What? Then what do I have to forgive you for?"

"Well I'm not completely innocent," he says, ducking his head. "But I didn't fuck anyone."

"So what? You got blow jobs from them?"

He stays quiet.

Bingo.

"I see," I mutter with scorn.

"Lana—"

"Evie and I would like to be left alone now, if you don't mind," I say stiffly. "Thank you for her."

He sighs, sounding tired. "I was hurt too, you know, it wasn't just you."

"Yeah, it sounds like it," I reply. "You didn't see me doing anything with other men."

"What the fuck was Wyatt then?" he growls. "You were trying to move on and deal with the pain, the same as me. I'm a man with a high sex drive. I'd never cheat on you, but we weren't exactly together. Still, I didn't want my dick in another pussy. Maybe you should think about what that means, trying to see it from my point of view."

He stands and walks toward the front door. "I could have any woman I want, Lana, but I only want you. I fuckin' love you. I'm not perfect, but neither are you, and we both need to want this to make it work. You need to have a long think about whether that's good enough for you, because I'm not gonna wait forever."

He leaves.

Only then do I allow the tears to flow.

"I didn't come into the clubhouse with ulterior motives," I tell Sin as he walks into my apartment and sits down like he owns the place.

"I know that, Lana," he says gently. "But you have to admit, it looked bad. We didn't know you were an author and you came to stay with us to look after Clover when you clearly didn't need the money. But if I didn't think you were telling the truth, this would be a whole different kind of visit."

"Faye needed me," I say with a shrug. "And Tracker and Anna were there. I write on my own schedule, so I didn't have a shitload of work to do or anything. It was like I was taking a break."

Sin glances down at Evie, eyes widening. "I see Tracker's been here."

I nod, smiling. "Yeah, earlier today."

He studies me, making me squirm, then leans forward, his elbows on his knees. "Tracker's hurting. He won't admit it, of course, but his actions speak for him. He drinks more. He fights more. He gets in everyone's face. He's lost the easiness about him. Basically, I want the old Tracker back. And you're going to get him for me."

"Sin—"

"Do you love him?"

"Yes, but—"

"Do you want him to move on with another bitch?" he asks boldly.

"No, of course not, but—"

"He's a man, Lana. A wild one. But for you, he showed you a side most of us will never see. Put everything behind the two of you, go work shit out. For all our sakes," he says, standing up. "Not every man will drop three grand on a puppy just so an ex-girlfriend won't feel lonely, and so she will be protected in the future." He shakes his head. "Thoughtful bastard."

He gets up to go. "Oh, and one more thing," he adds as he walks out my front door. "Faye wants a signed book."

When I hear his bike pull away, I look at Evie and sigh. "Wonder who else will drop by today?"

Sin is right, but he's also wrong.

Yes, I love Tracker.

But how am I supposed to just move on and forget every-thing that happened? I'd kept things from him, but he made me feel like shit when he pushed me away without giving me a few minutes to explain. I hurt him; he hurt me back. Is that love?

And if it is, do I want to be a part of it again?

TWENTY-SEVEN

OUT of all the people I thought I'd see today, the man in front of me wasn't one of them.

"Lana?" he says, eyes widening.

Staring into the eyes of my high school crush, I square my shoulders and force a smile on my now strained face. "William, hi."

I glance around the shopping mall, hoping someone will save me, but no one appears, just my luck.

"How are you? You look amazing," he says, smiling. "It's been years. Do you still keep in touch with anyone from school?"

Just Allie, if you could count her.

"No," I say. "Didn't have many friends in school, if you don't remember."

He suddenly looks a little sheepish. "I was a douche in school, I'm sorry. I did like you though. Allyson was a little obsessive with me back then. Wonder what became of her. We broke up straight after high school."

I don't have to wonder—unfortunately I know firsthand.

Shrugging my shoulders, I say, "Who knows?"

"Do you want to grab a coffee or something sometime?" he asks, smiling down at me.

"Oh. Ummm."

"Just as friends," he corrects himself, but looks slightly disappointed at my answer.

"I don't think so," I say, being honest with him. "I don't think my boyfriend would be happy with that."

Plus, I have no plans to see you ever again.

"Right," he murmurs. "Of course you'd be taken. I'm glad you're well, Lana. Your man, he's a lucky one."

We say an awkward good-bye, then part ways.

Seeing William makes me miss Tracker. I don't want to go backward; I want to go forward.

And Tracker is my future.

If I have to fight for him, I will.

Tracker and Arrow are standing next to their bikes outside the clubhouse. They must have just come back from somewhere. They both stare at me as I get out of my car and approach them.

"Hey, Lana," Arrow says, eyes crinkling, then he leaves me alone with Tracker.

"Hey," I say, looking into the blue eyes that I miss every second of every day. "Can we talk?"

"Got a call about you today," he says, an unreadable expression on his face.

"A call about what?" I ask, shifting on my feet.

"Someone saw you out with a guy," he says, jaw clenching so tight it looks painful.

"Are you kidding me?" I ask. "I was at the mall and ran into someone I knew in high school."

"Who?" he asks, studying me.

"Some guy. William. I had a crush on him back in the day and he screwed me over," I snap.

"Do you want me to beat the shit out of him?" he asks casually, like he is asking me what I wanted for lunch. "You should have called me. What's his full name?"

"Umm, no. But thank you for offering," I tell him.

"Offer still stands," he says, smiling a little.

"Who saw me? Do you have spies everywhere, or have you got someone following me? That's a little stalkerish, don't you think?" I say, annoyed.

Tracker avoids the question. Instead, he nods. "You wanna go inside, or you wanna go for a ride?"

I eye his bike longingly and he chuckles. "Ride it is."

On the back of his bike, my arms wrapped around his chest, I close my eyes and feel like I'm home. We ride for over an hour before coming to a stop at a scenic view, overlooking the ocean.

"I don't like that you let other women touch you. You had to have known in the back of your mind that we would want to get back together," I blurt out as soon as we're both off his Harley.

He rubs the back of his neck. "I wasn't thinking, Lana, I was just feeling. Hurting. I wanted to forget, and I guess I told myself we weren't really together, so it wasn't cheating."

I narrow my eyes at his convenient logic.

"I know I fucked up," he adds. "I told you. I'll never ever turn to another woman, no matter what happens between us. It was fucked-up and not the mentality I want to use. Some bikers do cheat, but I'm not one of them, at least not with you. Never with you. I don't even want anyone else, okay? I guess it was almost like trying to go back to what my life was like before you entered it, but it was bullshit because I don't want to go back. You're my life now, and I wouldn't have it any other way."

"Okay," I say slowly. "I hooked up with someone too, so you can't be mad, going by the rules you made."

He smirks. "No, you didn't. You're not that type of woman, Lana."

I throw my hands up in the air. "See. How is this fair? I'm a good woman, so I get screwed over and am just supposed to forgive you for everything?"

"I forgive you too," he says. "For keeping shit from me. We're also going to have a long talk about anything else you've been keeping to yourself. I want to know everything. And now I'm directly asking you, so you can't get away with your sneaky little omissions."

I open my mouth, then close it when I can't think of anything to say. "I think that's everything. Oh, except I actually went to high school with Allie. She was a bitch then, just like she is now."

"No shit?" he says, looking surprised. "Why didn't you say anything?"

I shrug, looking down. Then explain my history about Allie and William in detail. "She didn't remember me at first. She made my life a living hell, so I didn't want her to have something else over me."

He comes up behind me, wrapping his arms around me. He presses his lips against my neck, and says, "Fuck her. You're ten times the woman she'll ever be. God, I've missed your smell."

"Don't push me away again like that, Tracker," I warn. "If we fight, then we fight, but the way you just cut me out? It really hurt. You were an asshole and I didn't deserve it. If you're going to do shit like that again, then I don't want to do this with you."

"I know," he whispers. "I'm sorry, okay? And I never say sorry, so know how much I mean it. I can be a dick, all right? But fuck, only you have the power to hurt me like that, and I didn't handle it very well."

"You think?" I all but growl.

"I said I'm sorry," he says in a gentle tone filled with regret. "It won't happen again. I don't know what the fuck else I can say to make you forgive me." He pauses. "Don't even think about getting even though. I'll kill any fucker you try and let near you."

My lip twitches at that. The thought never even crossed my mind, but it's interesting that it did his. "If you even look at another woman—"

"I didn't even look at another woman, I only wanted you," he says. "I closed my eyes and pretended it was you. Trust me, she's nowhere near as good as you, so it didn't fucking work, then I pushed her off me. I knew I'd fucked up right then and there."

I elbow him in the stomach. "I hate you! You're such a pig, Tracker!"

"Just being honest," he grumbles. "Fuck, I can't win, can I?"

"Not when some other bitch had her mouth on you! Did she lick over your piercing like I like to do?" I ask harshly, even the thought of it infuriating me further.

"Lana—"

"I seriously hate you," I yell, cutting him off.

"Well, I love you enough for the both of us. Now give me a

kiss," he demands. "Haven't had those lips in too fuckin' long. I've been dreaming of them, Lana."

"No."

"Yes," he growls, cupping my face in his hands. "Don't tell me no unless you mean it."

"Did you kiss anyone else?" I ask, looking him right in the eye.

"No," he says quietly, tightening his hold on me. "One blow job. One. That's it, I swear it. And I regret it. I was just so angry, Lana. I didn't even come. I pushed her off me and went to my room, feeling fuckin' disgusted with myself."

"You *will* regret it when I'm done with you," I vow.

He chuckles. "My bloodthirsty woman."

"Still don't like you," I snap. "You better have gotten tested since you had some random woman's mouth all over you."

"I did. I wouldn't put you in danger. I'll always be honest with you, even when the truth hurts," he says. "I don't want any lies between us. I don't want to hurt you either. I don't like seeing the pain in your eyes."

"We messed up," I say on a sigh. "Both of us."

"It doesn't mean it's too late," he says, turning me around and kissing my mouth. "This will never be done with. Never. We're not perfect, but as long as we aren't giving up, then fuck it, we can make it work."

"That easy, huh?"

"No, not easy, I just want you that much, so I'm willing to put up with all the shit I know you're gonna throw my way."

We kiss.

Lots.

Then head back to my apartment and make love.

*   *   *

For the first time ever, I turn Tracker down for sex.

We're in my kitchen, and I've just finished cooking breakfast.

"Why not?" he asks, not sounding angry, just curious.

I look at Evie. "I'm not having sex in front of her. Scar her for life!"

He looks down at Evie and calls her a cock block, sounding amused.

"Do you want to come to Rift tonight? I think Faye is going."

"What about Anna?" I ask.

"Not sure," he replies. "You'll have to call and ask her."

"I will."

"Did you have to put a pink sparkly collar on the dog? She's meant to be a man killer, not a fairy princess," he comments, staring down at Evie.

"She can be a guard dog and look good at the same time," I reply, making him close his eyes and shake his head at me.

"You're a pain in the ass."

"Rethinking us getting back together already?" I tease.

"Never."

"Good answer."

"It's the truth," he says, crouching down to pat Evie. "I better get going, had a missed call from Sin. I'll come pick you up tonight."

He kisses me, his mouth lingering. "Love you, baby."

"Love you too," I reply dreamily.

"Call me if you need anything."

"What if I need something now?" I ask, playing coy.

He looks down at Evie.

"In the bedroom," I suggest. "Meet you there."

I start running to my room, but he catches me and throws me over his shoulder. "As if your short legs could outrun me."

"I have long legs for my height!" I argue.

He chuckles. "Compared to mine?"

"Maybe I wanted to get caught."

He slaps my ass, the sound echoing throughout the room. "I know you wanted to get caught."

"Now that you have me, what are you going to do with me?" I ask, putting on my best sultry tone.

"Hmmmm," he murmurs, throwing me down on the bed. He glances at the mirrors on my bedroom sliding doors. "I think I'm gonna fuck you from behind, watching your face and pretty tits in the mirror."

I clamp my thighs together. Yeah, I might like this idea.

"And then what?" I probe.

"Then, I'm gonna pull out, go down on you, tasting your sweet pussy. After you come, I'm gonna lie you down on your side, sliding into you until both of us come again," he says in a low tone. "Then I'm gonna get back to the clubhouse before Sin kills me."

Two hours later, Tracker leaves.

There's my exercise for the day.

TWENTY-EIGHT

ANNA, Faye, Jess, and I are at the clubhouse, cooking a huge dinner for the men. Several members from other chapters are visiting, and we want to be good hosts. Faye got the call first from Sin.

"Yes, they're all here with me," she says into her phone, sounding worried. She looks us over. "Anna, Jess, Lana, and me." She pauses. "All right."

She looks up at us. "We're not allowed to leave the clubhouse under any circumstances."

"Why?" Anna asks, putting down the potato peeler. "What's happened now?"

"No idea," Faye replies. "The men are still coming to visit, so let's get this food made. I'll grab my gun in case anything does happen."

"Clover?" I ask.

"She's protected," Faye replies.

We watch her with wide eyes as she leaves to get her gun.

The woman is badass.

I look to Anna. "What are you going to get? Knives?"

She laughs, and pulls some brass knuckles out of her bag. "I have these babies."

I roll my eyes. "Where the hell did you get those?"

Faye walks back into the kitchen. "I'll go talk to Blade and whoever else is here. Lana, can you speak to Vinnie? He's in his room last I saw."

I walk to Vinnie's door and knock. No answer. I try again but nothing. Turning the doorknob, I find the door unlocked, so I open it and peer inside. The bedroom is empty, so he must be in the bathroom.

"Vinnie?" I call out. I knock on the bathroom door, but there's no answer. Turning the knob, I find it locked. What the hell is going on? I rush back out to the women.

"His bathroom door is locked but there's no answer," I say. "Something feels wrong."

We all share a look.

"Anna, get Blade. He's out front working on his bike."

Anna nods and runs to the front yard, her brass knuckles in her hand.

"It could be nothing," Jess says, glancing to Faye.

"I guess we'll find out," Faye replies, walking to Vinnie's room with her gun in her hand. "Jess, call Sin and tell him to get here now just in case. I have a bad feeling too."

Jess nods and grabs her phone as Faye and I enter Vinnie's room.

"Fuck," Faye bites out, her tone laced with panic.

"What?" I ask, following her gaze. "Shit."

There was blood.

Sliding from under the bathroom door.

We both run to the door, trying to open it, banging on it, trying to kick it down—everything to no avail.

"Is there a window we could get in from?" I ask. Tracker's bathroom has a window I could fit through; maybe Vinnie's is the same. All I'd have to do is push out the screen.

Anna runs in with Blade.

"What the fuck is going on?" he asks.

We point to the blood. "Can you kick this door open? We need to get to him, now!"

We all move aside as Blade kicks open the door. It takes three tries, his huge biker boots denting the door until it finally gives.

What we see when we open the door shocks the hell out of all of us.

It isn't Vinnie inside his bathroom.

It's Allie.

And she's dead.

The men arrive.

Vinnie rides up on his bike—apparently he was with Sin the whole time, not in his room. But the question is, who killed Allie, and how did they get into the clubhouse?

The men are pissed. On edge. Wondering who was behind this shit.

They check the entire compound from top to bottom, and someone takes Allie's body away. The bathroom is cleaned by a professional. Then the men head to the off-limits room to have a club meeting, or church, as they call it.

Guests from other chapters start to arrive, and when they hear what happened, they vow to help with whatever they can.

The party atmosphere isn't there anymore, of course, it's more a business, we-have-shit-to-get-done vibe, but we still make sure everyone is taken care of, well fed, and watered.

When I finally sit down, I start to process Allie's death and seeing her lying like that on the floor. Blood was gushing from her head, like she'd been hit with a crowbar or another sharp object. Her eyes were half-open and staring blankly ahead. Shit. I didn't like the woman, but that didn't mean I wanted to see her hurt, or dead. Did someone kill her, or did she slip and fall? Feeling guilty over all my uncharitable thoughts over the years, I stare down at my hands, wondering what Tracker was going through right now. At one point, I knew he cared for her, maybe even loved her. She'd been living here for so long, all of the men were used to having her around. I scan the room. How was everyone dealing with this?

After what feels like hours, Tracker resurfaces, looking tired and angry. He stands in front of me, and I rest my head on his thigh. He runs his hand through my hair, cupping my head against him.

"Come take a shower with me," he says, his voice rough. I stand and walk with him to his bathroom. When he stands there, looking a little lost, I undress him and turn the shower on. When the temperature is right, I lead him inside, then undress myself and join him.

"Are you okay?" I ask, picking up the soap and washing his body.

"Fuck." He sighs. "I didn't love her but . . . Christ, Lana. I didn't even know where she was all this time. She was killed because of us, and she wasn't protected by us. I don't even know what to feel. She hurt you, so there's no way in hell I'd want her back in the clubhouse, but I didn't want her dead."

"I know," I tell him softly. "I know. No one expected something like this."

He lets his back sink down the wall, until he's sitting on the tiled floor.

I sit next to him, rest my head on his shoulder, the water droplets raining on us.

Bitch or not, Allie was Wind Dragons.

And everyone is feeling her death.

A few days after Allie's funeral, the club gets some information. Zach, one of the members from another chapter and Rake's friend, found out that Allie was staying with another man after she was kicked out of the clubhouse. And that man is the vice president of the Kings of Hell MC. Slowly the puzzle is being pieced together. Did Allie turn to them? Or did the man seduce her? She might have gone to them for revenge, knowing the Wind Dragons didn't like the Kings of Hell in their territory, or maybe it was a coincidence? I seriously doubt the latter, but hope it wasn't the former.

"So what are you going to do about the Kings of Hell?" I ask Tracker.

"We organized a meet with them tonight. They haven't even told us what they want, why they're here, so first we find that out. Go from there," he answers, putting on his boots, then glancing up at me.

"You doing okay with all this?"

I nod. "Yeah, I mean, as well as any civilian can."

That gets a small smile out of him. "You aren't a civilian anymore, Lana, you're my old lady."

"Right," I reply, running my hand down my arm. "I'm okay. I'm here for you, whatever you need, whatever the club needs. I'm all in."

He stands and places his hands on each side of my face. "What I need is for you to stay safe. Don't leave here unless you're with two of the men. Two, all right? At least until we know more. Tonight while we're at the meet, this place will be on lockdown. No one leaves and no one comes. So prepare for that."

I nod again. "All right, I can do that."

"Good girl," he says, sounding relieved. "Let's hope these fuckers weren't behind Allie's death. Bringing her here like that? Sends a message that they want a war. And if they want one, they're going to get one."

I shiver at the tone of his voice.

"Be safe," I tell him, brow furrowing. "Don't assume anything. We don't know the truth of what really happened yet."

"I'll play it smart," he says, grinning. "This isn't my first rodeo, Lana, but fuck you're cute for caring so much and offering up advice."

I roll my eyes. I wasn't trying to be cute. "I need you with me, Tracker, you hear me? You better come back to me in one piece."

"Baby," he says, eyes softening. "It's just a talk tonight, nothing will happen. We want to be safe, make sure all the women and kids are taken care of."

"I know."

"What are you going to do all day?" he asks, bringing me against his chest.

"Write," I say. "Help Faye with whatever needs to be done for tonight. Worry about you."

"Lana," he murmurs, kissing the top of my head. "Stop being so damn cute or you're gonna get fucked again."

"How is that a punishment?" I reply. "I'm going to be as cute as I can right now."

He pulls back and grins. "Fuck, I love you."

"Love you too," I whisper.

He pushes my hair back behind my ear. "Stay here."

"I will. What about Evie?"

"I'll pick her up from your apartment and bring her back here with me."

"Okay."

One more kiss and then he's gone.

TWENTY-NINE

HAT evening, Faye, Anna, and I are running around making sure all the women and kids have everything they need. The atmosphere is relaxed—the men told everyone not to worry, that they were just being overly protective, and everyone is taking them at their word. When the men all return, looking bleak, I think something has happened. Tracker brings Evie to me, then tells me to wait in his room.

"Is everything okay?" I ask Tracker when he comes to bed.

He undresses and slides into the sheets naked. "Their VP fucked Allie, but they deny killing her, or hurting her in any way. Say they're not here to start any shit, and they want peace with us."

I feel confused. "None of this makes sense. How do you know they're telling the truth?"

"We don't," he replies, sounding tired. "We're going to have to wait and see. Get one step ahead of them. Don't worry about anything, Lana, we have a plan and everything is under control. All you have to worry about is pleasing your man."

I slap his chest. "Jerk."

He chuckles. "You know, no matter how messed up shit gets, knowing I'm coming home to you makes everything worth it."

I snuggle into him and tease, "That's because all I do is worry about pleasing my man."

"Damn straight," he replies, and I can hear the smile in his voice.

"So what is the plan you guys have about the MC?" I ask.

He kisses my brow. "Can't tell you everything, Lana, you know this."

"I know," I grumble back. "I just can't stop thinking about Allie lying there . . ."

"I wish you never saw it," he says, stroking my jawline. "Wanted to hide you from all the bad shit."

"You can't hide me from everything," I say quietly. "It's just a part of this world. Not just the biker world, but the world in general. We're surrounded by bad people, doing bad shit. The men in this MC are good men, and I think you're damn amazing, so I'll always stand by you."

He rolls on top of me and kisses me. "You see me?"

I nod. "Yeah. I see all of you."

I take his hand and lead it to my pussy.

"Feeling horny tonight, are we, baby? Did the thought of me out there facing down those other men turn you on? Because you know I'm one of the baddest motherfuckers out there?"

"Yes," I reply, gasping as his fingers make contact. "I'm feeling fearless."

"Hmmmm."

He lifts up my T-shirt—which really is his T-shirt—and slides my panties down. His cock is rock-hard, and I like that it's that way without me even touching him, just from our words and our bodies being pressed against each other. Baring my breasts, he leisurely sucks one nipple, then the other, making me wetter. His thumb presses on my clit the same time he slides inside of me.

"Fuck," he curses. "Feels better every damn time. Don't know how the fuck that's possible, but it's the truth."

He takes his time, fucking me with a slow rhythm, a bump and grind that has me dripping wet and begging for more.

"What does it feel like when you come?" I ask Tracker after we make love. Well, it was more like fucking, but that was one in the same for me now. I love how intense and rough he can get one second, sweet and gentle the next.

"Hmmm," he rumbles. "It starts with the rhythm I get into, finding one that works perfectly for me, then it builds, and keeps building until I can't take it anymore, traveling along my shaft until it explodes inside you. Just before I come, the base of my cock is so fuckin' hard, there's nothing like it. The buildup is crazy, the explosion is the culmination of so much tension. The feeling of the tension moving from my balls to then squirting my hot come into you is second to none. I fuckin' love it."

His explanation is hot, and honest. I love that I can ask him these questions and that he answers them without hiding anything.

"You know sometimes as soon as you slide into me I can almost tell what mood you're in, going by how hard you are, how rough you're going to be. It's so sexy," I admit, looking down and biting my lower lip.

He lifts my face up with a gentle pull. "Don't be shy to tell me things like that. That was fuckin' sexy coming out of your mouth."

"Yeah?"

"Yeah," he says, grinning. "I read your book, remember? I know the thoughts that swim in your head. I know how naughty you can be, and I love it. Don't be shy with me, baby; talk to me. I'll show you your every fantasy, every sexual desire. Maybe I should read that book again, and play out every sex scene with you."

My breath hitches. "R-really?"

"My baby likes that," he says, lips pressed against my neck. "Some of those scenes got me so hard, knowing it was you who wrote those words, you thinking about it. Christ, Lana. What else have you got going on in that mind of yours?"

I lick my lips. "Maybe you should read more of my books and find out."

"I will," he says, rolling me into him so my head is on his chest. "Now sleep. I'll probably wake you in the night with my mouth on your pussy."

The next day, I walk into the living room looking for Tracker when I find him talking to none other than my father.

"Hi," I say awkwardly, looking from one man to the other.

"'Mornin' baby," Tracker says softly, then turns his eyes to my dad, his face going hard. "Your father, and I use that term loosely, wants to talk with you. It's up to you whether you let him. I can always kick his ass out."

My dad pleads with me with his eyes.

"It's fine."

Tracker comes to me. "Call out if you need me, all right?"

I nod, and he leaves the room, but not before giving me a possessive kiss.

I sit down on the couch, then motion for my dad to do the same.

"What do you want to talk about?" I ask him, threading my fingers together and resting them on my lap.

"I was wondering if I could take you out for dinner," he says, clearing his throat. "Slowly get to know you a little better, maybe?"

He wants to get to know me, now? I have to ask why. Is it my connection to the club? Or is it just an old man full of regrets for his life choices?

"When?" I find myself asking.

"How about next week sometime? Or whenever is convenient for you," he says quickly, looking hopeful. "You know, I wanted to do something nice for you. So I was going to pay for the apartment you're living in—instead of renting it you would own it. But when I went to talk to the landlord about it, he said he'd already sold it. Tracker bought it and put it in your name."

My jaw drops. "He did what?"

My dad nods, smiling ruefully. "That apartment is fully paid for, and in your name. Have you checked your bank account? The money you paid for rent will still be in there, untouched."

"Holy shit," I blurt out. "I can't believe he did that." I look at my dad. "And you didn't need to try to do that for me. That's too much. I never wanted anything from you, except you. Yes, there were times Mom and I struggled financially, and I hated that you were rich but didn't help her out, but I still would never ask anything from you."

His face ages before my eyes at my confession. "I really am a selfish fuck, aren't I?"

Kind of, but I didn't say anything.

"Anything you want, Lana," he murmurs. "It's yours."

I think it over. "I want Mom to be able to retire early. She works so hard, every day. Always has. I paid off her house for her. She does so much for me, always made sure I had whatever I needed. Now I'd like to repay her in some way."

A thoughtful look comes over his face. "She won't quit her job, and she's too proud to accept anything I offer. How about a large retirement fund for her?"

I nod. "Sounds good."

"The fact that you asked for something for her and not you, says to me just how well she raised you," he says, looking down at his hands. "I wish to God I had some part in that, but I didn't. All I can do is try having you in my life now, as little or as much as you'll give, and I'll be grateful."

I nod stiffly.

It's time for me to forgive.

To let go of the past hurt and to live in the present.

"Oh, wow," I say, starting to feel emotional. "Dinner sounds great . . . Dad."

THIRTY

WHAT happens in the next book? Tell me, now," Faye demands, looking at the laptop screen over her shoulder. "Does Alexander die? Or does he come back and kidnap Kylie?"

I save my work and close the laptop, spinning on my chair to face her. "Faye, give it a rest, I'm not ruining the story for you."

She pouts. "But . . . why not? Come on! Aren't there any perks of knowing an author?"

"Free signed books. Advance copies. The fear of knowing everything you do and say could end up in a book."

She grimaces. "Pretend I didn't tell you earlier how annoying my mother-in-law is."

We both laugh. "Too late, might already be in there."

"You should name a character after me," she suggests. "Faye is an awesome name. It means fairy."

I roll my eyes. "Fine, I'll name my next heroine Faye."

"Sweet! Can you name the dude Dex? I can't see me fucking anyone else, even in print."

I still. "Holy shit that was a cute line."

"I have my moments." She shrugs, then pauses. "You can use that line. In fact, you should probably take notes from me."

"I'll get right on that," I reply dryly.

"The book should be called *The Biker Queen*," she continues, waving her hand through the air. She then looks at me. "What do you think?"

"I think you should write the book yourself," I suggest. "It could be awesome."

She nods. "Good idea. Maybe they'll make it into a movie."

I nod, on the verge of laughter. "Make sure you tell Sin beforehand though, or what happened with Tracker might happen to you."

Her eyes go wide. "You're at the stage where you can joke about that? Awesome! Because I had a few jokes I was keeping to myself, not wanting to hurt your feelings."

I scrub my hand down my face. "Seriously?"

"Yeah," she says. "Crap. I better go get Clover from school."

I look at the time. "She doesn't finish for another thirty minutes."

She grins sheepishly. "I know. I just like to be there early, just in case."

"Thirty minutes early?" I ask with wide eyes. "What do you go there and do?"

"Sit outside her classroom."

I smirk. "Is this why I heard Arrow calling you a psycho mother the other day?"

She scowls, eyes narrowing slightly. "Yes. The bastard. Wait until he has a kid, then he'll understand."

Anna walks into the room. "The men are in a bad mood."

"Yeah." Faye sighs. "They're trying to find out what happened to Allie, get to the bottom of it, but hitting dead ends at every turn. They've been gathering info on the Kings of Hell, but besides the drugs, we've found nothing. And they're just as curious about us as we are about them. Apparently one of them has the hots for Lana, which is why they were watching her that time."

My cheeks heat. "W-what?"

"Yeah," Faye says, grinning wide. "I thought Tracker was gonna combust when he heard that. He wanted to head over to the Kings of Hell clubhouse and beat the shit out of whoever is coveting his precious Lana."

I throw her a look. "Maybe you should be the author. I'm sure that's an exaggerated story."

She shrugs. "It's romantic though. Biker romance at its finest. You should write that in too."

Anna shakes her head, making a face. "You're crazy."

"Crazy like a fox," Faye retorts, then grins at Anna. "Wanna head to the gym? Could use a sparring session."

Anna sighs. "Just got my period, so not pregnant, so why the hell not?"

Faye looks to me. "Wanna learn some moves? They're great for real life and the bedroom."

How can I say no to that? "What about Clover?"

"I'll ask Dex to get her," she says, pulling out her phone and ringing him.

"Okay."

I stand up. "Show me."

Of course the men walk into the gym while Faye has me pinned to the ground, straddling me.

"I'm so hard right now," I hear Rake say, then "Ouch," as one of the men must have hit him.

"Oh come on, don't pretend you're not," he says to Tracker, then looks at Anna. "I'm pretending you're not even here."

"Appreciated," Anna replies in a dry tone.

Tracker walks over to us and looks down, smiling. "Learning a few moves, are you?"

Faye lets me up. "She's small but fast."

"I think I have a long way to go," I say, raising on my tiptoes to kiss my man. "But it's kind of fun. Exhilarating."

"Rake's right. I am turned on right now," he admits, grinding his pelvis into me. "But then again, you breathe and I get turned on."

"Get a room!" Anna calls out.

"Or a couch!" Rake joins in. "So we can all watch."

"You said you weren't going to bring that up again, you bastard!" I yell.

"Rake," Tracker growls. "Leave my woman alone or we're getting in that ring."

I roll my eyes. "Are you guys here for anything other than to annoy us and disrupt a very educational experience for me?"

Sin walks in and we all look to him. "President of the Kings of Hell is here at our gates. Claiming he wants to talk. He's alone."

The men all share glances.

"Where's Clover?" Faye asks, looking worried.

"She's at my mom's," he says. "Safe, don't worry."

"I don't like it," Arrow announces, looking to Anna. "The women are in here."

"We have guns," Faye says. "He's alone. Two of you hold him at gunpoint while he talks."

"Faye," Sin growls. "Stay here with the women. Don't fucking move."

"Yes, sir," she replies, saluting him.

Tracker kisses my mouth. "Stay here."

Arrow does the same to Anna. "Don't separate."

The men leave, closing the gym door.

Anna and I look to Faye for guidance. "Let's get armed just in case," she tells us, walking over and lifting a board in the floor. I glance inside, to see it's full of weapons.

It's on.

"It wasn't them," Sin announces. "Took balls for him to walk in here, unarmed and alone, wanting us to know they didn't touch Allie, and they're not here to get in our shit."

I'm pretty sure everyone was thinking the same question.

Who the hell killed Allie then, and why?

Tracker holds my hand, rubbing his thumb along my knuckles. When I look down at his hands, I notice that they're red and swollen. "Who did you hit?" I ask.

He glances down at his hands as if only just realizing he had marks on them. "Someone got in the way of my fist."

"Who?"

Rake chuckles. "This morning Tracker ran into the guy from the Kings who wants you. Let's just say he won't bother looking in your direction again."

I gasp. "You didn't."

"Why?" he replies. "You like having men panting after you, is that it? He should have known better than to want someone who's mine, and now he does."

I actually felt sorry for the guy. He didn't even approach me.

"You're so . . . mean!" I whisper.

"You're mine," he replies simply. "People need to know."

"Caveman," I utter.

"Only when it comes to you."

There is no winning with this man.

I find that with the right angle, speed, and rhythm, I can make Tracker come again soon after he's just come. He'd just finished thirty minutes ago, and he's ready to do so again.

"Fuck, Lana," he grits out. "You really know how to work me, don't you?"

I smile seductively.

I'd once asked Tracker what goes through his mind when we're making love. Does he have any sweet thoughts? Or is it all hot, tight, wet-pussy thoughts? As a writer and as his lover, I wanted to know. His response was a classic one.

"When I'm rock-hard, I'm like a shark. Concentrating and going in for the kill. I don't think much of anything besides reaching my goal."

Tonight, I was the same. Well besides the rock-hard part. But I wanted to blow his mind, so I was concentrating on doing just that. I'm on top, straddling him. He has his hands on my ass, squeezing tightly as I ride him into oblivion.

"Right there," he groans. "Fuck. Yes. Lana."

I lift my hips up and push back down on him, over and over again. The feeling of him inside me is one that will never get old. Being connected to him, it's like this is where I'm meant to be.

We're animals, living off our base instincts.

I belong to him, and he belongs to me.

Nothing else matters in this moment except each other, pleasure, and our connection. Tracker is a man who both respects me and protects me. He's an alpha male, but he also knows how to listen, how to take how I'm feeling into consideration. He's a shade of gray, no white or black.

I lean down and kiss his mouth, but he soon takes over, kissing me with a passion that should frighten me.

But it doesn't, it fuels me.

His want, his need, his obsession fuels my own.

We're bound, Tracker and I.

Whether that's a good or a bad thing is yet to be seen.

THIRTY-ONE

T HE guy who Tracker hit, from the Kings of Hell MC, his name is Zed. And he is standing right in front of me at Rift.

"Hello," he says, grinning at me.

"Hi," I say, staring at his black eye. "Sorry my man hit you."

He laughs. "I would've done the same if you were mine."

I look around. "Do the Wind Dragons know you're here?"

He nods. "We're here for a peace-meet-up kind of thing. We're going to prove we can all get along here with no issues."

I didn't get it, but whatever. "You know if Tracker sees you talking to me there will be no peace."

He smiles again. I don't think he's the sharpest tool in the shed. "Tracker's out front talking with our prez. Maybe we could sneak in a quick dance?"

The man has a death wish.

"No, thank you," I say. "But thanks for the offer."

"What she means is, fuck off," Anna says, coming to stand next to me. "She's just too nice to say it."

"But you're not?"

She shakes her head. "Nope. I like doing it."

"Are you taken?"

She grins, flashing her teeth. "Yeah, by Arrow. If you want to live you'll step away, because I don't want my man going back to prison."

Zed leaves, but I don't miss the twitch of his mouth.

"Men are weird," I announce.

"The Kings of Hell are weird," she replies. "Talon's coming here tonight too. Whose stupid idea was this? Someone is gonna get killed."

"Hopefully it's one of the Kings," I mutter under my breath, making Anna laugh.

"You really are Wind Dragons, you know that, right?" she says. "I love you, Lana."

"Love you too, Anna Bell," I reply. "We should hug. This is a hugging moment."

We do.

Tightly.

"I'm joining this hug," Faye announces, wrapping an arm around each of us.

"Everything okay?" Sin asks, walking up to his wife.

"Yeah," we all reply at the same time.

Sin looks over all of us. "Didn't know I have three wives."

Faye pulls away from us and goes to her man's side. "Everything okay?"

Sin nods. "Yeah, everything is okay. We have a few leads on Allie's death, so we're going to see what we can come up with. Until then, stay close, don't separate, and always have someone with you when you leave the clubhouse."

"We know," Faye says. "We're being careful."

"Good," he says. "Now let's try getting through this meeting without someone dying. Whose idea was this again?"

Anna smirks. "Not ours."

"Fuck," Sin mutters. "I need a drink."

"I'll order a round," Faye says. "I think we all need a damn drink."

Surprisingly, the rest of the night progresses without incident. As the Kings head out, Tracker tells me that tonight was actually for a reason—they'd set some kind of trap.

"Are you going to dance with me?" I ask him, running my fingers down his arm.

"I will." He grins. "When a good song comes on."

"What's wrong with this song?" I ask.

"You like this music?" he asks, raising an eyebrow. It was a Beyoncé song—"Drunk in Love."

I shrug. "It's good to dance to."

"I haven't heard you listen to anyone except Ed Sheeran, Sam Smith, and First Aid Kit. I seriously know the lyrics to all their songs," he grumbles. "You listen to their albums on repeat."

"You love it."

"No, I love you, so I put up with it. There's a difference."

He can be so damn sweet sometimes!

We dance for a few songs and then he disappears outside with the men. Talon arrives and dances with Anna for one song while Arrow stands on the side looking like he wants to murder Talon with his bare hands.

Faye comes and stands next to me, her eyes not leaving a pretty blonde. It's then that I remember where I've seen her before. She's the woman Tracker was with while we were broken up.

"What is she doing here?" I ask through clenched teeth.

Faye winces. "She asked to see Tracker."

"Did she now?" I say slowly, enunciating each word.

Tracker comes back inside the club and I watch as the woman runs up to him to greet him. Tracker actually takes a step back from her, which mollifies me a little, clearing the red haze that was clouding my vision, but when she puts her hand on his chest, all bets are off.

I approach the two of them, standing next to Tracker, deciding to put him on the spot.

"Who is this?" I ask, glancing at him with a fake smile.

His jaw clenches, and I don't miss him cringing. "No one."

"Why does No One have her hand on my man's chest?" I ask, turning to face the woman.

The bitch gives me a smug look. "He wasn't your man when he—"

I cut her off. "Yes, when he put his cock in your mouth, closed his eyes, and pretended it was me. I know. We were broken up then, now we're not."

The woman's eyes widen. "I see."

Tracker looks down at her. "I'm taken. Won't be happening again, all right? You should go."

He uses a gentle tone, which I actually appreciate from him because she doesn't need to be treated like shit. She was good enough for him to let her give him head.

Her face has a look I don't like on it, but she leaves and I let her without saying anything further.

Tracker holds me. "You done?"

"I thought I behaved quite well under the circumstances," I say, lifting my chin up.

His mouth twitches as he cups my chin between his thumb and index finger. "You have nothing to worry about, okay?"

I nod.

"Whether you're around or not, I'm not looking to fuck up what we have."

"Good," I say softly.

"You know everyone is staring at us right now, being nosy bastards, right?"

I turn and scan the room. Yes, all eyes are on us. I turn back around to him with my head held high. "Who cares?"

He throws back his head and laughs. "You like fighting and fucking in public!"

I gasp. "That's it!"

He laughs some more and picks me up, bride-style, carrying me outside while I squirm.

"Where are we going?" I ask.

He ignores me and asks Blade for the keys to the club's four-wheel drive.

Unlocking the doors, he puts me down in the backseat and gets in, closing the door behind him.

"What do you think you're doing?" I ask, amused as he tries to fit his big self into the space.

"Gonna fuck you," he says. "Sit on my lap, you're gonna ride me."

"Bossy."

"You love me bossy—I bet you're wet right now," he says huskily, trailing his finger down my bare thigh.

I am; damn him.

Leaning back against the leather of the backseat, he undoes his belt, then his jean button and zipper and pulls his pants down enough to expose his cock and balls. "Jump on."

I slide my panties down my legs then straddle his lap with my dress and bra still on. He holds his cock while I slide down on it until he's fully inside me, and then I start to move, slowly at first, then I pick up the pace. Tracker pushes my hair out of my face and kisses me, from my lips to my jaw, to my neck and up again.

"You're mine, Tracker," I whisper against his mouth. "You always say I'm yours, but you're mine too."

"I know, baby," he says back, his eyes heavy-lidded. "Always yours from the moment I saw you."

I place my hands on his shoulders and use them as leverage to push up and down, working us both into a frenzy.

"Good answer."

We come together, me panting his name.

"Do we have to go back in?" I ask him, as I slide off him, picking up my panties and trying to clean myself up. "I'm not putting these back on."

He takes them from me and shoves them in his pocket. "They're mine now."

"Perv."

"You love it," he says, tenderly touching my lower lip with his thumb. "We can go home if you want. Need to check in with Sin first, but should be fine. Unless you want to stay and dance with Faye and Anna?"

"With no panties on?" I ask, raised eyebrows. "Would that turn you on? To know I don't have anything on underneath and only you know it?"

He licks his bottom lip. "You always turn me on, Lana."

"Answer the question," I push.

"Yeah, of course it would. Unless another man comes near you and touches your ass or something, because then I'm going to lose my shit."

I bring his face down to mine for easy kissing access. "Let's go dance for a few songs, then leave."

He shakes his head. "What the fuck have I created?"

"Someone who's perfect for you?" I tease. "Or maybe you just brought out the real me."

He sucks on my bottom lip. "I'll take you any way you come, you know this."

He rests his forehead on mine.

I kiss his lips.

Then we dance and go home.

THIRTY-TWO

TRACKER

WE didn't want to do it, but we didn't really have a choice. While everyone was at Rift tonight, we had cameras installed throughout the clubhouse. If whoever killed Allie comes back to fuck with us again, tonight or in the future, we want to know who the fucker is. It isn't the Kings of Hell MC, although it would be so easy to blame them, especially after we knew of their VP's association with Allie. Apparently though, the bastard was infatuated with her and wanted whoever killed her dead too.

Fuck.

We had Vinnie and Talon search the place the Kings of Hell are staying at, a warehouse about an hour from here, just to make sure. They came up with nothing. Yeah, the bastards look clean. Until they give us a reason, we'll let them live.

The worst part though is that it looked like someone inside the clubhouse had something to do with it, or in the very least helped someone get inside.

I hope like hell that isn't the case.

Sin's on edge, Arrow's on the verge of beating the truth out of anyone in his path, and I want to make sure Lana is safe no matter what the cost.

And after that, I want to marry her.

"Tracker," Sin calls, walking up to me.

"Yeah?" I'm standing by my bike, about to come inside.

"Need to talk to you about something."

"What?" I ask, not liking the sound of this.

"We need to leave the clubhouse to catch this bastard. Last time we were all out except a couple of the men, and all the women were home. I don't know any other way unless we leave again. We'll be close by, of course, but I think we should tell everyone we're going on a run. Let no one except us know the truth."

"You want to use the women as bait?" I ask, jaw clenching. "What the fuck, Sin?"

"You think I like it?" He curses. "It's this, or we wait, watching over our shoulders until we find out the truth of what happened."

"Christ," I utter. "Maybe you should at least tell Faye. She can protect the women and it will be better if she knows what's going on."

Sin looks down. "Will you be okay with that? Faye knowing and not Lana?"

"I trust Faye will protect Lana," I say. "I think I'll feel better knowing she knows and will have the other women's backs."

"She is pretty badass," Sin comments with a smirk that doesn't reach his eyes. "I'll tell Faye what's going on, but no one else. We need this situation controlled. Not that I don't trust my men. I trust you, Rake, Arrow, Irish, and Vinnie with my life. I just need everyone's reactions to be real, I don't want anyone to know what's going on. I'm going to re-create the scene. Start there."

"Smart," I say. "Fuck, let's get this done with. Anything you need, brother."

He puts his hand on my shoulder. "I know."

We need to find the bastard who dared to fuck with us right under our noses.

THIRTY-THREE

LANA

THE men are going on a run. It's been a week since we were at Rift, and nothing eventful has happened. I've been escorted to school and back, and have pretty much moved into the clubhouse, Evie in tow. Tracker thought it would be safer for me to be here, surrounded by him and the other club members. I feel safer here too, even though this is where Allie was found. I know the people around me won't hesitate to save my life. That's the kind of bond the members have. They're a family. A family not of blood but of choice. Some would say that's more powerful.

"Lana!" Clover says, running into my room. I pick her up in my arms and swing her around.

"Hello, princess," I tell her, kissing her plump cheek. "How are you?"

"Good," she replies. "I'm staying at Nana's tonight."

"Are you now? How fun," I tell her, putting her down.

"We're gonna bake cookies."

"Save one for me, will you?"

She nods. "I'll make you a chocolate one."

"Perfect."

"Uncle Tracker said you like the chocolate ones," she says, grinning.

"Uncle Tracker is right; I do."

I love that he notices all these small details.

"There you are, Clo," Faye says, coming in. "You ready to go to your nana's?"

She nods and waves to me. "'Bye, Lana!"

"'Bye, sweetie."

Faye looks at me and wrinkles her nose. "I'll be back. Going to drop her off with Sin."

"I'll be here," I say, joining Evie on my bed and opening my laptop. I've typed one chapter when Tracker walks in.

"We'll be leaving in an hour," he says, lying down next to me. "Come here."

I move my laptop and snuggle up next to him. "You're going for three nights, right?"

He nods. "Yeah. Prospects are staying behind to keep an eye on things. Anything you need, tell them."

"Okay," I reply. "We'll be fine."

His arms tighten around me. "You better be. You know I love you and will do anything to protect you, right?"

"I know," I reply. "I trust you."

His grip becomes almost painful.

"Tracker."

"Sorry," he says, easing up. "I just want to hold you until I have to go. Why don't you tell me all about your new book?"

I tell him about it, then answer all his questions.

When he leaves, his kiss is slow and gentle.

Lingering.

But when he leaves, I'm left with a bad feeling.

TRACKER

The women are fine.

Lana is fine.

Nothing is going to happen.

I repeat these three sentences over and over again. Did we make a mistake with this plan? What aren't we seeing?

If something happens to Lana . . .

I'll never forgive myself.

Sin is watching the surveillance cameras. We're inside a hotel, said we were stopping for the night. Talon is staying close to the clubhouse and is ready in case anything happens.

Now, we wait.

When we see a figure walking into Vinnie's room, and into the bathroom where we found Allie dead, we're confused. What is he doing? Just checking out the scene of the crime? But then he speaks, and what he says is more evidence than we ever thought we'd get.

"I'm so fuckin' sorry, Allie," he says, crouching down on his knees and touching the floor. "I loved you, I'm sorry. I didn't mean to hit you that hard. I was so angry."

He exhales deeply. "You were mine. I'd rather you be dead than let anyone else have you."

Fuck.

Looks like we found our killer.

*   *   *

LANA

The morning after Tracker leaves, I wake up to yelling. Throwing the sheets off me, I open the door and run out of the room, Evie at my feet. It takes me a few seconds to process the scene in front of me. Arrow has Blade pinned against the wall by his neck. He's surrounded by all the other men in the MC. Tracker, Sin, Trace, Rake, Irish, Ronan, and Vinnie. They're all watching with avid interest, through narrowed eyes or with arms crossed over their chests.

Arrow rears back and punches Blade in the face.

I whimper, as blood starts to drip.

Why are they doing this?

How could they just stand there and watch?

Tracker sees me and snaps his head to the door. "Inside, Lana. Now."

I listen to him. I know from his tone he isn't fucking around. I step back into the door, bumping into a tired-looking Faye and a confused-looking Anna.

"Why is Arrow beating the shit out of Blade?" she gasps. "What the fuck happened?"

I have no answers.

Faye grabs our arms and pulls us into the kitchen.

"Sit," she commands. "We'll wait until they come inside."

Sin walks in first. Scans the room, then pulls his wife by his side. "We need to talk."

Clearly.

"We set up cameras in here. We saw Blade going into Vinnie's bathroom, staring at where Allie's body was found. He was mumbling shit over and over, how sorry he was."

"What the fuck?" Faye gasps. "Blade?"

Sin explains what happened. Apparently Blade and Allie were sleeping together. He said he loved her. When he saw her on the back of one of the Kings of Hell members' bikes, he lost it. Allie had snuck into the clubhouse to get something. She and Blade got into it. He hit her over the head and tried to frame Vinnie, by leaving her on his bathroom floor. Apparently back in the day, Vinnie had a small thing for Allie, so it might have looked suspicious if the men didn't trust Vinnie and Vinnie was with them at the time of Allie's death. Blade had locked the door and closed it, locking her in from the outside.

We all listen with wide eyes and shocked expressions.

"What's going to happen to him?" I ask, trying to process everything.

"We're handling it," Sin grunts. "You all stay out of it, you hear me?"

I swallow.

Blade?

How many times did he drive me around, keep me company, or have a laugh with me?

Countless times.

Surely they wouldn't . . . kill him, would they?

Anna is blinking profusely, as if trying to sort out her thoughts. I look at Faye, whose eyes are on her husband.

I don't like this.

I hear yelling from outside.

I block it out.

I go back into our room and bury myself under the covers.

I slide my earbuds in, letting the music soothe, trying to push out the vision of Blade, someone I trusted, being punished for his crimes.

I wake up held in strong arms.

Tracker pulls my earbuds out and turns me to look at him. "Sin said he told you everything."

I nod. "What happened to him?"

He cringes. "Babe—"

"Shit, Tracker." I breathe. "He really killed her?"

He nods. "He confessed."

"Everyone trusted him," I say quietly.

"I know," he replies, a look of devastation flashing through his eyes. "I trusted him to protect you, over and over again. He also said he was with Allie when she beat you inside your house. He was there, Lana. I'll never forgive that, ever. And he paid for what he did, or in your case, didn't do."

Betrayal spreads through my veins.

He watched her beat me? From behind? Sneaking up on me so I had no way to defend myself?

Shit.

"It's all over now," he whispers.

I swallow. "I guess you're right."

"Tough with prospects," he admits. "Never know who they really are until they're tested. Won't be leaving you with one again. Only full-fledged members."

"Tracker—"

"You're keeping it together well, baby, proud of you. You know we set cameras up in here and left you guys alone; I felt like we were using you as bait. Fuckin' hated it; didn't sleep a wink last night. Only thing that kept me sane was that Talon was close by if need be, and Sin was watching the live footage." He pauses. "Sad part was Blade looked . . . gutted over Allie. He went into that bathroom and cried. He killed her, then fuckin' cried about it."

He swallows hard, trying to salvage some control.

"Must have been hard to watch."

"It was. He must have been a bit unstable to do that. Or maybe he thought there would be no ramifications. The fact that he tried to pin it on Vinnie, a brother, shows he has no loyalty."

"Did you know Blade and Allie were sleeping together?" I ask.

He shakes his head. "No clue. She must have been sneaking around with him when I got with you. I don't know how she got him to come with her when she broke into your house. The two of them together . . . two psychos."

"I'm sorry," I whisper.

"I was just thinking about you, Lana. Knew Faye would have your back. She stayed up all night walking around the house, keeping an eye on everyone."

"Faye knew, but we didn't?" I ask, feeling a little hurt over it. "What if something else had happened? Wouldn't it have been better if we knew what to expect?"

Tracker's eyes soften. "Knew Faye would look after you. Didn't want to worry you. Sometimes you need to trust my decisions, all right? I always have you in my mind. First priority."

"I do trust you."

"Good. Now give me those lips," he demands.

I kiss his lips softy and gently.

I'm doing something I never thought I'd be doing.

Having dinner with my mom and dad.

Together.

It's weird, yet nice.

"How's school going?" my dad asks.

"Good," I reply. "Between school and writing, I'm keeping busy."

"And Tracker," my mom adds, eyes filled with mirth. "When will the two of you be getting married?"

I almost choke on my mouthful of wine. "Not just yet."

"Guess I'll be waiting awhile to be a grandmother then," she sulks.

Dad, on the other hand, looks relieved but stays quiet.

"So you were good friends with the old president?" I ask him.

He nods. "Yes, Jim and I were really close. He was a good man."

"Sin is a good club president."

Dad nods. "Yes, he is."

"Where is Tracker tonight?" Mom asks, sipping her drink.

"He had some club business to attend to," I say. "He'll be back later to pick me up."

We talk all night. It's nice, but it makes me wonder, *What if?* What if my dad chose to stay with us instead of his career?

At the end of the day, I guess it doesn't really matter.

I'm living in the now, and life is good.

THIRTY-FOUR

D O I have to do this?" Tracker growls. "Do you know how much shit I'm going to get for it?"

I do know, but I don't care. He said he'd do it, and now he has to.

"We're here, you may as well just get it done with. Plus, you look fucking sexy right now."

"Christ, woman, the things I do for you," he says with a defeated sigh. "This right here proves my love for you. I wouldn't do this shit for anyone else."

"I know," I tell him. "And I appreciate it."

"You better," he scowls, fiddling with the hat on his head.

I bite my lip, trying not to grin at his predicament. He is so uncomfortable. Tracker knows he's good-looking, but I know doing something like this isn't really him. He uses his charm to get women, but I don't actually think he's vain. He's just confident, and this really isn't his style. Still, I can't help but admire him. His ripped body, his tattoos, the V of his hips, he is phenomenal. Don't get me started on his six-pack, because I could write a whole book on how amazing it is.

"You're the one who chased away Wyatt, now you can fill his shoes," I say, gesturing for the photographer to continue with the photo shoot. "We only need a few more shots. Please, Tracker."

"Wyatt was a fuckhead," he says, flexing his biceps enticingly.

"Yeah, he wouldn't even return my call when I needed him for another cover."

"Good, he's smarter than he looks."

"Well then stop complaining," I say, trying not to laugh.

Tracker rubs the back of his neck, then does as he's told, following the photographer's orders. My new book is a cowboy romance, so Tracker is bare-chested with a cowboy hat, jeans, and chaps, along with the boots to match.

He looks fucking sexy.

His blond hair is down, hitting his shoulders in slight waves, the stubble on his face thicker than usual.

Delicious.

Women will buy my book for this cover alone.

He flexes his muscles, then changes position to rub one hand down his abs. I'm getting turned on by just looking at him, and I can't wait to bring him to bed after this, still dressed in this outfit.

I still can't believe that he's mine.

All mine.

Holding his hat with one hand, he slips his thumb into his belt loop, flashing me a dirty look before turning seductive for the camera.

The camera loves him.

And so do I.

He continues to pose, throwing me looks in between, letting me know he isn't happy but is doing this for me. I'd normally have Wyatt with a female model for my covers but I wasn't going to watch some model slide up to Tracker, so he's going to be on there solo.

The cover is going to be ab-licious.

We wrap up the photo shoot and he comes straight for me. "I think I look better as a biker than a cowboy."

"I think you look good as anything," I say, running my hand down his chest.

He glances down at me knowingly. "You're wet for me as a cowboy, aren't you?"

"Of course I am, you look . . . wow. Tracker you look sexy. Hotter than any male cover model I've ever seen."

"Wyatt included?" he asks dryly.

"Million times better than Wyatt," I tell him, licking my bottom lip seductively. "In fact . . ." I continue, "I really want to save a horse right now."

"What?" he asks, frowning.

"I want to save a horse by riding a cowboy."

His lips twitch. "Baby, if you wanna fuck me, just say so."

We don't make it home.

I ride him in the car, bouncing up and down on him until we both come so hard we almost pass out.

When we do get home, all the brothers are standing out front, waiting to give Tracker shit. The whistles and catcalls start.

"Now I'm gonna have to kick all their asses in the ring to prove a point," Tracker grumbles, but winks at me playfully.

"Holy mother of shit!" Faye yells when she sees him. Fanning herself she walks up to him. "Hello there, cowboy!"

Sin grabs her, throws her over his shoulder, and leaves the room.

"It's not my fault he's so hot!" she calls out, earning her a smack on her ass. "Ouch! That hurt."

"See," I tell Tracker. "It's not just me."

He glances around, seeing Anna and Jess staring at him too, along with the random women Rake is with.

"Is this how it feels to be a woman? Seen as a piece of meat?" he asks, a contemplative look on his face. "I don't know how I feel about it."

"Next cover you can be a sexy highlander in a kilt," I announce, almost swooning at just the thought of it.

"Fucking hell," he mutters.

"Or a Viking. You totally look like one."

"Lana."

"Yes?"

"You're lucky you're beautiful, because you're a pain in the ass."

I get ready for bed, brushing Evie and letting her outside, before bringing her back in to sleep. After she's sorted, I have a long shower and dress in my pajamas. I'm just getting into bed when I hear Tracker come home, the front door unlocking and then relocking.

"Chapter ten," Tracker says, walking into our room with my book in his hand.

"What about it?" I asked. "And hello to you too."

He smiles sheepishly, leans down and brushes a quick kiss on my mouth. "Hey, baby."

"Hi. Now, what about chapter ten?" I ask. "And weren't you at Rift? What the hell are you doing carrying my book around with you everywhere you go?"

"I want to do it to you. Right now," he says, narrowing his eyes on the page. "Sounds hot. And I started it and couldn't stop, so I've been taking it around with me."

Sweetest biker in the world.

Curious, I peer over the page, seeing what scene he is talking about.

"You would," I mutter, taking off my glasses and putting them on our side table. Tracker officially moved in with me last week, although we still spend a lot of our time at the clubhouse. It's nice having our own space; much more private. Tracker admitted that he loved this apartment, he only said he didn't because at the time he wanted me to move into the clubhouse with him, which I kind of figured out anyway.

"You wrote a threesome scene."

"I did," I reply slowly.

"Does that mean that's on your bucket list? Because I don't think I'd handle that very well," he admits. "Well I'd handle a third woman better than a third guy." He pauses. "I'd probably kill the guy."

I throw my pillow at him. "Nice try."

He chuckles. "Hey, you're the one writing these scenes. It's putting ideas in my already dirty head."

"Just because I write them doesn't mean I want to reenact all of them. Sometimes it's hot to just fantasize."

"Hmmmm. I'm gonna write my own sex scene," he says, rubbing his chin. He grabs my laptop and starts to type. Curious, I can't help but watch him.

She waits for me in bed, naked, legs spread. Her pussy is glistening, and my mouth waters, wanting to taste her.

No, devour her.

Possession runs through my veins. She is mine. I'll kill anyone who tries to take her from me.

"Tracker," she whispers, flashing me a seductive smile.

"Been waiting for me, have you?" I ask, starting to undress myself while unable to take my eyes from her body.

How did I get so lucky? With the blood on my hands, with the things I've done. The way I've treated women in the past. Used them. But Lana, she is mine. She is loyal as fuck, smart as hell, and only has eyes for me.

"Always," she replies. "Wet at just the thought of you being inside me, so hurry."

I smile down at her, all teeth. "Greedy little thing, aren't you? Demanding. You should know that it's me who makes the rules here."

She clamps her thighs together. She enjoys being controlled; I know it and I use it against her.

Now undressed, I stroke my cock and watch her, making her squirm just a little while longer. Lowering to my knees, I spread her creamy thighs and bury my face in her without a word.

She tastes like honey, sweet.

A scent that's all mine and no other man will ever know.

"That's actually pretty damn hot, Tracker," I say, feeling impressed. "Sexy biker writer. Is there anything you can't do?"

"Get my woman to have a threesome?" he jokes. I giggle and pull my laptop away from him and sit on his lap in its place.

"I love you."

"I love you too," he says, expression softening as he scans my face. "You've ruined me for other women, just like you said you would. You're my end."

Sweeter words were never spoken.

EPILOGUE

"YOUR boobs are huge," I tell a very pregnant Anna. Her IVF treatment had worked, and she is expecting her first bundle of joy. "How many hands do you think it will take to cover one? I think like four of mine."

She grins. "Two male hands."

"Yeah, if the hands belonged to Hagrid," I say, referring to the Harry Potter character. "Or some other giant male creature."

She laughs, her whole body shaking. "Two of Arrow's works fine."

"What are you doing here anyway? Shouldn't you be at home relaxing?" I ask her, gesturing to the bar around us. It was an early night at Rift, people are hanging out, not all drunk just yet.

"Couldn't miss this," she murmurs.

Miss what?

"Have you decided on a baby name?" I ask.

She rubs her protruding stomach. "If it's a girl, I want to call her Alana."

"What?" I whisper.

She smiles. "Didn't want two Lanas, so I thought Alana would work."

"Anna—"

"Don't get all soft on me, Lana," she replies. "These hormones are pissing me the fuck off. I cry for everything."

"Suck it up, Anna," I say in a hard voice. "See. All you need is some tough love."

She laughs at that. "You and tough love? Don't mix."

I roll my eyes. "Don't underestimate me, bitch."

She looks up. "I know you better than that, don't worry."

Tracker comes up behind me and nuzzles my neck from behind. "There you are."

I smile at his presence.

Ed Sheeran's "Thinking Out Loud" starts to play and I smile wider.

I freaking love this song!

I've never even heard them play a slow song at Rift before.

"This song is for Lana," the man says into the microphone, causing me to gasp.

Tracker's hands tighten their grip on my waist as he spins me around and kisses me. When he pulls away, he reaches into his pocket and pulls the most beautiful ring I've ever seen out of a black velvet box.

"Marry me," he whispers into my ear. "Make me the happiest man in the world."

"Of course I'll marry you!" I yell, putting my hand out. He slides the huge diamond onto my fourth finger, and stares down at it in approval. It fits perfectly.

"It's beautiful, Tracker," I tell him. "I love it."

"I love *you*, Lana," he says, kissing my lips. "And I'm keeping you."

He rests his forehead against mine. "Can we go home and fuck now? I need to be inside you."

I smirk at the romantic moment being over. "I'm sure there's an empty room somewhere around here. . . ."

He grins, shaking his head. "You were made for me, Lana, fuckin' made for me."

I feel the exact same way.